Chizellé T. Archie
ENTERPRISES

HIS GRACE, *His Blood,* HIS MERCY!

HIS GRACE, *His Blood,* HIS MERCY!

CHIZELLÉ T. ARCHIE

His Grace, His Blood, His Mercy!

Copyright © 2015 by Chizellé T. Archie

This book is a work of fiction. Places, events, and situations in this story are purely fictional. Any resemblances to actual persons, living or dead, is coincidental.

No part of this book may be reproduced, stored in a retrieval system, or transmitted by any means without the written permission of the author.

ISBN: 978-0-9861840-0-0

Dedications

Daddy you did it again! Only you were the one to give me the strength, when you knew I had none, to do what you called me to do. You gave me the power to write when there was nothing to write, in those moments of weariness, the moments of loneliness, tiredness… just when I was plain ol' scared. You knew! Thank you!

༒

To my Diamonds, my Diamonds in Training, yes all of you…

༒

My assistant, my love, my joy, the reason I do what I do, Freedom Jah'an, Mommy couldn't make it without you!

༒

Angela Denise "Ankie" Wilcox Jackson, my cheerleader, my promoter, my sistermanager! This one is for you! Miss and Love you…

What is Grace?

According to dictionary.com, "grace" is defined as the manifestation of favor by a superior. It can also be defined as the freely given, unmerited favor and love of God.

In other words, **grace is getting what you <u>do not</u> deserve**.

Example of God's Grace:

The grace of God is unearned; it's freely given to you by God, although you don't deserve it. An example of God's grace is the gift of eternal life.

For it is by grace you have been saved, through faith—and this not from yourselves, it is the gift of God— not by works, so that no one can boast (Ephesians 2:8-9).

What is Mercy?

According to dictionary.com, the term "mercy" can be defined as having a disposition of compassion or forbearance (to refrain from something).

In other words, **mercy is not getting what you *do* deserve.**

Example of God's Mercy:

Mercy is an act of being spared from judgment. When we hear, "thank you Lord for mercy" this is the same as saying, "thank you Lord for not giving me what I deserve, for withholding judgment and punishment from me."

It is of the Lord's mercies that we are not consumed, because his compassions fail not. They are new every morning…" (Lamentations 3:22-23).

The Blood

We all know that blood is biologically part of our body. However, blood is also intimately associated with the vital element of the individual as a person. That is why we give to the Blood of Christ all the adoration due to Christ Himself.

Our blood is naturally meant to be inside the body. Hence, every time we bleed, it is something of an unnatural or catastrophic nature. Many illnesses, for example, are perceived by bleeding caused by some malfunction in the body. Bleeding is almost a sign of alarm, which because of its violence, calls attention to the fact that something is terribly wrong with the person.

Looking at this bloodshed, we should note that the mercy of God wanted all that Blood to be shed with unheard-of abundance. All the blood in the Body of Our Lord Jesus Christ was shed, as if to show that He gave us everything, without holding back even one drop, because of His immense desire to save us. One drop of His blood would have sufficed, yet He shed all His blood to the point that the last drops were mixed with water that left His side when Longinus pierced His Heart with the lance. He wanted to hold nothing back in order to redeem us.

Let me sum this up for you; because of His Grace, He loves us so much that He shows His favor to us by giving us the things we KNOW we DO NOT deserve. Through His Mercy, He also loves us just as much by holding back ALL the things WE DO deserve, especially when we have done everything to deserve it! BUT, because of His Blood which was shed for us all, He still loved us just that much to die on the cross that we may have eternal life!

#atweetablemoment

Foreword

HIV- It's amazing how those three little letters, when paired together, can cause such a huge effect on our society, our community, our world. HIV- three letters that cause so much fear and discrimination. These three letters that have changed the face of society; they rip us apart and in turn brings us together. Every patient I meet always says the same thing "why me?" or "I never thought I could get this", but HIV does not discriminate, it affects people of every age, every class, every race, and every gender. It is white, black, yellow, young, old, rich, and poor. It affects ALL of us!

I am still not sure why God has called me to be an HIV medical provider for youth, but He has, and I am so grateful for the strength to help care for children and teenagers inflicted with HIV. Living in Atlanta, GA it is hard to escape the epidemic; it's everywhere, yet hardly ever talked about. We see an ever increasing amount of newly diagnosed adolescents entering into care for HIV/AIDS for the first time, and each year they are coming to us younger and younger and in more and more numbers.

Children are growing up too fast in our society, between technology making us more connected to others than ever, and lack of parenting or supervision; teens are making their sexual debut younger. However, teenagers don't have the maturity or developmental ability to understand the risks that are associated with sexual intercourse and the possible long-term implications of choosing the wrong partner.

Working as a pediatric infectious disease specialist in Atlanta, where the epidemic is at an all-time high has been both challenging and rewarding. Just in the past four years we have doubled our patient numbers, averaging 10-12 newly HIV+ youth per week. If this rate continues that means within the next year we could see an additional 500-600 cases just in our clinic.

What does this mean for our community, our state, and our nation? Why aren't we talking about this more? The conversation about HIV prevention and transmission has disappeared from our society. For some reason, it's seen as a disease of the 1980s and 1990s and people don't think that it is still happening (and in such high numbers) in 2014. However, that is not the truth, the truth is, HIV is here, it is staying, and it will only continue to spread if we don't start talking and doing something about it. Yes, treatment has come a long way since the early stages of this epidemic and individuals living with HIV/AIDS can live a long time while on treatment. However, it's the individuals that don't even know they have HIV that are the most risky. Of all the cases of HIV in America only about 80% actually know their status, that means there are 20% of people living with HIV and have NO idea they are infected! Scary thought!! And of all new infections recorded in the United States, in 2012 about 50% were among youth 13 - 25 years of age; an even scarier thought. But the most scary statistic is that an African-American male living in Atlanta, GA who makes his sexual debut at age 18 (and a lot make it much younger than this) that individual has a 60% chance of becoming HIV infected by age 30. These statistics are frightening and they must stop! This is the generation that must make it stop.

HIV is an exhausting disease; it exhausts the patients inflicted with it, their loved ones, their partners, our medical system and those providers and nurses who have been called to help. But it is with tolerance, compassion and love that we trek through it. In combating HIV, you are not only combating a disease, but the stigma, shame, judgment and fear of others. People's initial reaction to HIV is always based in fear, however, in order to combat fear and prejudices we have to educate. We need to start the conversation with our youth at home and in the schools. We need to empower them through education, to make good decisions and have an awareness of the risk. We need to stop hating and stigmatizing those living with HIV/AIDs and love them as we love ourselves. I know God has placed me on this earth in order to help those youth and young adults navigate the scary waters of living with HIV. Through tolerance, compassion and love I have been granted the incredible gift to watch teenagers enter into care at the lowest point in their life, at their breaking point and at their weakest, and through time and faith raise above all disparities and finish school, maintain good health, make better sexual decisions, and move on to college and professional lives. HIV doesn't need to break an individual, it doesn't affect the soul, but for so many it does. We need to treat the mind, body and soul in order to help the person living with such a stigmatizing disease rise above it. I believe so much in this generation of young people; they are resourceful, intelligent, and diligent. I believe in this generation, we could see the end of new HIV cases, but we need to start talking about it again to empower people to get tested, to get care, and to stay in care!

Ashley D. Boylan MPH, PA-C
Grady Infectious Disease Program
Pediatric and Adolescent HIV Specialist
Atlanta, GA

Chapter One

Gabrielle Grace Cartiér, is the name...

Summer is almost over and with all the fun I'm having, still can't wait to get back to school. All the rage is about how eighth grade is the best, to me, it's only just saying goodbye little girl, and hello womanhood! So far thirteen hasn't been that bad, matter of fact; it's all to the good, it would be better if my mother wasn't always on my case. It's hard being the daughter of Victoria Bouviér, but you might know her as Diamond.

    I have so much to live up to. The pressure is unbelievable. Everyone expects me to be this great whatever, but I'm just a regular teenager, wanting to live a regular life, but one thing that has worked in my favor is that I happen to have the body of a woman twice my age, and for what it's worth, it has me thinking about things other thirteen year olds just might not be thinking about yet. Right now I stand approximately sixty-one inches, just a little under my mother. Oh, and I happen to have the skin shade of honey, chestnut cocoa puffs, which only illuminate my piercing light brown eyes. My hair, yes, it's whipped, all the time, thanks to the Chi, but lets not forget the good genes. Yes, you know I'm part Creole, so, to say that, my hair is about as straight as straight can get. No chemicals, all mine! My body is getting out of control, my breasts are a lot larger than most girls; a 34-B! I was nine when Aunt Flo paid me her first visit, and since then, three things have been on my mind, boys, sex, and sex.

Like any other day, today it's on my mind constantly, and with only one week of summer vacation left, it's got to happen. I refuse to go back to school the only girl still holding the "V" card. I'm sooo over telling lie after lie, about what it's like, how it felt, did I like it. You know all that crazy talk, and on that note, it's about time. In order for this to happen it'll mean I'll have to finally prove to my first love, Drew, who just so happens to be six-four, twenty-three years old, skin as smooth as Hershey's chocolate; you know the dark and creamy kind. Yes it's my mission, to show him what I'm made of. Oh did I forget? He's the owner of Club Etcetera in Midtown. Every girl I know would jump at the chance to get with him, but he's checking for me. I have to show him I'm worth it. Many times I've chickened out, but not this time. Let another girl have him, NOT! You must not know who I am… I'm Gabrielle Grace Cartiér, pronounced (car-tee-yah) don't get it twisted.

For a hot minute, I log onto Facebook, seven more friend requests. One is from a dude that goes to my school; not interested! Ignore! My BFF, Quinn, keeps telling me it's the "older, more mature" guys I should be interested in. She says, "If you got to ask the parents for the car, then later for you." More than likely his Momma's car has a curfew, and it's probably two hours before his. That's Chapter 3 in the Rule Book. Chapter 1, Rule #1 – 'You must have your own car, because he who walks, walks alone.' Rule #2 – 'You must have your own money, because if you can't feed me, you don't need me.', and Rule #3 – 'You must have your gear correct, because if I'm fly, you gots to be fly, not Ol' National Flea Market fly, Lenox Mall fly.' See, it's a straight violation to be caught with someone that's rocking last year's kicks, by doing that, you can get five tickets from the fashion police, and I just can't let that happen.

Umm, got a message, it's Drew. Haven't talked to him in a while, tried calling him a couple of times, but he doesn't answer, hopefully this time he'll tell me what's really up.

Andrew Harrison
July 16 at 9:52 AM
Got your calls couldn't get back. What up, can you get out later? Don't be playn, ain't with them games.

Seeing his name just does something to me, maybe it's because it's been a week since I've seen him. Before I left, he was tight with me, pissed. I told him it wasn't my idea; it was my Dad's. Tried to let him know I had no plans of kicking it with anyone else, but he didn't believe me, he just said he'll see me when I get back.

Gabrielle Prettyeyes Cartiér
July 16 at 9:54 AM
Yeah, I can. Where should I be?

I'm so hoping Quinn is over her grandma's. Let me call her real quick.

"What's up girl?"

"Nothing."

"Need a favor. Can you take me to the mall?"

"Why? Don't tell me, you talked to Drew."

"Yeah, sort of, more like a message, he wants me to get out."

"Bout what time?"

"Don't know yet."

"Check right quick, I'll tell Grams I need to borrow the car."

"K. Hold on."

Andrew Harrison
July 16 at 10:08 AM

Phipps, by Versace round 6. Don't have me waitn. If you ain't putting it down don't even come.

Yes! It's going down. Getting chill bumps just thinking about it.

"Quinn, what about 5:15?"

"You know at eight, lights out for Grams, so it should be all good."

"Thanks. Now I just have to—"

"You gon' do it this time?"

"Well, yeah, especially because when I left, he was heated, so maybe if I show him I'm serious he'll believe that I wasn't messing around while I was gone."

"We'll see. You said that last time."

"Anyway… see you later."

I did say that, and I know he wants to, and so do I. Tonight… I'm losing it.

His Grace, His Blood, His Mercy!

Oh yeah, it's Tuesday, and both parents have late meetings, so all I have to do is tell my Mom I'm going to Quinn's, but it all depends what mood she's in. Since we got back, she's changed, doesn't help my Dad, Marcel, is away all the time.

First things first, what do I wear? He's made it clear he loves me in the True Religions, but for what I'm trying to pull off, I need something a little—I need a dress. Got it! The yellow ruffled peasant dress, with the multicolored ankle wrap floral espadrilles. I know he'll like this one, its itty-bitty and cute! This must happen, and not to mention, he is a *real* man, and not a lit-tle boy.

ℰℴ

It's five thirty, don't think I forgot anything. All of my chores are done, even a little extra so that Mommy Dearest won't have anything to complain about. Her going off on me because I didn't clean my room is the last thing I need. Between her and my dad, restriction is no joke! As long as she thinks I'm with Quinn, I'm straight.

So my make-up is on fleek, thanks to my Uncle Lucy. It's because of him I have priority at the MAC counter! Though I do notice I'm going to have to double up on the Proactive, lately the zits have been in full effect.

Soon as I hit the car, Quinn makes the joke that he'll smell me before he sees me; could this be a good thing or a bad thing? Guessing too much perfume, oh well, I'm sure he'll like it. Suddenly the car gets quiet, and I already know what she's about to say.

I beat her to it, "I know what I'm doing, I got this."

"Don't doubt that, you're a smart girl, but I still want you to make sure he has—"

"Yeah, I know—condoms."

"That too."

"Well then what?"

We both burst out laughing at the same time.

"You know, brushed his teeth."

"Girl, you know it's nothing like a brotha kissing on you with yesterday's breath," she says.

Still laughing, I say, "I would hope so, but if not I have the Doublemint on standby."

She cracks up, because as the Rule Book states Doublemint is a "real woman's" gum, and because of this I read her mind. And just like most dudes, he thinks Big Red is what's up. Ewww.

We're here. We get a spot near Twist; oh how I wish I was old enough to get in. Already tried… The fake IDs gave us away, but it's cool, I have no problems getting into Etcetera, and just as sure as I'm profiling on Drew's side, there will be no need for the fake stuff, straight VIP access.

Seems like I've been sitting forever, I look up and here he is, looking so good. Come to think of it, that's the first thing I noticed about him, his swag. Every time I see him, he has on a fresh pair of Jordan's. Don't think he's ever worn the same shoes twice. So I won't seem overly anxious, slowly I stand up and give him a hug, and as soon as I do, the insides of my stomach feels like somebody's doing cartwheels ninety miles a minute.

"What up shawty?" he asks.

Blushing, I say, "You."

In that smooth tone, he replies, "Well that's wassup then."

Somehow, I was hoping he would show me more affection.

"You ready to go?" he asks.

I nod. "Yes, where are we going?"

"You said you was ready right?"

Hesitating, I respond, "Yes, but you do have–"

"I got that, but we might go by my boy's spot first."

I stop for a minute, "So we're not going to a hotel?"

He doesn't answer. We just head to the car.

Wow, I'm finally about to be inducted in what we call the "real woman's society." Just in time for school. Now I'll really be the baddest chick on campus. Not that I have any worries or anything. The only thing I'm tripping over now is that I just wished Momma would let me shop in Victoria's Secret like everybody else. She acts like I'm still a lil' girl. Little does she know, I'm wearing the PINK panties and bra set Quinn bought for me.

He wastes no time switching the station from HOT 107.9, to August Alsina. Now that's what I'm talking about, and really, did he put on my song, *"I Luv This"*? Wow, it's a lot different from riding with you know who. Anything beats listening to Lord, Lord, Lord, you shole been good to me, and ugh, if I hear one more holy-rolly song I'm going to scream. I swear the station stays on 102.5! If she had any idea he was in my iPod on heavy rotation, she would all but kill me. It's like she is so into the church, it's not funny, scriptures for everything. The only thing she listens to is Gospel. I'm beginning to think she knows Marvin Sapp personally. Her theme song is *"My Testimony"* I can hear her now singing "…so glad I made it." Track 9, I know it by memory! What am I thinking? I'm supposed to be focusing on one thing, giving "it" up. I sneak a peek at him, and I promise this dude is looking sooo hot right about now. Just at this moment I get a text from Quinn.

7/16/14 Tue
Quinn: Handle ur biz
6:04 PM
   7/16/14 Tue
   Me: Lol
   6:05 PM
7/16/14 PM
Quinn: I'm 4 real. Don't 4get what I told u!
6:06 PM
   7/16/14 Tue
   Me: k. I'm str8t!!
   6:07 PM

Drew asks who am I texting so much. What?!! Hold on Mr. The way he sounds as if he has a jealous streak. I knew it! He is so into me. This only makes me more ready to let him know just how much I care for him. Right now I feel like I'm on top of the world.

✧

Forty-five minutes later we manage to get through traffic on Lenox Road. We eventually wind up on Piedmont at what looks to be a hole in the wall. A sign is blinking $29.00. Are you kidding me?!! He must not know who I am! Is he crazy? I'm sorry but I never pictured my first time being at some sleazy MOTEL, I always thought of it being more five star-ish. As much as I hate some of the things momma tells me, there are still some things she's taught me that will never change, such as anything under four star is not even worth my time, and this here looks to be more around two, so… that would be a NO!

Whew! He was just testing me. He had to be. Driving a 750i, I know he can afford a better room than that. After minutes of going back and forth, he caves in and we end up at the Wingate. Now this is more like it.

It takes him a while to come back to the car. I was just about to start getting nervous. I've been playing this over in my head for some time, and I'm not about to let anything mess it up. A few minutes later I'm standing in room 104.

I'm starting to feel really comfortable as if this is our own private suite. I sit on the king bed, look around and take it all in. First, he adjusts the temperature, and then turns on the TV. Thank you, I didn't want to say anything but it's like super cold in here. He takes off his shirt, puts it on the back of the chair, and after that, he plops across the bed. He lets on he wants me to lie across the bed with him, and without giving it a second thought I do. Moments pass, and next thing I know he's rubbing my thighs. I don't stop him. It really feels good. My heart begins to beat a bit faster, but I don't worry. This is why I'm here, right? I lean over to kiss him, he returns the gesture. Umm a little wet, but it's okay. Quinn says, the wetter the lips, the better the kiss, and yes he does have Big Red breath! I'm so trippin', because he asks if I want a piece. That would be a no. Before I know it, I'm touching his penis, that's now hard as a rock. I think to myself oh my goodness. A cold feeling goes through me.

"Oh, that ain't nothin'," he says.

I take a deep breath, because I get a flashback about the dude Quinn told me about, that was soooo big even she wanted to cry, but I don't flinch.

"May I see it?" I ask.

Did I just say that?

Immediately he gets up, unbuttons his pants, mmm, mmm, mmm, Calvin Klein boxers. He looks good in just underwear. The more he undresses, it's sinking in, this is really about to happen. He pulls me up from the bed, pulls me closer to him. We kiss even harder. By this time I'm beginning to feel something I've never felt before. Sorta feels as though my "private area" as momma calls it, is throbbing. A lot, a whole lot. Quinn didn't say anything about this, but anyway, I like it, and I'm still doing this. He reaches around to take off my bra; he slowly looks me up and down, like he just hit the mega million jackpot. He kisses my breast! Now there's a wet feeling in my panties. I do remember Quinn talking about this, she says, when this happens, it's a good thing, because it will be a lot easier once he goes inside. It's not supposed to hurt that bad, she says.

"You ready?" he asks.

Breathing hard, I say, "Yes."

Just as we pull back the sheets, a memory of the last time I was in a hotel crosses my mind. Ironically it was with my mother, she was in one bed and I was in the other, the feeling wasn't quite like this though. My heart is pounding.

After several rounds of the touchy kissy, I look him directly in his eyes, and for some reason they seem distant. It's like I can see straight through him, and for a moment there is a weird feeling, like I'm the only one into what's about to go down. Holding himself above me, he pushes my leg apart to make more room, and then he takes the other leg and does the same thing. Placing his weight on top of me, he begins to kiss me on my neck so hard that I am sure it will leave a mark the size of a plum. I can feel his hardness pressing up against me, ooh he smells so good, he began to moan saying, "Damn you taste good." I melt. Then all of a sudden I get an overwhelming feeling that this is not how I wanted this to be. Before I know it I am no longer moist, I'm as dry as the Grand Canyon.

"Please stop," I say.

"Stop!" "What?!"

He's getting so upset. This is not the same person from earlier.

He continues, "Oh, hell no, you're 'bout to give this up. You got me out here like this, and all you can say is stop! Oh, you 'bouts to come correct. Girl you must be crazy!"

It's not long that tears begin to swell in my eyes, and he's still propped above me waiting for me to get myself together, just so we can finish what we've started.

"Drew, this is not how I want to do this."

Angrily, he says, "Well, how do you wanna do it then? Right now, you have two choices, slow or fast; you make the decision."

"Before we go any further, can I ask you a question?"

He looks at me with pure disgust. "What is it?"

"Do you love me?"

He pauses, and looks at me like I'm crazy for real, but to my surprise he answers, "Yeah, I do, so now what?"

The more he's on top of me, the harder I cry. I continue to ask him to get up. He doesn't move. I look over towards the mirror, and I get a glimpse of my naked body under this man, and I don't like what I see.

He keeps pushing. "Look, I'ma ask you one mo' time. What up? You gon' do this or what? I told you don't come with no lil' girl games. You said you was ready, but now you want to bag out like some lil' girl in middle school."

Right here I realize that lying doesn't always work in your favor. In hopes that this will make him move, I blurt out, "I'm in middle school."

"What! You—"

Pleading, I say, "I thought you knew that by now. You said you knew everything about me. You said you really cared, and that you loved me."

"Chick, I was goin' by your profile. It said you was born in 1994. Man, how old are you for real?"

Still crying, I say, "I'm thirteen; about to be fourteen."

"Thirteen!! Girl you 'bout to get me put in jail! Get up, get yo shit."

I've never seen him this angry. While he is putting his underwear on, I notice, he wasn't wearing a condom.

"Were you going to have sex with me without a condom?" I ask.

The look in his eyes is so frightening. "What you think? If you was a real woman that wouldn't even matter to you. I don't have to cover myself to prove a point. I don't even like rubbers."

I remember what daddy said, 'If he doesn't respect himself he won't respect you.'

He grabs his keys to the car, looks over at me, and says, "You better call yo girl to come get you. You ain't worth me takin' you nowhere."

His Grace, His Blood, His Mercy!

No he didn't. I know he's not going to leave me here like this? I was wrong. He did! But not before letting me know he wanted his money back for the room. I can't stop crying. I get my things together. I feel horrible.

So what am I to do now? My mother would go straight Brooklyn if she knew I was even here, my only choice is to call Quinn. But where is my cell phone?

Chapter Two

Gabrielle, Big Pimpin' is Facebook approved...

What may seem like an eternity, I finally contact Quinn, and thank goodness, some man turned my phone in to the front desk. When I let on to where I am, she knows exactly where to come; just so happens she and Lil' Kevin came here before. She affectionately calls him Lil' for a reason. We stay laughing about that.

My phone is blowing up. It's him. Really? Does he think I would give him a thought after what he pulled on me? After a couple of times my heart really wants to answer it, but my mind tells me to push ignore. Quinn senses my frustration.

"Girl, what's up with ol' boy?"

"Why you ask?"

"Well, first of all I shouldn't be the one picking you up. He should, and you know the tank."

Okay, whenever she says this, I already know I need to hand over some gas money. It's like I got it like that. Sometimes I feel as though I'm walking around with a stamp on my forehead that says "FriendTM."

"Na'll it ain't nothing like that, like I said on the phone when I called you, he just got real pissed off at me because I didn't give in."

I look over at her, and I swear her head is spinning around like that girl in The Exorcist.

"What! You didn't do it? What's your problem girl, every time you say you gon' do it, then you wind up chickening out. I keep telling you, ain't no brother gon' keep dealing with that. One day you gon' have to put your guards down, and go ahead and do what you gotta do."

"Yeah, I know."

"Yeah, you know I'm right, before you know it you'll be labeled as a teaser, and trust me you don't want that."

For a second I imagine that thought, and it's not pretty. She's right; the day is going to come where I'm going to have to prove myself.

꩜

Seven fifteen on Sunday morning and just as every Sunday morning momma wakes me blasting T.D.Jakes. I've heard him so many times, I find myself saying in my Jakes voice, "Get ready, get ready, get ready!" If I didn't know, I would really think he was our Pastor. She's watches him on a regular, and you know if she misses him, you best to believe it's on the DVR. I'm willing to bet she has the Potter's House prayer line

His Grace, His Blood, His Mercy!

on speed dial! Matter of fact she does… I remember seeing it in her contact list under "Prayer Call." That figures. Our church though, it's cool. One thing about it, there are a lot of cute guys that go there. My friends are always asking to come to church with me just to see. Not get the word, to scope out the scenery. Well who can blame them? Personally, I don't find any of them to be my type. It is this one guy that keeps sweating me, but I'm not feeling him like that. Pretty boy, bow ties, plaid pants, sweater vest, not to mention the blazer. It's like 95 degrees outside. Who does that?

In Teen church this morning, another minister is preaching; right off I'm digging him. He opens up cracking jokes, quoting words from T-Pain's, "Buy You a Drank", he asks us the question, why when a man buys a girl a drink he automatically thinks she should stay with him the rest of the night? We all laugh. I'm so feeling him right now; overall I think he's good. He's not boring; he's actually kept my attention, unlike some of these old stuffy preachers that always have to growl and sweat to get the church pumped up. I realize he's hit on a lot of the same things my daddy talks about, like how a lady should always be classy, that she should demand respect at all times. If a man gets the idea that a woman has no respect for herself, then why would he respect her? He and momma are forever reminding me that women are to be treated like a diamond, and not a cubic zirconium. Humph, why am I feeling some kind of way? Drew seemed like he respected me at first. Okay, clear your mind Gabby, not in church. Wish I could stop thinking about it; wish I could stop thinking about him.

As soon as church is over, and just as I am trying to clear my mind of all impure thoughts of the opposite sex, blazer boy comes over to me. I can't help but die laughing on the inside, because even the way he walks… everything screams weak link! He opens his mouth; full of braces. OMG, he even has the colored wires. Blue of course. He tries to say hello, but in between the stuttering and the mush-mouth I can hardly understand him.

"Hhh, Hi, I'm Albert Dunagan."

I'm in church, I know better, but the boy is killing me.

I smile. "Hi, I'm Gabrielle."

He reaches out to me with that misunderstood, whether I should shake her hand or hug her look. We go with shaking hands. He clears his throat, as to not stutter this time, but he does, but at least this time I'm not laughing inside.

"I know who you are. You go to Benetton Prep, right?"

I'm trippin', because just as he is asking me this, I remember I've seen him somewhere before. Just hoping it's not my school.

"Yes I do."

He gives that sheepish grin as if to say… yeah baby.

He continues, "I thought so, because I've seen you around. Math team right?"

What! Is he a stalker?

Before I know it, I ask him, "How old are you?"

He responds, "Fourteen."

Really. Way too young! Rule# 7 – 'Never date a guy your age.' The rule is at least half your age, and fooling with Quinn, you can add plus five to that.

While we're standing here making small talk, my mother beckons for me. I'm guessing service is out for her, and it looks as though she's been crying. Let me guess. It's me. She tells me all the time, I keep her on her knees. She comes over and hugs blazer boy. He returns the gesture. He acts like he knows her personally. I tell him see you later, he does the same. As we're walking away, he dashes back, gets my attention, hands me a piece of paper, and says the dreaded words, "Call me sometime." Not!!

All the way to the car I have to listen to momma go on and on about how Albert is a nice respectful young man, and that she and his mother Sheila are sorors. She says he's a child prodigy like me, and I need to make friends with other young people like this, especially since it's not that many of us. And, oh uhn-uhn, did I hear her correctly, did she say he lives a couple of streets over from us? You gots to be kidding me. Brookhaven is way too small.

All day my phone has been going crazy. I've gotten more friend requests today than ever. I've even gotten request from people I have never seen in my life. Right now I'm holding it down with 727 friends, 426 followers on Twitter, and the Instagram is off the chain. Posted a collage the other day, got 111 likes. Selfies are right up my alley. I pull out the tablet and before I can get signed in good, another message.
Rishard Big Pimpin McCants
134 mutual friends
Shawty, what's good wit ya? Nice pic.
Okay. He is fhy! Confirm.
As soon as I accept his request I get an invite to join the group "The 4-2-0 Crew". I click 'Join', and immediately the chat window pops up.

Rishard Big Pimpin McCants: wuzzup lady

Gabrielle Prettyeyes Cartiér: nothn much and u

Rishard Big Pimpin McCants: u wuz up

Gabrielle Prettyeyes Cartiér: ☺ Thnx

Rishard Big Pimpin McCants: u r welcome

Gabrielle Prettyeyes Cartiér: kool

Rishard Big Pimpin McCants: u get my request

Gabrielle Prettyeyes Cartiér: Yeah I got it. What's it about

Rishard Big Pimpin McCants: wuz ur number

Gabrielle Prettyeyes Cartiér: Kmsl

Rishard Big Pimpin McCants: wuz so funny

Gabrielle Prettyeyes Cartiér: U might be a serial killer

Rishard Big Pimpin McCants: naw I'm gud u saw my pic, do I look like I'm a killa lmbo

While he's talking crazy, my phone rings, it's my other bestie, Angel. She's so not what her name says. If she wasn't my girl, I would think she was the devil's pawn.

I scream, "Holla!"

Laughing, "Hey girl," she says back.

"What you up to?" she asks.

"Oh me? The usual, on Facebook, chatting with some fool."

"What you mean?"

"Some guy named 'Big Pimpin'."

She cracks up laughing.

"You know how to pull 'em don't you?"

"Yeah, I got it like that. So what's up?"

"Not much, just getting ready for tomorrow. I'm so dreading going back."

"Not me. I can't wait. Believe it or not, I'm so psyched about my new Honors classes."

"Yeah you would be. Smarty pants. Who looks forward to even harder classes than what they have to take regularly? Only a geek."

"Now you know… don't be saying that out loud. From what I've heard, nobody's checking for a super-smart chick."

We say it together. "The dumber the betterrr!"

"But whatever, Gabby you make straight A's."

For a minute that gives me a rush, because I love myself some Chemistry.

"Well yeah you're right, but you're not that far behind."

"What because of that boring Honors English class? I only did that to impress—"

"Yeah, I know, Niko."

"Yes ma'am, Niko."

Laughing so hard, I say, "Well, I guess it didn't work, huh?"

"Guess not. Dude wasn't studying me."

I look over, and the message alert is going off. He's still on here?

"Girl this dude is really crazy. I thought by now he would've realized I wasn't responding for a reason."

"What does he want? He isn't a stalker is he?"

I giggle, "No I hope not, but he is cute though."

I talk to Angel, and chat with him at the same time. I notice the time on my phone, 8:15. I need to get my things ready for in the morning.

Rishard Big Pimpin McCants: u there

Rishard Big Pimpin McCants: smh oh so dat's how it is

Gabrielle Prettyeyes Cartiér: I'm here, I was talking to my girl for a sec, sorry

Rishard Big Pimpin McCants: it's like dat huh?

I hurry up and let Angel know that he isn't a stalker, but he is definitely a little strange.

"Girl, he asked me for my number?"

"How does he look?"

"Go to my page, and look at his picture. His name is Rishard Big Pimpin' McCants."

"Alright, I'm checking."

Rishard Big Pimpin McCants: so wuz up u gon give me the number or what? Your pics are hot! **#bomb.com #cuteashell**

Now that's funny. It won't hurt though, the least I can do is not like his voice, and block him out after that.

Gabrielle Prettyeyes Cartiér: Rotfl it's on my profile. U didn't c it?

Rishard Big Pimpin McCants: I'm calling, u betta not be lying

This dude had better be for real.

"Girl, he is hot!" Angel yells.

"I know right, and he's nineteen."

Before I count to ten, there's an incoming call.

"Hey Angel, let me hit you back. It's him calling."

"Mr. Big Pimpin'? Oh, Drew ain't going for that."

I can't tell her that it may be over.

"See you tomorrow girl, and oh yeah, come correct."

"You know it. Your girl is always on fleek, even if-it-is in a uniform."

I switch the call.

I hesitate to say hello. Rule Book states, Chapter 2, Rule #1 – 'Never seem too ready.' Makes you look easy.

"Wuz up?"

His Grace, His Blood, His Mercy!

I pause again. "Hello."
"Wuz up Ms. Gabrielle?"
"Nothing Mr. Big Pimpin'."
"Ohhh, you got jokes."
"No jokes over here."
"So, you are a Kendrick Lamar fan, huh?"
"Yes."
"What you know about that?'
"Oh he's the truth, now."
"Okay dat's wassup."
"What about you? Who are you into?
"Nobody in particular, right now I'm on that August Alsina."
"He's alright. What you listening to? 'No Love'?"
We laugh.
"Really, Ms. Lady, you ain't even ready."
I'm thinking, did he get the Drew memo already? Teaser…
"Thanks for joining the group," he says.
"No problem, it seems like it's a lot of people in the group."
"Yeah, we trying to get it kicked off, me and some of my boys from round the way. You know some other people that might wanna get in?"
"Not sure, I'll have to check. What's it all about?"
"The name speaks for itself."
"What you mean?"

Before I can finish my conversation, Momma barges in. I guess the sign on the door that reads "House of Gabrielle" doesn't mean anything. Of course the first thing to come out of her mouth is, "Do you have anything else better you can be doing besides on that phone?"

Yada, yada, yada, how can she ask this? She bought the phone. She had to know I would use it for more than just talking, hence the unlimited text messaging plan, and who needs a computer anymore? Isn't that what an iPhone is for? I hurriedly try and hang him up before she goes off.

Here she goes. "Gabrielle, you really need to get your priorities straight. I'm tired of coming in to every room in this house, and you are face down on that phone. I'm beginning to regret I caved in and got it. Your daddy constantly complained that you didn't need it."

Angrily I say, "He never wants me to have anything."

"No, that's not the case. He wants you to understand the true value of money. Better yet, why am I explaining anything to you? What I say goes. That's it."

I mumble under my breath, "What about you? What do you think? Never mind don't answer that."

"Like-I-said, I don't have to explain anything to you young lady. The main thing is I said off the phone, internet, all of that, it's time you get your things ready for in the morning. First day of school, and this year will be even better, and I expect nothing less from you than any other year."

How did I know she was going to come in here and give me the First Day of School speech? I've just about memorized it. It's a good thing I make straight A's, because otherwise, I don't think I could stand it. She's getting totally out of control. Sometimes I wish we didn't have all of this, the money, the cars, none of it, because if I was a regular girl then maybe she would have other worries, and she wouldn't pay so much attention to me.

His Grace, His Blood, His Mercy!

I'm not even worrying about Cruella Deville, because my mind is on other things. Pumped up doesn't even begin to describe my excitement. I get goose bumps just thinking about all the new things ahead of me this year. It's going to be so good. It's said if you wish upon a star then your wish will come true, tonight I'm wishing big. Most of all, I hope Drew forgives me, because I really do love him. I've got to make it up to him. That's if he even cares. Oh yeah, school, I got this.

༄

Once I'm done, I call Quinn, she doesn't go back to school until next week, she's super excited because she'll be a junior this year. She goes to Columbia High. Now let me tell you about Quinn, my girl has a body that has been banging ever since I met her. She has always looked as if she was my big sister, really big sister at that. In a pair of jeans, the dudes can't even pay attention for looking at her and what I joke her about, the Kim Kardashian booty! No waistline at all. I guess she is somewhere along the lines about 5'7", really light-skinned; I call her light bright, you know what I mean, could use a little sun. As pretty as her real hair is, a girl just has to have the weave; the curly kind, the wavy kind, the oh-so-not-curly kind, whatever, she will have it on any given day. Her motto is: Always switch it up. Regular is boring. Weave is the spice of life.

Hopefully she will move over here permanently. After her mom died she's been split between Grams and her Aunt who has six other children. From what I can tell Grams is pretty well off herself, not doing bad at all. Actually Grams still driving, and she has some cool old lady friends, and from what I've seen, a couple of cool ol' man friends too. Grams don't play. Maybe that's why Quinn's aunt Skyye and Grams are constantly going at it. Major beef. I asked mom before could she stay with us, just so she wouldn't have to deal with all the drama, but it wasn't happening. To me she has never really cared much for Quinn. She thinks she fast. Whatever! She's my shero. But Grams, oh she loves herself some Grams. I believe this is the only reason she trusts me with Quinn. We've been best friends since second grade. She has never known either of her parents. Her father died soon after her mother, so it's like I inherited the sister I never had. The one good thing is that I get to hang out in the DEC every now and then, when her aunt lets me.

I call twice, her phone is off. That's normal, every month the phone is off, don't know why, she has a little gig at the wing spot. Maybe one of her sponsors didn't pay it. That explains why I haven't heard from her today. Soon as I get comfortable, a 212 area code comes up, it's my dad Malcolm. I figured he would call before I go back to school. I hesitate answering because I'm still mad that he didn't make it to my last recital. He claims he was in the hospital. Lately, that's his excuse for everything.

In my nasty voice I answer, "Hello."
"Hello baby girl."
He sounds weak.
One word, "Hey."
"Are you all ready for another year?" he asks.
I pause and take a deep breath, "Yes sir."

"Gabby, I know you are still mad at me, but I am very sorry. I haven't been feeling well lately, and I can't seem to shake this sickness."

"Don't tell me, you've been in the hospital again?"

"Well to be honest, yes, I'm actually here now. I just wanted to call you because I spoke with your mother earlier this week, and she told me school starts tomorrow. I didn't want to miss calling you. I am so proud of you, and I know you will do a great just as you have thus far."

OMG, really man, kill it with the sob story dude. He has missed out on so much, what does he want from me?

As much as I don't want to, "I say, thank you. Sorry you are not feeling good. What did they say is wrong with you?"

"I have pneumonia, and it has really taken a toll on me."

I feel bad. But I don't want him to know it.

"Did they give you medicine?"

"Yes they have. It seems to be working, but I just need to get my strength up. How are you? I heard you had a great summer."

"Yes I did. It was so much fun."

Just that fast I forget I'm supposed to be angry with him, but he's my *real* daddy; I love him, and I don't want him to be sick.

"I'm glad."

I can hardly understand him for the coughing.

Quietly I say, "I love you."

I can hear a silence over the phone, minus the beeping alarms in the background.

"I love you too princess. I hope you have a good first day. Daddy has to go. The nurse is here to check my vitals. Be sweet, I'll talk to you soon."

Before I close my eyes, I say a prayer that God will look after my dad so that he can get better, because even if he has missed out on a couple of things, he has been here for me more than most people I know. I can say I'm blessed to have two fathers in my life.

Just before I get into a deep sleep, momma comes in to kiss me goodnight, and so does my dad, Marcel. They both let me know how proud they are to have me as their daughter; in which I would hate to let them down, but it would advisable for all parties that they give a girl some breathing room!

Chapter Three

Gabrielle, Shh! No talking in class...

Back to school it is, and the first day I get homework. It's not long I realize my favorite teacher is MIA. Where is Mrs. Walker? She's been here all this time, and I've looked so forward to taking History from her. My counselor and I specifically chose International Relations & Conflict Honors: 20th & 21st Centuries because of her. She's the best. Just like any other time, it's beginning to feel a little weird being in a class full of eleventh graders. But you get used to it after a while.

Today this geeky lil' man, named Mr. Cromwell, shows up talking about he's going to be our instructor for the year, and if we have any concerns, we can address them with the counselor. He proceeds to give his entire bio, so he has a BA and a MA in English, a MS in International Relations, and a certificate in Intelligence Analytics, and most of all I see that he has taught at the John Hopkins Center for Talented Youth. Wow, pretty impressive, so now everyone turns to me. What am I supposed to do? One dude yells out, "Smart girl, in a couple of years that's going to be you right?" Everyone tends to think the little geeky eighth grader is a little strange. I admit, sometimes I miss my other friends, but it's not my fault I was born as what some would say, "Einstein's protégé". At four years old, my parents had my IQ measured, in which I scored at 170. When most toddlers should be getting used to walking and talking, by age 2, I was already calculating basic arithmetic. Momma is always making jokes of how by the time I could walk, I was figuring out the square root of pi, and because of this, I have been offered admission to some of the best Universities in the country. But Momma has pushed very hard for me to stay in "regular" school, so that I can have a "normal" life, and have "normal" friends.

Sometimes I wish I was an average girl, and then maybe people would stop looking at me like I'm a freak. For example, it's this lady my mom knows, I promise she asks me for the numbers to the lottery every single time she sees us. She tries to play it off by giving me a hug, and then she whispers, "Hey baby, I know you got the numbers this week." Really lady? One time after church, we saw her at Publix, and she pulled the usual, by this time Momma had walked away, and I couldn't help myself. She asked, and I just couldn't resist. I gave her the numbers from the sermon our Pastor had preached that day. Psalm 139: 7-14. I know I was wrong, but I had to give her the mega ball number, so I gave her the number three, one for the Father, one for the Son, and one for the Holy Spirit. Pow! Don't think she won, but it was fun though.

His Grace, His Blood, His Mercy!

Listening at Mr. Cromwell give his credits, I'm thinking it probably wouldn't be so bad if he didn't have this ridiculous Phil Collins look. In my opinion, if your hair is receding to the point where it begins at the middle of your head, let it go I say! I've been wondering the same thing about Stevie Wonder for the longest. I mean really? I know he's blind and all, but he can feel! He has got to know it's time to let it go. Seriously, don't think I'm going to be able to handle this for the whole year without cracking some type of jokes, but the more I zone in to what he's saying, I start to think this may just be a good year.

I'm not in class for a full thirty minutes, and Jordan is already texting me about this year's party. I'm thinking "Dag girl can we get back to school good first?" Jordan is this girl that's been harassing me about joining our group for the last two years. You would think after the second turn down she would get the point. She's cool and all, but she just doesn't fit into the whole GEMS (Gorgeous, Elegant, Mature, and Sophisticated) persona. Right now it's only six deserving young ladies that's deemed worthy enough to come close to being a GEM and that's Angel, Dionne, Jazmine, Bree, Sarah, Lorna, and yours truly, Gabs!

I get a tap on my shoulder, "Excuse me young lady, what's your name again?"

Reluctantly I answer, "Gabrielle."

"Last name?"

I'm like, look Mister, you got me pegged the wrong way.

Before I know it, I say, "Cartiér".

I can hear those clowns behind me laughing.

"Well, Ms. Cartiér, is it? So you are aware I have a NO tolerance policy for any of the smartphones, the not–so smartphones, any kind of technology that warrants communication between you and another student in or out of this class. Do I make myself clear?"

Aahm, oops, Phil/Stevie whichever, has lost his mind. I know he didn't just go off on me like that. I wasn't even the one texting. That shyster Jordan knows better not to even think of asking me anything about becoming a GEM after this.

Eventually, he decides to get off of his throne and off of me, just in time to pass out the syllabus for the year. Looks like we will be incorporating a lot of website learning, in which I'm cool with that. Ironically, this week will be more so introductions, along with studying via textbook "population growth" "human rights" "citizenship" "state" "ethnicity" "globalizations" "nation-state", and via website I am to read up on "Major Relations of the World Ranked by Number", as well as the "CIA Fact book."

Yeah baby! It may be hope for Mr. Cromwell, oops excuse me, Phil after all. By the time he gets done with his extensive presentation, I look around and some of the class is about as lost as they could be. I glance over at Kim and of course the girl's taking notes faster than the speed of lighting. Between she and I the entire class will be depending on us, well me should I say, because she's not giving up anything. Before class is out, three people have already let on that this class is going to be BORING! Not me… I'm ready. Bring it!

His Grace, His Blood, His Mercy!

9:55 and the bell rings. I survived the Phil effect, only one hundred and seventy-nine more days to go. On the way to my locker, Jordan is still asking me about this year's party, although I must say, last year's party was the truth. Oh we were so turnt up! So this year has to be better than all the rest. It isn't two minutes before she walks away that I get a glimpse of a girl I have never seen here on campus before. She looks to be every bit of 5'6", long black straight hair, flat-ironed to perfection. Either she's got a banging stylist, or the Dominican's hooking it up, one of the two. Whichever one it is, I know it's tight, but she'll never know it.

Lucky me. Of all the lockers in this place, hers has to be two down from me. And why does it seem like every boy in this school is drooling after her? Wait a minute! It's not even going down like that. She gives me a look as if to say, and who are you? Little does she know, I've got this on lock.

Paying so much attention to whatever her name is, although I do think I heard someone call her Danessa. I don't even realize it, but I'm about to be late for AP Chemistry, my favorite class. And yet another new teacher this year; word around the school is that she's no joke. Ms. Lucinda Hunter was a Professor at Georgia Tech, but decided she wanted to do high school for a change. Whew! It's a good thing I attended Dukes' TIP program over the summer, I believe she's going to be off the chain. Now that I think of it, it was one of the best things to ever happen to me. Still can't believe I was actually working in an actual Organic Chem lab designing compounds. Can't wait to complete our experiment! Some of my classmates may never know that experience, and plus I have the best mentor ever, Ms. Abbey Paige. Surely, it was something I will never forget. So ready for next summer, but I won't let these people around here know that, I'm already labeled as the "Chem geek". Which in all honesty I don't mind, because it allowed me to learn even more, and to see so many other gifted students there really challenged me. I guess my making a 2279 also helped. Both math and science has always been my thing, so okay Ms. Hunter, let's go…

I walk in the class and the chill is unbelievable. No, what is unbelievable is that skirt she's wearing. Last I heard the hippie days were long gone. Fashion tip 101: It's called the DIY No-Sew-Skirt. One minute that's all it'll take. We can pull the YouTube video up, go in the bathroom, and voila, come back and the lady is back in style! This is a Preparatory School not a Monastery. IJS

As far as the syllabus goes, looks like we're going to be studying, structure of matter, properties of matter, chemical reactions and rates, thermodynamics, and equilibrium, in which most of this is nothing new. I see we are going to have at least 20 exams; this is including the 4 review exams, 16 labs, with several having a guided lab, and one bonus lab that counts for 50% of our grade. According to this, we can earn extra credit, not that I need it, it's just that I'm a lover of all things chemistry, and… Tory Burch.

Before I know it, my phone is vibrating in the bottom of my purse. Not sure if I'll be put on blast like History Phil did me last period, but I take a chance anyway. Text alert. Hope it's Drew. Nope, it's Big Pimpin', nevertheless, I get a rush.

8/4/14 Mon
Rishard: wut up
10:20 AM
    8/4/14 Mon
    Me: n class
    10:20 AM
8/4/14 Mon
Rishard: u didn't call back
10:21 AM
    8/4/14 Mon
    Me: went to sleep
    10:22 AM
8/4/14 Mon
Rishard: it's like dat
10:24 AM
    8/4/14 Mon
    Me: U know I had school today
    10:26 AM
8/4/14 Mon
Rishard: ok school girl
10:27 AM
    8/4/14 Mon
    Me: whateva
    10:28 AM

Something told me not to try it! Ms. Lady is going off, and she has taken my phone! Wrong answer Boo! She tells me she will have it for the remainder of class, and if she has to take it again then she is going to have to let my mother know, and that would be a neg-a-tive!

Chizellé T. Archie

For this to be my favorite class, I can't even focus. Momma tried taking my phone once, and that was a disaster. It seems like I'm missing out on so much of my life right now. Every second I'm away, a new story on Facebook is added in the newsfeed. Well, since it doesn't look like I'll be getting it back, so back to Princess Leia. Per the syllabus, class is scheduled for 52 minutes. Why do I feel like I have 49 minutes left? I look around and most of the class must have thought this was a free day. Glad I'm prepared. Supplies on deck, graphing calculator, check; goggles, check; lab notebook, check.

Be ye ready at all times, is what I've been told most of my life. This is one time where it pays off. Ms. Hunter decides she is going to do an okee-doke on us, and give us an ice-breaker, just to see if we've been paying attention up to this point. The way she looks at me, with those beady eyes, it's like she has it out for me and it's only day one. I'm used to this; I've had several instructors challenge me. Some people just can't get used to the idea of having a thirteen-year old around that's smarter than the average college professor. It's funny though. She gives a handout with one question. We have fifteen minutes to answer. I answer it in less than five. I amaze myself at what I can do sometimes. She's looking like, WTH? Her temples are flaring. No seriously, she's pissed. So many times I've wondered why Momma would continue to subject me to this. Keeping me here in a classroom setting, doing school work she knows is clearly basic to me. Her reasoning is that she wants me to grow up with my peers, be around students in my age range. Really, Momma? You've got to be kidding me. My teachers really want me around so that I can help them out. I will never forget, Ms. Bailey, my sixth grade English teacher actually had me helping her with the test questions. She tried to make it seem as though she was asking me in regular conversation, but I knew better. I was like, lady please!

So we get our next assignment, and it is to be paired off into lab partners. People are already looking at me as if I'm the little blue sign, "Walmart's Value of the Day". If anyone walked in this room right now, there's a line from my desk to the door with each of them wanting to be partnered up with me. Even the guy next to me with the plexi-glass glasses wants to be my partner. The twins Paris and London even ask. How about NO! What do they think I am stupid? Or do they just think they are going to get an easy "A". Nevertheless, I have to have a partner, so let me think… girl vs. boy. Ahhm, a whole semester with some chatty wanna-be, nope, I'm sorry. Gabby is going with Alex Henderson, the cutie sitting back of the class, in the corner, last row to the left, somewhere in the ball park of 5'10", grey eyes, light skinned, curly reddish-brown hair, with maybe anywhere from 30-35 freckles on his face. Really tried not to notice him so much, but it was hard not to. Couldn't ignore how he walked into the class with that Gucci backpack on, he had me at "Hello," and according to the Rule Book, his swag is mega. Got that Jay Z thang going on, and anyway he acts like I'm a regular classmate. Wish I could say the same about him. I guess that's why it's called chemistry. Note to self. To be put on "Hottie List."

"Hey what's up, I'm Alex?" he says.

Feeling all girlie inside, I answer, "Nothing, and you?"

"Just trying to get this thing kicked off. I'm on a mission, trying to get my GPA where I need it to be. College bound. So, I'm not crazy."

With a smile on my face widest as the Nile River, I say, "I can understand that."

He laughs, "Yeah right…"

We give our names to Ms. Hunter; she looks up as if to ask, "Are you serious?"

While we are standing waiting for her validation, we exchange numbers, and he whispers, "We need to hook up." I look at him like ohh yeahh… but then I remember Drew, so I say, "Just call me." With this sheepish grin, he replies, "Ok cool, by the way, you know you are cute for a little girl."

What!!! Did he call me a little girl? Uhn, uhn… No Mr., you got me all twisted. Anyway!

☙

By the time I get to my locker, my crew is already waiting for me. We do our iconic hot GEMS call. Altogether, with two snaps, we say, "Flawlesssss!" sealed with a "Smooches!!" So many girls have been dying to become GEMS it's not funny. I started the group two years ago. At first it was just Angel and I. We go way back, I'm talking about preschool. She's a "PK." Her dad's a Pastor, and if you know like I do; she's far from the "good girl" kinda like "not-so-good girl," can't tell her parents that though, she's got them wrapped around her fingers, much like I do. She lost her virginity last year to Da'Quan McElmore a.k.a. Da-Da, humph, he ain't hitting on two cents; LMBO! Nevertheless, Angel and Da-Da are still kicking it, although he tries to act like he's so much, I'm not impressed. I guess she thinks he's all that because his dad plays for the Falcons. Like I said, I'm not impressed. Get me a championship ring then I might be excited.

I'm trippin' because my girl Dionne is all psyched out because she just found out her transfer has been approved for the year, annnd her financial aid has been approved. Dionne is my home-girl that lives over off Donald Lee Hollowell b.k.a. Bankhead! Actually, she's from New York; Brooklyn to be exact. Can you say all the way BK? Just remembered she went with us the last time we went back to NY, when I saw my grandparents. We had so much fun, too much to be honest. It was all good until we got caught trying to catch the train to Queens to kick it with these Muslim dudes Aswan and Malik. Malik, Malik, Malik. I was so feeling him. He was actually one of the finest brothers up until I met my Drew. Her parents have pretty much been separated for the longest. Right now, she lives with her Dad; he drives for MARTA, and trust she really cashes in, her hustle is selling dag-on Breeze Cards, and trusts the girl gets her paper! I just feel sorry for her sometimes; because her dad is down on his luck a lot. I wish my father could help find him a job, but in the meantime, it's all good Dee will make a way; she's another Quinn. Hardcore! But the girls gear is always fye. She has this home-boy from around the way that stays hooking her up with the latest and flyest of everything. I've never seen anyone that has so much Michael Kors, Jimmy Choo, or Tory Burch, and they live in the hood!! The day she rocked that Louis Vuitton at the Honors Assembly, it was a given, she had to be a GEM. Keep in mind it was a runway bag! Ain't no anybody just gonna have that.

"It's so on," she screams. "Your girl is about to be rolling in this joint fo' real. I'm about to give Rasheed a call right now. Last I saw him; he had that new Michael Kors Satchel. I gots to have that one."

Right now I'm thinking, honey that bag is so at least $450. How much is your financial aid? Or better yet, how long is it going to take for that gold to turn Santo Gold? I will have to examine that to make sure it's actually Michael Kors, and not Mikey Kors.

"Oh, Jazmine doesn't do 'Street Release'." LOL! Leave it up to Jaz. This girl here is a trip, always speaking in third person. She really thinks of herself as this glorified fashion police, in which this could mainly be due to her mother being a Stylist at Barney's. It's always good to have a friend whose mom can get you into the most high profile fashion shows. The one time her mom came with that black lace Stella McCartney gown, I think my mom was like the mother ship has finally come in… From that point, they have been the best of friends. Mom bought it to wear to the Met Ball, and as much it costs, I don't blame her. Shoot that's like the Super Bowl to the fashion world, and you best know it, if there is such a thing, my mother Victoria Bouviér brought home the trophy.

Jaz continues to rag on Dee, but not long before Dee goes Brooklyn on her.

"Oh slow your roll!" Dionne blurts out. "How you just gonna think my bags are knock off?" Everyone looks at me!

೧

Saved by the bell. Third period it is; PE. Me, Lorna, and Bree are all taking PE together. Oh it's about to be on. Before I can put my things down, Bree is already cheezing in the

His Grace, His Blood, His Mercy!

Coach's face. If anybody hates dressing out for PE, it's her. We have always janked her about her being knock-kneed, could be why she mostly wears pants. On Chapel days, it's hilarious; this is the only time you will find her wearing a skirt. To me she doesn't look that bad, but the boys think otherwise. Oh she's pretty, thick, wavy jet-black hair, size four. She's forever bragging about her Native Indian heritage. What is it, one-fourth Cherokee? Granddaddy Winston is always saying everybody wants to be Cherokee. Just so happens out of all of us, she's the tallest. Plus, she's the Head Master's daughter, so you already know who gets the preferential treatment. We've been friends since fifth grade. Actually she was on the junior debate team, and at the time I was competing for Nationals. After school she'd ask to study with me, and before long we were both competing for the Tournament of Champions. Her plan is to go to Yale Law School. I can see that, because she's smart enough, doesn't really have much of a fashion sense, but she's cool.

"Gabrielle, how are you today?" Coach asks.

"I'm doing well Coach. Just getting ready for Track and Field, I can' wait."

By the look on his face he can't either. Last year we won Best All Around in our division. I love running. It's the few times I truly can be free. Free from all the pressure of being such a smart little girl. When I'm on the track, I forget all about having to think about this and that, I just run, and run I do. The 400's yes! I be killin' 'em. I realized a long time ago just how much I loved it when I was visiting my grandparents in BK and some of my friends would always challenge me to race them. I always won! Always! It was to the point they would actually put up money to see me race. Still to this day I think my Granddaddy Winston had a bet going on me. I was only seven, and he had a jersey made for me that reads "guépard" means cheetah in French. Since then I have been his little "guépard."

༄

PE was a breeze, didn't do today much though, still trippin' off of Lorna. First day of school, and she gets her period today! Dag that sucks, big time. She was really uncomfortable. We've all talked about it, so no biggy to me. I'm a vet in that area; keep a stash of "Always" in the locker. Never know when Aunt Flo may just show up. Come to think of it, who came up with that stupid name anyway? Aunt Flo. When it comes, it doesn't remind me anything of an Auntie of mine. Not nice at all, painful and just plain disgusting. I want to know why do we, girls have to deal with all that nasty crap, and all the boys have to deal with is getting a hard on in public. Go figure. Then we have to deal with it for over three days. Yuck! Whoever tied that into womanhood was on some other stuff.

Lorna is pretty cool though, her Dad plays for the Falcon's and you already know we love it during game time. They're in pre-season now, but I can't wait until the regular season, it's going to be so on. VIP suites, the works, he and my Dad Marcel hang out from time to time, whenever he's in town.

Oh heck no! What's up with this? Ol' girl seems to be putting her things in locker 531. That's the biggest locker in the school. I have been trying to get this locker for a minute now. We all have. Not sure if this is true, but rumor has it that

His Grace, His Blood, His Mercy!

when the school was built they mistakenly made one locker wayyy too big, like big enough for three people to share. How did she get it? Last I heard, Administration stated they were not allowing anyone to have it. Inquiring minds want to know, earlier today she was two down, but now what has happened since that time? Sarah will know. She gets all the info. Gotta love that chick. She keeps us well informed of everything. I've never seen someone that knows everything about a person just by speaking to them. We joke with her all the time. She's our modern day Miss Cleo. The girl swears she can tell your future, for a small minimal fee that is, ten dollars to be exact. I used to think she was playing, but once I started to see some of her things she told people were actually happening. I was like, oh ok. Just maybe she might be on to something. Now, the one person that has proven to be a thorn in all of our side is Sarah's little sister, Morgan, she's worse than Sarah, we can't do anything around her. She tells everything!! A seven-year-old tattletale… But we will not let her get in our way, at least we hope she doesn't. Nevertheless, I immediately put Sarah on to the locker situation, because right now I don't have time to deal with it. Bigger fish to fry. Need my phone back!

☙

Before heading to lunch, this dude Romerius, who thinks he's God's gift to this world, comes by my locker and hands me this invite to his party. Tells me it's a must I be there, well we know that, just didn't realize he knew it! It says it's supposed to at Etcetera. Ok then. Ahmmm I forgot just that quick, not sure if I'm welcome there.

Drew still hasn't called, texted, anything. Well I wouldn't know. Mrs. Darrington has my phone! Uugggh, this is so hard. I need my phone. I know by now I have several missed texts. Why did I even think that? Here comes Angel.

"Girl, what happened to your phone? It's all over the school, the smart girl's phone got taken away, and you know you had best get that back before–"

"Yeah I know. Who you telling?"

We both are thinking the same thing. My momma is crazy!

She keeps talking. "You get your invite? First party of the year?"

"Of course I got it. Duh. Just a little skeptical about it being at Etcetera."

"Why? He ain't still trippin' like that is he?"

"I would say so, he hasn't responded to any of my texts."

"Text him from my phone, he won't know, just say you are using my phone."

"Cool."

I am really hoping he would at least respond back, knowing it's me.

"Did you bring your lunch today, she asks."

We laugh, because we know I always have my lunch. Drago, my Mom's Chef fixes it for me every day. Today it's Tuna over wheat with pistachios, and can't forget the famous Drago salad. It's always something new. I've been begging this man to give me something unhealthy for the longest, it hasn't happened yet. Oh let me not forget the bottled water. My mother is also a health nut. I'm guessing she is in the gym right now, either that or on some business call.

Just as we head back to class, she yells, "Gab, it's him!"
I read the text.
"How can I help you?"
I respond. "It's me… Gabby. Y haven't u responded 2 me?"
He texts back. "Whose phn is this?"
Hurriedly I reply, "My girl Angel's."
No response back.

☙

This is not usual, but I'm so over this day! Right as the final bell rings, Dionne runs up to me and gives me today's list of requests. I'm cracking up, because it's only day one, and we've gotten nine requests to join the GEMS so far, this just may be the best initiation yet. Overall, I could say today went well just wish I could get Drew off my mind. If it's the last thing I do, I am going to get with him, and then, it will be just us two.

Dag, I just realized, my phone, not again, my teacher has it! I know Mom has been trying to call me to let me know she's on the way. Hopefully she'll know I'm in the regular spot. Better yet, I'll call from Angel's phone and tell her I lost it somehow, or I guess I can say I left it in my bag in my locker. Either way, this is not looking good.

Waiting I remember Romerius' invite, people have been talking about it all day, from what I hear, they are talking EPIC. Suddenly, someone taps me on my shoulder. Rishard! Where did he come from?! Ooh this boy is so fine.

"Hey you, looking good in your little school girl uniform."

I'm caught off guard, but I respond, "Hey, what's up?"

Knowing dag on well this dude does not attend this school, I don't know what to do. Mom is on the way here too. I'm nervous as all get out.

He continues, "So, did you get the invite from my little cousin Ro?"

I'm like, "Yeah, so is it his party or yours?" Regardless, I know now more than ever I need to be there. It's a must!

"It's the crews' party. You know the 4-2-0 Crew. Remember?"

I hurriedly say yes, as not to seem so blah.

"Lady I need you there, you and your girls. It's going to be the shiznyee!

Laughing I say, "Oh, so you now you Lil' Scrappy?"

"Naw boo, I'm me all day long. I just need you to make it, alright."

Before I know it, out of nowhere he point blank plants a kiss on me that just want wait. No, I'm serious. I'm so messed up now, panties and all.

Just then I see my mom turning in. As fast as I can, I say, "It's my mom—"

"Cool. It's ok. If you don't mind, I'll hit you up tonight."

I'm still trippin' from the kiss, I mumble, "Oh-oh-ok."

Again I remember my phone. I try yelling to him, but he's disappeared. I guess this

is what they mean when they say, "pulled a ninja."

Chapter Four

Victoria, like any other day, business as usual...

This must be one of the worst days I've had in a while… I don't even remember. Marcel being gone so much is really taking a toll on me. I never thought moving to Atlanta would prove to be such a lonely experience. In between church, Gabby, work, the foundation, amongst the other charity organizations, my life is nonstop. I have not had any time for just me. Demetrius is constantly telling me I need a break. The one good thing is that since the economy has turned around, business has picked up, and hopefully for the best.

Can you believe it, the one minute I try to sneak in a quick nap, my phone is going off. I try to act as if I don't hear it, but what if it's important? It'll have to wait. I knew it. Not going to happen. Somehow I find the strength to roll over and listen to the eight voicemails just before the one that sends me right over the edge. Mrs. Darrington, Gabs' principal, has asked that I call her at my earliest convenience. What in the world could they want now? We've already made our contribution for this quarter. My first mind is telling me to call her back, but the other one is pulling me back to the bed, saying lie down, and rest. Only because I know she's calling I do what any parent would do, I call back, and to my surprise it's not about a donation.

"Hello Mrs. Darrington, this is Victoria Bouviér, how are you this afternoon?"

In her kiss up voice, she says, "Well hello to you also Mrs. Bouviér. Hope I didn't disturb you, but I thought you may want to know that Gabrielle has had several issues this past week with having her phone out during class."

I'm hearing this, but I do not believe it. I know we have had one too many talks about that phone. Now she doesn't want me to flip out on her.

"In both her History and Chemistry classes the instructor has had to remove the phone from her at least twice. I'm sure she is well aware of the consequences that come along with having the teacher confiscate her phone. She's been given a warning thus far, and the next time she will receive five demerits, and then after that, she will have to attend detention, then if the situation has not resolved itself, she will have to attend Saturday school. I'm sure that it will not get to that point."

Here is where the Brooklyn chick wants to come out, but I pull it together; I do remember, that's not how a quote-unquote Godly woman should act. But, for this one minute I remember first and foremost I'm a Christian mother and I know there has to be somewhere in the bible where it talks about beating

His Grace, His Blood, His Mercy!

the hell out of your child; especially when you have told her to keep the phone put up at all times while you are in school.

Taking a slow deep breath, I respond. "Thank you so much Mrs. Darrington for informing me of Gabrielle's behavior. However, apparently this has happened before, in which I would have appreciated it if once it happened I would have been notified then, not several days later."

"I do understand, Mrs. Bouviér, but I wanted to allow her an opportunity to correct it herself."

"I appreciate that, but just so we are clear, I am the parent, and so that there are no misunderstandings, if in the future she gets out of line in anyway, I want to be contacted immediately. Again, I am thankful for you letting me know, and trust me this will not happen again."

"Have a wonderful day, Mrs. Bouviér, and again thank you for that generous donation."

"You're welcome, and you have a great day as well."

I'm not sure what has gotten into Gabby lately. Since the girl has turned thirteen, she's changed. Momma warned me. I don't recall being this way at thirteen. If it's not an iPhone, iPad, iPod, these children these days could care less about it. I remember when the phone would just ring, you would answer it, and maybe your parents had the *call-waiting* feature, to click over and have someone else on the line, but now… hell you can even see the people you are talking to! Facetime! Have it your way! But not today, her behind is mine; MY WAY!

It never stops, my phone is going off again, but this time it's a reminder. My four o'clock meeting today with John Hobbs of Atlanta University, which now is a multi-billion dollar endowment. I've been managing this fund for I know the last eight years; they are one of my largest investors, with a portfolio of over 3,000 different investments in stocks, bonds, venture capitals, real estate, and energy, along with other investments. Since I first began managing the fund, its value has basically tripled from 1.5 billion to now well over 6.9 billion. Even with the fall of the market we were still able to maintain. With management fees, and incentive fees, after everything is completed I stand to gain 56,105 million. I realize hedging is very risky, especially knowing I have 35% of our own internal capital invested, but I also know in this business you have to play to win, and in saying that I have been on a winning streak for some months now. The numbers prove it, 20% returns! Never in a million years would I think I would see the day where Diamond Management would have a total in assets of five billion. Yes Lord I thank you, but next to you, I know Marcel has been my greatest asset. I am so grateful that I have him here with me to share in all of it, although there was that time... Thinking back, 2011 was horrible, actually it was a very trying time for the market in general. Never thought of giving up, but it was a mess, 20-30 losses. I had just begun to really start seeing great returns. The Diamond Investment Fund definitely put the company in the Billion Dollar Club! Though I just don't get the feeling I used to get. Maybe it's because I have not been able to share a lot of my success with the one person who it all began with. I know I shouldn't be selfish, but I would be lying to myself if I didn't say that sometimes I wished we didn't have these billion dollar conglomerates. For some reason, it seems like that's all it's about. But when I begin to think that way, I remind myself that I fell in love with a man that has, and always will be a go getter. He loves what he does, and for the best part, he loves me. Right now, I just want him to come home.

☙

Two and a half hours later, I pick Gabby up from school. Just like any other day she seems as if everything in her world is A-ok, but I know different. I try to give her the chance to tell me before I take the liberty and turn into Mommy Dearest. I take one look at her, and suddenly I see her father all over her. I think back to his determination to go as far as he could to hide a lie! Even when I knew beyond a shadow of a doubt that he was not where he said he was… Okay Vic, come back. Woosa!

West Paces Ferry is backed up for some reason today. It has to be an accident; we have been sitting here for what seems like forever. I turn down the volume on the radio.

"Gabrielle, how was your day?" I give her the chance to NOT lie.

"It was ok."

"Just ok?"

I don't remember the last time this child said school was "just ok."

"Yes ma'am. I made an 'A' on my Chem exam. I made an 'A' on my quiz in Lit. Ummm, what else? Oh yes, I was asked to serve on the Student Board, again."

By listening to her, I can tell she is trying everything to avoid telling me.

"Have you talked to your father?"

A sudden silence hits the car. Maybe it's selective hearing. I will try this once more.

"Have you talked to your father this week? He called, and he says he's being discharged sometime tomorrow."

Coughing, clearing her throat. "No ma'am, I haven't talked to him."

"Maybe you should call him."

Sometimes I have to laugh at myself. No, now I'm laughing at her. This stupid look she is giving me.

"I will call him tonight, when I'm done with homework."

I can't resist. I pull an okee-doke on her. I come to a stop light. Push her number to dial her phone over the speakers in the car. Straight to voicemail.

"Gabrielle, I'm going to ask you this one time. Where is your phone?"

Lord have mercy, the girl is going as far as to look for it. She looks in her purse, even in her backpack.

"I left it at school."

I try to refrain from pulling the car over, but I'm afraid that the police at this cross walk will take me right to the people. Did she just lie to me like that?

"I talked to Mrs. Darrington today. Perhaps does she have your phone? Or does one of your instructors have it?"

She's probably hoping I am on a slow fall to hell as we speak. Out of nowhere she goes into this whole spill about how she was not on her phone, it was another student, but the teacher keeps saying it's her, and she feels that she is being treated unfairly. She feels as though their rights have been taken away! Excuse me! So now I'm raising Gabrielle Mathis? Although, Judge Mathis is fine now.

"Little girl, what do I look like to you? Do you think I was born yesterday?"

She mumbles under her breath, "No ma'am."

"Per Mrs. Darrington, you have been having this issue with your phone being taken away all this week, and I knew you didn't have it, but I wanted you to tell me. When did you start lying like this? I'm more disappointed than anything."

Whenever I say I'm disappointed that just about kills her.

"So… this is what we are going to do. Until you can prove to me that you are responsible enough to handle a phone, you WILL NOT have that one any longer. I will supply you with a company phone that is to be strictly used for emergency calls only. And if I find out that you are using it for anything outside of that then you belong to me. Do I make myself clear?"

"Yes ma'am."

Right at this moment, I'm so missing Marcel. If I could just get a hug or something, maybe that will make me feel better. Only one more day. He's been gone now for three weeks, but it feels more like three months. I'm looking forward to spending some quality time. We need it, we both have been crazy busy lately. I thought that by letting go of a lot of the responsibilities things would have eased up a bit. It has gotten more stressful. Well it could be that I need to go in for my three month checkup too.

My phone rings, its Demetrius. Business as usual. I answer and I can tell he is somewhere ordering something to eat. I promise this man is always patronizing somebody's eating establishment.

"Victoria, don't forget the meeting this evening at six. We've got to push this deal through. Plus, we've got to get ready for the Annual Charity Ball next month, as well as you have several women that are wanting to get you on their schedules for The Premiere Leaders Executive Conference. Oh yes, by the way, what do you plan to do about your trip to Washington?"

I'm so used to this now; I am like a sponge that soaks it all up. I will say, Demetrius has been my saving grace. He keeps it all together for me. He's been with me since we first moved here. It was hard to let Melissa go at first, but it was a mutual decision. After she got married, they had my Godson, Austin, and then Bailey, so it was best. I made sure they were well taken care of. Last I talked to her; she was doing the soccer mom thingy. I tried that. Umm, let's just say I'm not that Mom. I would love to be, but Good Jesus, with all the events Gabby has to attend, my schedule, Marcel's schedule; it's just way too much. I realized a long time ago, I needed a personal assistant, plus I needed someone that could help me balance out everything at home. Thank God for Samantha. She's a Godsend. Even though she's my go to girl for everything that I can't do, I still make it my business to be Mommy. I admit, while I'm traveling, it hurts that I can't be at all of Gabby's meetings, but trust me I am well informed. I trust her with my life.

"Demetrius, I will be at the meeting. I'm headed home now to drop off Gabby.

I'm sure this won't be a hard deal to get. They seemed very eager to go with my suggestions. Our last conference call went very well."

"Well, I'm getting a bite to eat before then. You know, I can't do business on an empty stomach."

Laughing, I reply, "You can't do much of anything on an empty stomach."

"Hey Gabby!" he yells over the speaker.

She's still upset about the phone thing I'm guessing. She will be just fine. There is no way I am going to let a thirteen year old rule me. She has me way wrong. I know I can be a tad bit overbearing at times, but I do this because I love her so much, and if anything ever happened to her, well I don't even want to think like that.

"Hey Gabby!", he shouts again. "Is she on that phone?"

I say loud as I can so that she can hear me, "She doesn't have it! She left it at school. She can't seem to live without it apparently; at least that's what her principal says."

She yells back in a tone I've never heard before, "Momma stop telling everybody my business!"

Don't know what has made my foot immediately hit the brakes, press the car in park, and turn around and knock the hell out of her. It could be my first reaction, or it could be the fact that I WILL NOT tolerate it now, or ever; her talking to me or any adult like that. Where did that come from? She has never done anything like that before. Even though I do realize she is at that age where Momma calls it, 'starting to smell herself', but Lord help me, if it is going to be like this… ooh baby. I settle back into my seat, get a quick glance in the rearview mirror, the tears are flowing like crazy down her face. I don't think she expected that. I didn't either.

"Victoria, Victor-i-a!" OMG, Demetrius is still on the phone. Does he ever stop?

"Yes I'm here. I had to handle a situation right fast."

He does this smooth like croon, "Ok Momma, come back. Breathe. Take a deep breath."

He's right. I'm not sure what happened, but that did something to me. My head is hurting something awful. Just as I'm pulling into the driveway, the phone beeps in, it's my honey! Suddenly it all seems better. Gabrielle, grabs her things jumps out of the car, throws her book bag over her shoulder and I think that's a slam of the door, maybe I could be wrong, knowing I just went Madea on her. But, I will deal with that in a minute.

The voice on the other end, says, "Hey you." It never fails, whenever he calls, it makes my entire world seem like it's all right. Goose bumps every time.

I breathe. "Hey sweetie."

"How are you today?" he asks.

I chime in. "I was doing great until about fifteen minutes ago."

"What happened fifteen minutes ago?"

"Gabby happened fifteen minutes ago. She yelled at me, and I'm not sure where it came from, all I know is that if–"

"Wait, wait, wait, wait, wait. She yelled?!" He never raises his voice. "What was that about? Don't tell me, the B-O-Y-S.'"

As much as I hate that thought, I'm actually glad to tell him no.

"So what was it?"

"The phone."

He chuckles. For some reason this really isn't all that funny to me. "The dreaded phone fight again. We discussed that before you even got that phone for her. I was against it from the beginning."

He is always so right. I just didn't think it would be this hard. She's always been such a good child. Never would I think some electronic device would bring so much discourse between us.

"Yes baby you are right, you were right. I'm starting to regret it." Did I just say that? What is wrong with me? It's not like me to be so understanding. Well it is him. He has this effect on me.

He goes on. "I will talk to her tomorrow when I get in, but now I'm calling to make sure my lady is good. I miss you a lot, and I can't wait to see you. These trips are wearing me down, and the more I am away from you, it only makes it worse."

What you say! He does it again. Reads my mind. This man, this man. Lord I thank you for him.

"Yes, I feel you. I was saying the same thing just yesterday."

"I'm trying to work on some things that will hopefully mean less travel. That way I can work more East Coast. Although you know the West Coast is our largest source."

"I know."

He senses the sadness in my voice.

"Hey how about tomorrow night, meet me at the Sheraton. Got a little something for you."

Oh he's definitely reading my mind. Q-Time it is. I look over at the clock, it's ten past five. My meeting.

"Sweetie, I have a six o'clock meeting with the Diaz'. Need to get the deal done."

In a reassuring tone, he sings, "That's my girl. Handle your business. Go get 'em' honey. Call you later. I love you."

My heart settles. Still feels like the day we crossed paths.

Peacefully I say. "I love you, too."

He ends by saying, "Give Gabs a kiss for me. Tell her I love her too."

※

Before heading out, I can't help but snatch some of that whatever Drago is cooking up, looks to be his famous Jalapeno Cilantro casserole. Having him has proved the next best thing next to sliced bread.

Gabrielle runs through to the kitchen, and says to me, "Have a good meeting Mom."

Who is that? That's not the same child I just dealt with. I say to her. "Thanks baby. I love you. We will talk later this evening if it's not too late. Samantha is here if you need her. Remember what I told you."

I hear the home phone ringing, while I'm walking out of the door, and at the same time my cell is ringing. It's Demetrius.

"I'm leaving now."

"Just checking. You know how you are."

"Well I had to change clothes."

"My point exactly; it was nothing wrong with what you had on before."

"Really, Demetrius?"

"Yes, really."

We go round and round about this all the time. He says he has never seen a woman that has as many clothes and shoes as I do. I think he exaggerates a bit, but as my CoCo motto goes "A girl should be two things, classy, and fabulous."

I finally pull into *Aria*, and allow this handsome gentleman in valet to take over the Tesla, my new toy. I think I've fallen in love with it just on the fact that once you get a first glance, its look can be so deceiving, an electrical powered beast! OMG, a full glass panoramic roof! Oh and I have to hit myself when I get a quick glance of the "red brake calipers", sometimes I don't know if I love this more than my S550… can't think like that. I miss my baby so much. Mmm, mmm, mmm, this is sad, I'm reminiscing over a car. Well everyone has their vices, and mine is a beautifully crafted luxury vehicle!

As I walk in I'm still thinking about how Daddy is still angry with me over the car, if it was up to him we would own nothing else but Benz'. The biggest fight came when my sweetie gave me a Bentley Continental Flying Spur for my tenth anniversary. Daddy lost it! Until Marcel had a customized GT convertible sent to him for his 60th birthday, and I promise since then, haven't heard too much from him. Not too much, only when he feels the need to let us know that it was actually given to HIM and not Momma. Even after all of this time, she still would prefer to drive her classic 500 SEL! The older the better…

Before I can be seated, Mrs. Diaz is waving me down, already at the table. That's what I'm talking about, an eager client, ready to invest. Seemingly, they have already ordered their drinks. Looks as though Mr. Diaz is sipping on a glass of Zinfandel, but it looks like the Mrs. is going at it pretty hard. She is already asking the waiter to send over another Kamikaze. Just after I am seated here comes Demetrius, ready, in full work flow mode!

☙

An hour and several drinks later, the Diaz' have agreed to invest in the Diamond Fund. Yes! This is why I do what I do. I absolutely love it when a deal comes through, and as far as Mr. Demetrius, oh he did that thing. He really was a great asset, in which he always is, but I think today he just was so much more focused. I truly believe that they are pleased with their decisions, so now we just have to let the third party do their thing.

I pull my phone out to check to see if I have any Gabs alerts, but to my pleasure there are none, there are only love texts from Marcel. You have got to love a man that is always doing wonderful things for you. The meeting is just now over, and he has sent me a text that says, "Congratulations babe, so proud of you, knew you would do it." Even though I've done this a few times now, it is just something about the way he makes me feel, even so many miles away. Lucky is what I am. Yes that's it. Lucky.

Chapter Five

Victoria, Teenager 101

I'm home a little later than I expected. Unbeknownst to me, Gabby's up waiting for me. Now that's funny, I was on my way to her. Still can't believe how she acted earlier.

As I put my things on the counter, I grab a glass of water out of the fridge. I try to resist, but I can't help it, I take a little bite off of some of Drago's apple tarts. My weakness.

"How did everything go?" she asks.

As to not let her know how surprised I am to hear her ask, I respond, "It went well, very well, I must say."

She continues, "So Momma, when did you say your conference was going to be?"

"That has not been confirmed as of yet, but actually it's Mid October. Why?"

With those eyes that always get me, she says, "Oh, no reason." It's here I start to have a conversation with myself, and I ask myself, *"Now self, do you believe this, or is the work of a teenagers mind?"* I go in harder. Plus this is most definitely not the same child from earlier, I don't think.

"Well it must be a reason you asked. You've never really cared about any of my functions, so why now?"

"She leans over to me, and puts her head on my shoulder, and says, "Mom I'm just interested, no big deal."

I'm like, really Gabrielle? My Mother puts it best. When it comes to a child, leave nothing unturned. Everything is a big deal.

I suddenly switch the subject, and ask her, "So what was that all about earlier young lady, did you think I had forgotten about that?"

Turning her head toward the floor she musters up enough to say, "Like, ahhm, well, Mom, you know it was just that I was a little frustrated from what happened at school today. I knew my phone shouldn't have been taken from me, and that I really tried to explain to Principal Darrington that I won't do it anymore; especially that Bree and I are girls and all. I thought she would have a little sympathy for me."

I look her in her eyes, and I try to explain this to her so that she really understands this in a motherly tone. I tell her, "Gabs, I understand that there are going to be times where you may feel that you have been wronged, and that everyone else is out to get you. I know that you may have felt you did the proper thing in explaining that you should not have gotten your phone taken. BUT, I am going to tell you this only once more, you will no longer have that phone until I say otherwise. Remember your phone is a company phone and I will know if you are not doing what you are supposed to do.

She yells at me, "A company phone! But Momma, all my—"

"Excuse me, so you're yelling at me?"

Hands flailing, eyebrows raised, she continues to pitch a fit, and over a damn phone. This is not happening. You would think I just told her we were moving to Augusta, Georgia. Well if that was the case then I could understand this blow up.

She screams, "You can't take my phone, Daddy gave it to me!"

I further find myself explaining, "First of all, it's not yours, it's mine! I'm only allowing you to use it!"

All of a sudden, I get an instantaneous headache! A hot and flushed feeling comes over me.

She puffs up, and takes several steps back from me, as if she has something she really wants to say. I plant my feet on the floor, and I find myself getting into a stance kinda like Laila Ali at this moment, because Lord Jesus, she don't want this! How does the saying go, *"I bought you in this world, and I will take you out."* She doesn't even have a clue. With all I've been through. On a day where I just made a few million dollars too! Uh, Uh, the girl storms out of the room, grumbling, "I'm going to my room!" I manage to pull this one deep down in the belly, because I have to remind her, and while doing it, I hear myself hollering at her, "Oh and just so you know, that room is not yours either, that's mine too!!" Her door slams! Before I know it, I'm doing a Flo-Jo, and I'm up the stairs. Whoever put these doors in, must have known I would one day have to tear them down!

Heart racing. I bam on the door, "Open this door!"

No response. I continue to beat on MY DOOR, like a mad woman, all at the same time, tears flowing, because I cannot believe that I am having a brawl with my thirteen-year old daughter. Where did this go wrong? Where did I go wrong?

After what seems like an eternity she opens the door with blood shot eyes. And yes I'm so ready to knock her from one side of this room to the next. But suddenly I look at her, my little girl, the one who has never really done anything out of order, never given me any trouble, and all I want to do is hug her, and then I'm reminded, *"Spare the rod, spoil the child"*… So in saying that, I go ham!

※

Somehow, last night seems like a memory. But, right now it's just what the doctor ordered. An eighty-minute hot stone massage, pure relaxation at its best. When I arrive he already has our itinerary planned. Seven o'clock couples massage, nine forty –five, a private dinner in the Café, and afterwards all it says is a surprise. His thoughtfulness is just mind-blowing; I mean he never leaves anything to chance.

I stand in awe, gazing out of the glorious bay window twenty two floors up. Each time we've been here we've always requested suite 2231. It always makes me feel like a home away from home, even if it is only for the weekend. I walk over to the Grand piano, run my fingers over the keys. I began to play *Nadia's Theme"* the song of "The Young and the Restless." I know this because; it's how far I got in high school. Momma laughs and says the lessons paid off. I don't think so, since I've never showed much interest in the piano since then.

Silence falls over the room. I feel him watching me. I turn around and there he is, standing in the door picture perfect.

His Grace, His Blood, His Mercy!

A tailored Grey Burberry Plaid Suit, white silk shirt, black Ferragamo oxfords, and to top it off the Fatknots purple paisley bow tie Gabby gave him for Father's Day last year. Lord have mercy! Still after all of this time, this man can send chills up my spine. Oh, is that an orchid I see in his hands? It is. I walk over to him, and I find myself in his arms, the safest place a woman would ever want to be.

With a kiss to the forehead, he whispers, "Je t'aime."

Damn he smells so good. What is that? Right now I'm so ready to have him next to me; my mind escapes any thoughts outside of that.

"Je t'aime plus," I tell him back.

I pull into him as if this is the last time that I will ever see him. I wish we could stay right here, but he has something else on his mind. He walks me over to the bed, runs his fingers up the back of my hair, and fondles my earlobe in the right spot. He's taking me there. I try to sneak a peek at the clock, six thirteen. We'll have time before our massages. He catches me looking, grabs my face with both hands, and puts his tongue so deep down my throat you'd think he's mining for diamonds. I can tell he has missed me.

This man is not stopping. He continues to kiss me up and down my neck, how much I have missed this. He's so good at this. Yes, he's been away more times than I can count, but umm, right now he is pulling out all of the stops. Right before I can get in a word, he places my legs in what feels like a figure eight position and makes love to me like never before. I'm pulling at whatever my hands can grab hold to. He's whispering in my ear how much he has missed me, which is driving me insane. Is it okay to call on Jesus right now, because trust me he lets me take the lead, and that I do. Slowly I strategically position myself above him, wrap my hands around it, guide it to where it needs to be, take one big breath, inhale, and I go for what I know. It's sooo hard; just how I like it. He moans, and so do I. I pick up a pace that I didn't even realize I had. I'm breathing faster as I hear him tell me he needs me which sends my body into a shuttering mess. Seems like my Kegel exercises are paying off. Just by the look on his face, I know they are.

Just as I'm arriving at a place that God and the Angels reside, his phone, that damn phone, has gone off more than usual, and rarely does he let it ring out loud, but I guess he was so excited to get to me he forgot to turn it off. Though I could swear there was a ringtone for one of the calls. No, couldn't be. He doesn't even believe in contact pictures, not even mine. May it be that I was just caught up in the moment? I know what I heard.

꿈

A few hours later, I'm so relaxed. Jay and Cree are two of the best masseuses in Atlanta. Marcel is feeling some type of way too.

"I was thinking I would have Franck put together a little something for us." He says while scanning the menu. "Are you okay with that?"

Blushing I reply, "Fine with me."

Of course I know he is going to go with the Gazpacho Soup to start. It's his favorite. Me, I think I will have the Asparagus

His Grace, His Blood, His Mercy!

Salad. Especially after a workout like I just had. I'm a little embarrassed to think that I might need two.

My phone vibrates, it's Demetrius, he never calls me when he knows Marcel and I are having couples weekend. I take one look at it, and put it back down. Whatever it is will have to wait. Marcel takes a sip of his wine.

"How was your trip?"

"Business as usual babe. You know how it is."

I take a look at him and I remember again just why I fell in love with him. Thinking back to the time in my life where I was at my lowest, and it seemed as God sent him to me at the perfect time. I didn't realize it then, but every day of my life I can't think of anyone else I would rather spend my life with. We toast to us. Sit and watch an older couple as the glide across the floor, so in love. I can only hope and pray that we make it that long. Just before he asks me to dance, my phone rings again. It's Malcolm. WTH! My first mind tells me not to answer, but something in me tells me something is not quite right.

"Baby it's Malcolm," I say.

He nods, giving me the right of way to go ahead and take the call.

"Yes Malcolm, what's up?"

First I don't hear anything, then for a moment I can tell, he's calling from inside of a hospital room. I know things went horribly wrong for us; I just still hate it when he's admitted.

A raspy voice on the other end says, "Victoria, I need you."

Trying to disguise my facial expression, I respond in a light tone, "Excuse me, could you repeat that?"

Again, he musters up the nerve, "Vic, I need you."

Now, here he comes on some other stupid stuff. I don't have time for this right now.

Judging by my actions I guess, Marcel, interrupts, "You good baby?"

"Yes baby, I'm good."

Malcolm presses. "I've been needing to talk to you for quite some time now, is now a good time?"

Hurriedly I respond, "Actually it's not, can we discuss this maybe later this week?"

A hushed silence comes through, along with a sigh of frustration. "Yeah that's cool."

I'm like, really Malcolm. Are you serious right now?

The phone goes dead.

After that foolishness, it doesn't take me long at all to get back to my Mr. Man. All I need is to just to get a quick look at this man sitting across from me, and I'm back. Thank you Lord. Never thought I could love someone so much that even the site of them makes me wanna hurry up, get through this meal, get back to where we left off. From the way he looks, he's thinking the exact same thing. Especially the way he slowly takes his tongue and runs it around the rim of that wine glass, as if he is about to go where no one has ever gone before. "Check please!!!"

Chapter Six

Quinn, its midnight, time to get it ready...

Rocking that Bey, "Partition," I'm lying here thinking about who and what I need to be doing before I go back to that hell hole of a school. Pretty much spent my whole check on those tacky ass uniforms. Grams can only help out as much as her Social Security check allows. It's a good thing I work at the Wing Spot on Candler. It helps keep a little money in my pocket. Plus, I got this little side kick job every other weekend at the movie theatre. But, what really helps is the cheese I get from what the Rule Book calls "Sponsors". Now, according to the Rule Book, a Sponsor is an individual who pays for your food, your clothing, your vacations, your extra- curricular activities, and may even pay for your alcohol. A sponsor also provides transportation when needed. So we are clear in some instances, depending how you roll, this could be male or female. So now I'm working four at a time. There is Derrick, the truck driver who just can't get enough of what he calls me, his midnight rider. Then, there is Claude, my French lover, I like to call him Papi, he is the owner of that Little French bistro in Downtown Decatur. Oh yes, there is my favorite, Rhasan, my Jamaican, all da way from King-ston! Hung like what!! Scared a sistah so bad the first time I vowed after him no more, but after a taste of the Oxtails, Peas, and rice Mon, Jerk Chicken, and the ackee fish, it was all over. Did I say that he works over at the car dealership in Tucker, also he works for Juelle on the side running product and he works part time for the car wash on the weekends. Then there is my little best kept secret, this fine ass brother that has been trying to get at me for a minute now. It's crazy, we haven't exchanged anything such as sex thus far, but he comes to the Spot regularly, and always leaves a fat tip for me. All I know is that he drives what looks to be a 2013 or 14 White Range Rover Sport. He says he prefers not to give me his number just yet; he calls it the thrill of the chase. Out of all of them, the one that has been most consistent when I really needed them, or even when I didn't has been Derrick. He's kept it with me 100 the entire time. Just while he's crossing my mind, my phone rings. It's him; Derrick.

"What's up midnight?" He says with that southern drawl. A mixture between Mississippi, Louisiana, all I know he sounds sexy as oh get out.

In my girlish voice, "Hey boo. Nothing, what's up with you?"

"You know out here in Cali trying to get it. You know I gots to keep the paper coming if I'm going to keep a smile on your face."

His Grace, His Blood, His Mercy!

"Well, I guess you are right. So when will you be back this way, it's about that time."

"Yeah, who you telling. Why you think I'm calling?"

My first mind why he's calling is because he wants the same thing I do. So I continue to mess with him, give him what he's calling for.

"So you miss me huh?"

"What?" He says before taking another breath. "Baby that box… It's hard out here for a brotha. A brotha don't want to be caught messing with these road lizards out here. Need something a little more, you know…"

While he's talking, my mind is already where he is, and so is my body. I assume what I call the 1-800 sex line position. In a chair sitting straight up, hair all over my head, watching an old episode of the Game, but he doesn't know it. I get my midnight rider voice on, and go for it. Rule #35 – 'Never let them Know Everything.'

He whispers, "What ya wearing?"

Know I'm lying, I respond, "A pair of Victoria Secret's lace thongs."

"What color?"

"Black." I could say turquoise right now, he wouldn't care.

"Mmmm." He moans, and it's quite funny because I do too.

This grape lollipop somehow helps me get into the mood. So I go in.

"What you want me to do for you tonight?" Like I don't know, really?!

"I want you from the back tonight."

A give off a sheepish laugh. "So you want it doggy style?"

In that smooth voice, he answers, "Yes baby, you know what I like."

I continue, sounding like the girl in Coming to America, "Whateva you like."

He moans again.

I tell him, "Give it to me Daddy."

"You like it baby?"

I'm like, "Yes."

"Tell me you need me baby."

Oh, I can do that… no doubt.

"I need you ba-by."

"I hear him wearing it out. His voice is fading away.

"I take it there. You want Black horse, or White horse?"

Quietly he mumbles. "Black horse. Slow."

I know at this moment it won't be long. I let out a gasp, as if I am mounting myself on top of him, and then I ask, "Is it wet enough?"

He barely replies, "Don't do that to me, you know it's going to make me–"

Right here I hear him ask, "What you want baby?"

It's right here I say, "The new Michael Kors bag."

He's there, and he says, "Damn babe, you are the bomb. I'll send you the money in the morning."

All I get is dead silence, then a click.

I'm so good, I even amaze myself.

಍

Two thirty in the morning and my Aunt Skyye is still not home. Probably somewhere I guess you can say chasing the paper too, huh? Everything I know I learned from her. Even though a lot of people disagree with the way she gets hers, I'm good. It has proved to be no problems for me. If anything she has been the co-author of the Rule Book. I once asked her to teach me how to be like her, and at first she hesitated because she says she never wanted me to be like my mother; her twin. She died giving birth to me. My grandmother and everyone else has told me she died from what else, what we all black folks have the big "C," but hers was fast. I hate I never got to know her. Hell, I never got to know my Dad either. Bastard! He has never tried to reach out to me. He has never once tried to meet me. I've been looking for him forever. The last time I asked Gram's she broke down and cried, she told me my dad had died, and it was really useless for me to keep looking for him. He was killed by some stupid thugs on the street; . They robbed him, beat him to death, and then burned him; left him to die. I guess the little girl in me still hopes and prays that he is not dead. Maybe this will help me not be the way I am. But, for now I do what I do, and thanks to Aunt Skyye and her man Tiger they both been real good to me.

Chapter Seven

Drew, The Turn Up is real...

I turn into the parking lot, bumpin' that T.I. and Iggy Azalea. Everybody in the "A" is on this joint. Shiitt, "Mediocre" oh its fhyy now, and that's one lil' honey that can get it, I swear she can! Right now–if she want it. I know T.I. thought about hittin' dat a couple of times. Yes suh, fine as hell. Ion know now, it's a toss-up between her and my gul Nicki. Na'll, I can't even front like that, I'm still Team Nicki, I ain't gon' even lie. Now dat's who can get it.

   I promise doe, every time I pull in here to the club it never fails, something comes over me. I can't believe it, it's been five years already, and I'm still rolling strong. Plenty dudes I know clubs ain't last this long at all, and look at me. Shuttin' it down every night. We even goin' bigger tonight. Turn down for what!! Tonight we got the "All White Party." Some fellas from my old hood got this organization and in an effort to give back, they are puttin' on this event to say thank you to everyone that has supported them through the years. Can you say honeys and mo' honeys.

Before I can get in, I swear my man hits me up every time. I wish he would just get his stuff together. Mr. Walt has been hanging out here for a long time. I've asked him several times to let me help him out, even offered him a job, he always says no, but as long as I can share a lil' something with him he's good to go. So as usual, I hook him up, nothing big, just a lil' something to tie him over. Some people just satisfied being satisfied.

Spring Street was packed, felt like I was just chillin' for hours, finally made it back from makin' a deposit. Dropped two hundred seventeen g's, and that was for the last four days. I've already got my upfront money from the fellas. Everything from this point is cover and the bar, and of course the best part.

I cut 'em a deal, especially since one of 'em is one of my better suppliers. I'm talkin' top supplier. As a matter of fact, soon as I walk in, I see my boy, Zorro, stocking the bar. Tonight's gonna be a good night. We got 'em covered, fully stocked. Everything from Jose' Cuervo, Hennessy, the Black, that Jay Z new drink, D'usse. 'Course we got the Goose, Ciroc, you know we gots the Crown, can't leave that out, even got that Johnny Walker Red and Black. And I had to make sho' we had a lil' somethin' for my more chronologically advanced crowd, had to have the Michael Collins, Dewars, and that Tanqueray. That's just to name a few. Zorro let on the other night he took home three hundred in tips. That's pretty good if you ask me.

Damn, my phone has been blowing up from that lil' crazy chick that almost got me caught up. Being honest doe, Ion even think it was so much that she was a lil' cutie, I think I just was pissed off because I could tell she hadn't been opened up yet. A brotha didn't need dat on his mind. A newbie… na'll, wouldn't ever be able to get rid of that headache. I was feeling her doe. It's somethin' 'bout her for real. Enough so, that I ain't quite ready to just be done wit her like dat. Just can't let her know it. In the meantime, she got enough home girls around her to take up her slack. I'll get to her later, and by then she'll be good and ready.

Passin' through to the office, I catch the eye of this honey at the bar. Can't quite peg her. I'm usually good at reading these women. Even though I am only twenty-three, I have had my share. The old women are crazy about me, and the younger ones equally the same. The only shit I hate is that these little chicks, they be wantin' too much from a brotha. They need their hair done, they nails done, they feet done, even had one chick ask me to pay for her an azz job! What?!! I did it. And I must say that was the best I have ever paid for. LMAO! No fo' real, I thought at first it was going to be like all jiggly and shit, but to my surprise, it was as real as the next chick, even better. Gettin' a flashback right now, mmm the way she twerk that thang, send a brotha into spasms. She didn't know it though, but oh I've got my money back several times over. She loves the "X", and these hoes already know, now I aint payin' for your habit. You stupid enough to get caught up, oh you gon' pay for it. You can even get your other dude to pay for it, either which way, I'm gettin' mine.

She looks my way, let me guess, just broke up wit her man, feelin' all lonely, played, and emotional. Really ain't in the mood for the "depressed girl" today. It is two thirty in the afternoon. I play as if I don't see her checking me out. I walk behind the bar, just a, "Hello". They hate it. I continue as if I am looking for something.

She comes back. "Hello, to you too, sir."

I notice an accent. Mmm ain't nothin' like a Caribbean girl.

"What you drinking?"

Under his breath, Zorro mumbles, "Her sorrows."

We laugh together so that she has no clue we are laughing at her.

"Blue Cosmopolitan."

"Oh, so you are a Vodka girl, huh?"

"Not so much as I just love my country. Curacao"

Ok so I'm weak for the ladies that aren't from over here. Eddie Murphy put it best, you get you an "Umfufu" you are in there. Right 'til these crazy azz women in the states get to 'em.

I flirt more. "Have you been here long?"

"Actually, I moved here about a year ago with my boyfriend, and…"

Ah hell, here we go, I don't even have the energy for this right now. I wrap it up.

"So did you guys just break up?"

"Yes, we did, a week ago."

I put myself into the Friend Zone for a minute, just long enough to shut dis down. "I'm so sorry to hear that. I know you must really be hurting now. Trust me it'll get better in time. My advice to you, let your heart heal, but just know that we are here every day. I'll make sure Zorro takes care of you. The first drink is on the house." Please know paper before the poo-na-na, any day.

His Grace, His Blood, His Mercy!

❦

Not too long before I need to be back at the club. I take a quick minute to drop a call to this lil' chick to see if she wants to come through tonight. Better yet if it's cool for me to drop by, that way I can get a quickie. She's every man's dream; drama free! For the most part she got her own thang goin' on, she'on be sweatin' a brotha day in and day out, she knows exactly what she wants, and in the words of my gul Joseline, she love da beefcake. We just got that understandin'. She knows when I call what I need, and when she calls I know what she need. I'm in that kinda mood tonight.

Sippin' on some Crown, I scroll through my contacts, and I come across her name, and immediately I get stiff because I know if she's in, it's 'bout to go down.

The sexy voice on the other end welcomes me, "Hey, Mr. DJ."

I laugh because she says I got all the right beats and moves.

I respond, "Hey sexy, u busy?"

"For you, never!"

That's what I'm talkin' 'bout. Make a brotha feel good. Even tho' I know she mean dat doe.

"Ok then. Can I get a little me time then?"

"I'm here."

Man, why can't they all just cooperate like that? I mean no questions; nothin', just automatically know wassup. Just as I'm hangin' up wit her, my dude Pimpin' hits me up. I bet I know what for.

8/25/14 Mon
Pimpin: What up?
7:45 PM
    8/25/14 Mon
    Me: Headed out
    7:48 PM
8/25/14 Mon
Pimpin: Running low
7:48 PM
    8/25/14 Mon
    Me: I got u baby… Chef's palace
    7:49 PM
8/25/14 Mon
Pimpin: Fo sho'!
7:49 PM
8/25/14 Mon
Pimpin: U gud?
7:53 PM
    8/25/14 Mon
    Me: U kno I'm all gud …
    7:54 PM

I jump in the shower right quick. Get my things togetha. And I'm out dis bit. Throw on some Eric Roberson, light a Perdermo, and let it flow.

༄

Just as I already knew, it was gonna be good. Real good. Right now I should be on my way to da club, but I can't leave without one mo' round. She just got it like that. Make me wanna say forget it, Dre'll handle it. Just as I'm lyin' here tryin' to catch my breath, she comes back for more; even wetter and hotter than before. She's like a mad woman. As if she has somethin' to prove, in which if she know like I do, she'on have to prove nothin'. She whispers to me, that she wants to give her DJ something to think about when I'm round what she calls the "groupies." Out the blue all I hear is "Until Then, (Imagine)" Jill Scott, she just stands over me, begins to dance, slow winding, just how I like it. Yeaah, yes suh, I'm looking, but my mind is like brang it… skin so smooth, and just the right amount of perspiration, against the light make that body look like it's glistenin'. No she didn't! She turned around and I all see is azz for days. I sit straight up, can't go anotha minute longer, I grab hold to her, pull her to me, spread her mother nature as wide as I can, and slowly plant my face between her golden bronze thighs. She wails out my name, which only gives me the green light to pass go, I do, and with my unadulterated skills, she grabs my head, and pulls me closer in. She looks me in my eyes as if to say it… Don't say it. Before she can, I intentionally put her on top of it, have her turn to the back, and let her go for what she knows. And she goes and goes, and goes…

※

Glad Pimpin' didn't waste no time. That was nothin' to break him off an ounce. He'll take care it just like dat. Dat's one thang 'bout him, he is for real a hard worker, actually one of my best. I never had to question his loyalty. Believe it or not I trust him more than some of my family.

Chizellé T. Archie

By the time I do make it to the club, it's on and poppin'. Wall-to-wall; standin' room only. Honey's everywhere. Looks like a scene from R Kelly's "Step In The Name of Love" video. I head straight to the bar where I know it's goin' down. So many peeps I got to press my way through. Just before I make it, there is this chick that's just standing here looking at me as if she got some shit on her mind. As loud as the music is, she comes to me with some bullshit 'bout how I never called her back, and how I did her wrong, how I stood her up. The crazy part about it is that I'm looking at this broad like, do I know you? I try to keep it square, but she won't let it go. I'm talking about neck-rolling, all that "crazy chick" shit. I try hard as I can to ignore her, but she gon' make a brotha kindly have Mr. Big escort her azz up outta here. I keep walking and she falls back. Well it seems like she did anyway. Might wanna watch her, 'cause she the kind that'll have her other dude flat yo' tires, somethin' stupid like that. But, she is fine as hell. I'm just tryin' to remember the damn gul name.

Chapter Eight

Gabby, sometimes texting is not good…

Almost a month into school and I still haven't done it! This is crazy! And if that dude Albert calls me one more time, I'm going to go off! I've been trying to be nice, but I'm like really dude? What is so funny is that he would probably be a pretty cool guy if he would just chill trying to be so holy. Then I might, just might, give him some play. I'm hard up and all, but not like that. Well, I can't lie, the way things are going, it might be better to lose it to him, then maybe afterwards we can pray and ask God for forgiveness! Now that's not cool Gabby, you need to grow up… Anyway, he has texted me at least three times tonight, and I'm so iggin' him. He is the epitome of an RTO, you would think he would eventually get the picture. I'm not texting back, so if it was me, I would just STOP, but I can't just kick him to the curb, I might need him later. The Rule Book states, 'Never take them out of rotation. Always keep a spare.' In my case I need a few, because my body's doing all kind of crazy stuff.

Never thought I would say this, but I'm so about to get over Drew. I've texted him so many times it's not funny. He'll text back sometime, but it's only one word text like, yeah, no, cool, uh-huh, real short like. I told him I was coming to the party at the club, but he didn't reply back. For some reason I think he is so through with me, and Rishard, oh he has been on me tough. From the way it's looking, not sure if this holding out for Drew thing is really what's up. I might not be able to go too much longer. Speak of the devil. Rishard hits me up on Messenger.

Rishard: Heyyy sexy
Me: U crazy boy
Rishard: Wyd
Me: nothn jus homework
Rishard: U always doin homework
Me: Ikr
Rishard: Wht u wearin to the party, sumn hot I kno
Me: Why? I dunno yet
Rishard: u r comin doe
Me: It's a possibility

The Rule Book states, "Always keep 'em guessing. Never give up too much." I'll surprise him.

Rishard: So wuz up 4real
Me: abt
Rishard: u know wht abt, me n u
Me: didn't know it was me n u
Rishard: u da one trippn. U kno how I feel

His Grace, His Blood, His Mercy!

Me: ☺☺
Rishard: <3 <3
Me: Yeah right
Rishard: 4 real doe I want u …
Me: how
Rishard: sign into skype
Me: MOS
Rishard: cool send me a pic whn she leave
Me: k

༒

I fell asleep and didn't even realize it. Its twelve o'clock at night and the first thing I wake up to is Wendy Williams, she kills me with "Hot Topics" that lady is forever talking about some-body, and she has me hooked. She keeps me posted on all the gossip! I'm still trying to figure out if Jay Z and Beyoncé really are on the outs. I doubt it. They got too much money to call it quits. And I know Jay already got plans for Blu Ivy , and the group… "Seeds of Destiny's Children." But knowing him, she'll be solo, kick the other ones to the curb, and next you know, sold out tours everywhere! Now Rhianna and Chris Brown, oh that's another story all by itself. That madness! And what's up with T. I. and Tiny? Noooo! Say it ain't so!!! Well if that is true, she better look out, because Dionne is looking for him. That girl knows she loves herself some T.I., and for the record I'm secretly stalking Floyd Mayweather. Ladies back up! Looks like all of young Hollywood as they call it, is trippin'trippin'. Now the day that Nick Cannon and Mariah break up, that will be a trip! Kevin Hart will have a field day with that one. That's his boo! Mariah, that is. Kevin just doesn't have the money Nick has so to speak. I can hear him now, "Ahmm Mariah, baby, you know I love you, but you got to know how my checking and my savings work. If we gone be in this thing, you got to understand there will be days when we gon' have to take from the savings to put over into the checking, and then, just maybe then, it may just go through, but in the meantime can you let hold a brottha somethn." Then Nick will be in the background saying, "I told you, you shoulda left his broke ass alone, but you gon' learn today!" Oooh kmsl... I need to go to sleep, but as sleepy as I am, I can't go, so I text Rishard.

>**8/29/14 Fri**
>**Me: U up**
>**12:17AM**

8/29/14 Fri
Rishard: yep
12:17AM

>**8/29/14 Fri**
>**Me: Wyd**
>**12:18AM**

8/29/14
Rishard: Thinkn bout' u. What happen 2 my pic?
12:19AM

>**8/29/14 Fri**
>**Me: U got a pic of me already**
>**12:20AM**

8/29/14 Fri
Rishard: u know wht I'm talkn bout', let me c it Snap chat …
12:20AM

    8/29/14 Fri
    Me: c what
    12:22AM

8/29/14 Fri
Rishard: don't play, u kno dat gud gud
12:25AM

    8/29/14 Fri
    Me: U r crazy
    12:26AM

8/29/14 Fri
Rishard: no 4 real let me c
12:27AM

    8/29/14 Fri
    Me: FaceTime
    12:28AM
    8/29/14 Fri
    Me: u on yet
    12:28AM

8/29/14 Fri
Rishard: yep
12:30AM

That boy is crazy, I'm still trippin' that I showed him my breast over the phone, but what's really a trip is that I saw his manhood! Oh I can't wait to tell Quinn, he is not "Lil" at all. From what I can tell he is packing big time. That's why I like

FaceTime, when you creeping, it's a lot easier than Skype. If you -know- who knew I was on the phone she would call in the cavalry. I swear that woman has been so off the chain. I don't know what's up with her anymore. I need to call my Uncle Lucy, maybe he can find out for me. He will do anything for me. Anything!

☙

The last day of school before Labor Day, and I feel like I have been in school for a minute now. So looking forward to the three day weekend, everyone knows I love school and all, but I'm just starting to get so bored already. Momma doesn't know, but I have been secretly practicing for the Mensa membership. Prayerfully, I will get accepted. I know with my IQ I should have no problem. I've been tested over and over, but Momma just wants to keep me in a normal environment, she keeps saying, she wants me to be around "normal" children my age, but seriously I don't feel like a "normal" child most times. There is nothing about me normal. None of my friends get to participate in Dukes program, when there; I am around people like myself. I feel like I fit in.

On the way to school, Momma reminds me for the umpteenth time that she will be back in town no later than Tuesday afternoon. Her flight arrives at seven, so Sam will be picking me up this evening. Of course, Dad will in later next week, blah, blah, blah, I know it back and forth. I act as if I am sooo sad. I actually put on a little pout, just so she can feel better. I do feel for her sometimes, because there are times when she comes back from these trips, she is so beat, but I realize why she is doing it. How can I forget it? She makes me know it every chance she gets. She's doing it for me. So that I won't have to struggle as an adult, she doesn't want me to want for anything. Ok lady, I get it.

She tells me, "Gabby, I love you. I hope you have a wonderful weekend. Please know if I had it my way, I wouldn't be gone as much. I hate leaving you like this, but you know this is Momma's job; I have to do what I have to do. When I get back, we will do what we do best."

Now, she's talking my language. I already know where she is going with this, but little does she know. I have a little shopping spree planned already.

I answer, "I know Momma, and I thank you for everything. I know you love me."

She adds, "Very much, and by the way Samantha knows you are having a girls weekend, so she is prepared. I hope!

"Momma, you know we are good. Sam never has any problems out of us, but Momma, I forgot to ask is it okay if Quinn stays over too? Gram's said it was, I just forgot to ask earlier."

Knowing how she feels, this can take a drastic turn.

Surprisingly, she responds, "That's fine. But…

"I knew it!" here it comes.

"You had best make sure her fast tail doesn't be having any thuggish lil' boys calling my house."

I give her a look like really Ma'? Knowing I already know what's up. Because baby, it's about to go down.

I grab my backpack, jump out of the car, and give her a kiss. She kisses me back. Oh God, did anyone see that? I am so too old for that.

In English Lit this morning, I couldn't keep my eyes open to save my life. I am going to get enough of watching Wendy Williams at night. This is not good on a girls look. Feels like I have bags under my eyes for days. Plus chatting it up with Rishard didn't help either. I feel like just going to sleep standing right here in my locker, but I know I can't do that. Just as I put my book up, I notice Ms. Thang coming up next to me. I don't know what it is about her, but I just don't like her. I overhear Alex asking her if she is going to the party tomorrow. I break my neck trying to listen for the answer. Wh-? Did I hear her say? Na'll. I know she didn't just say what I thought I heard her say. I walk over toward them as to try to hear this again. Call me nosy I don't even care.

Alex asks her, "So how you pull that off?"

She laughs, "What you mean? You don't think I can pull somebody like him? Look at me."

I want to gag at this moment. Who does she really think she is? Me?

He laughs back, and says, "Girl you trippin' do you think the dude that owns Club Etc. got time for some high school chick? You might be fly and all, but you are not even in his league."

She responds. "Trust me, I know he does. We kicking it like that. We have been for a minute now."

I'm sick right now. I want to throw up everything I have eaten for breakfast. I know this ain't true. By this time, the halls are starting to get filled even more. I can see him give her a pound, as to say that's what's up then. She precedes to put her Louis Vuitton on her shoulder, flick what looks to be I know 18 inches of Peruvian hair, and walks over to her locker. If I could just drop dead for a little while… this girl just said she is with Drew. My man!!! The man I have been waiting for all this time! OHN!! I send out a S.O.S. text to all the girls to meet at lunchtime. (shit on top of shit). I am heartbroken.

༄

I somehow make it through my morning classes. I'm still not believing what I've heard. According to Sarah, she says she overheard her saying something to that effect a few weeks ago, but she just didn't want to bring it to me, because she hadn't gotten the final go ahead. Any other time that would totally go against the GEMS Bylaws, but in this case, I can see where she was coming from. I'm not mad at Sarah, but I wander how many of the other girls knew. I guess this explains why he has been so short with me.

All day everybody has been buzzing about tomorrow night's party. Oh yeah, I have been trippin' so much about the Drew and D'Sharee saga, I actually forgot whose party it is. While I'm thinking of it, I ask my teacher may I be excused. Earlier I got a couple of texts from Rishard. I need to text him back. To risk not getting caught, and my phone being taken away, it will be best I did it from there.

08/29/14 Fri
Me: hey u, got ur text, was in class
1:15PM

8/29/14 Fri
Rishard: it's cool. Jus holln at ya
1:15PM
    8/29/14 Fri
    Me: K. hey guess what …
    1:15PM
8/29/14 Fri
Rishard: ?
1:16PM
    8/29/14 Fri
    Me: I want u …☺☺
    1:16PM
8/29/14 Fri
Rishard: ???!!!
1:17PM
    8/29/14 Fri
    Me: Will ttyl. Headn bck to class
    1:18pm
8/29/14 Fri
Rishard: gud smarty pants
1:18PM

Just before I go back I can't help but send Drew a text. I have to.

8/29/14 Fri
Me: Hi Drew. How r u?
1:22pm

I try to wait for a response, but I've got to get back. By the time I make it back into the class, they have started the review for the test. Not worried, I got this. My phone is buzzing, but

I can't answer right now. It's killing me to know if it's him texting me back. The teacher calls on me to give one of the answers. I really don't like it when she puts me on the spot like that. My classmates always make fun of me anyway. If I'm not Doogie Howser, the girl version, then I'm either some other crazy name. My phone buzzes again. Now, I'm even more anxious to know if it's him.

Class is finally out. I rush to look at my phone. 2 missed texts. The first is from him. Not exactly what I want to hear.

8/29/14 Fri
Drew: Don't u have a class u need to be in lil girl? Fall back.
1:38PM

My heart drops. Oh so it's like that?
The next text is from whom else, Albert. Really?
8/29/2014 Fri
ChurchBoy: Hope you have had a good day! Be blessed.
1:50PM

I promise that boy is on some other stuff. Where they do that at? He is just way too nice. At least act like you got a rough neck, even if you aren't. Dag!

I don't respond. The crew is at the lockers. Even her! I know she is a senior and all, and I can respect the fact I misled him into thinking I was lot older, but when I look at her, then I look at myself, I'm like, what does he see in her? I'm way better looking, my hair is real, my breasts are real, everything about her says fake! Some people would call me a hater; I don't look at it like that. IJS.

Jaz comes up in full mode, hyping up the party. Even now more than ever I'm psyched, especially now I know Ms. Thang will most definitely be there.

Jaz yells, "Now, Jaz will surely be the baddest 'B' in the place on tomorrow night, and you know that, because Jazmine doesn't do anything small."

We all burst out laughing, because we know how she rolls. She's likely to come in there with some peacock feathers on knowing her.

Dionne burst out, "I'm sure you will, looking like a Saturday night special!"

Jaz rolls her eyes, but with two snaps up, turns and says, "And you know it! Got the black Versace dress on lock! Turn up!"

Bree chimes in, "IKR, girl it's about to be off the hook. I think half of the school is going. I have this cute little hot pink pencil skirt."

Before she goes any further, we are like Bree, a skirt? With those knock-knees, be for real. After she thinks about it, she laughs, and says, "Oh yeah, that's right."

She continues with a dismayed look on her face, "I hope Momma lets me stay over, you know she's really funny about sleepovers. And if I get caught, she will kill me." Well that being said, I don't think Bree will be going. Mrs. Darrington does not play.

I know Sarah, and Lorna won't be there. Sarah and her family will be leaving to go to Savannah for the holiday, so looks like it will be just me and my girls Angel, Dionne, Jaz, and oh yes! Quinn!

Chapter Nine

Marcel, diamonds have always outweighed gold...

My meeting with the investors has gone longer than I thought. I don't know if my body can keep up. I'm on the west coast so much; it's like when I get back to Atlanta I'm tired all the time. I just would dare let Victoria know any of this, because she has so much of her own going on. I am so proud of her. The way she has taken the company by storm amazes me. Basically she is running the entire empire. The Bouviér Dynasty! I laugh to myself. Mother would love it. I miss her so much. Although it's been seven years, it seems like just yesterday she died. Don't think I've been the same since. Not sure if I ever will. Every time I look into Victoria's eyes, I see a part of her. She is so much like Mother.

My partner Roberto calls me to tell me that everything is all-good. Yes! That's what I'm talking about. Merci Père céleste. Je loue votre saint nom ! I need to call my love and share the good news with her, but oh yes I forgot, she's headed to D.C. It's like we are always on opposite ends of the earth. I'll still call, and if I don't get her, I'll leave her a message.

Thank goodness, she answers. Oh, I love hearing her voice, makes me want to catch a red eye to D.C.

"Hello baby. How is your trip thus far?"

She sings, "Heyyy Mr. Bouviér, I'm great and you?"

I love it when she plays with me like that; gives me something to look forward to.

"How was the flight, comfortable I hope?"

"It was good, relaxing, you know that. Myron got me here right on time."

"Oh he knows better."

We both laugh. I hear a knock at the door.

"Hold on baby," she says.

I put a call into Myah to make something happen for me. Victoria is staying at the Four Seasons, so I need a hook up until I make it there. Plan to surprise her.

"I'm back sweetheart. That was room service."

"Cool. Hey love what's your itinerary?"

She responds, "Busy as heck! I know I have a dinner meeting tonight at seven, then after that I was thinking of coming back to the room, cuddling up with a good book. Lately, I have just had so much on my plate, I just wanted to relax."

I'm not sure who is tired the most, me or her, but I need to see her. I need her.

"I understand love. I can relate. It's like we are always on auto pilot, and we are passing each other in the air."

She chuckles. "You are so right. I feel that way most days. I miss you so much it's unbelievable."

"Say that again." I ask her.

"Say what?"

"Tell me you miss me."

In that sweet seductive voice, she says it, "I miss you."

Immediately I tell her, I love her, and that I will talk to her later this evening.

I end by saying, "Call me after your meeting."

"I will. Love you!"

☙

Thanks to my man Geoffrey, he was able to swing it. Usually it takes anywhere from a couple to three hours to charter a jet, but my man is a miracle worker. He's got me scheduled, and I'm about to pull out headed to D.C. to see my lady luck.

I love the CJ3, the ride is so smooth, and of course it doesn't take long at all to get settled in so that I can soon began sipping on a glass of Hennessey. After today, I need it. I must admit, I didn't think this one was going to go through. We have been trying to get this cat to go in for a minute now. I guess I've dealt with diamonds for so long; it's hard to go with the unfamiliar. This new venture has really been risky, but who would've known that gold would prove to be so profitable. Man, we about to kill 'em, but keeping that in mind, it's going to be very costly as well. As of yesterday it hit a record high of $1,910 for an ounce. It's just this thing of just not knowing how well it is going to perform, and whether there will be another crisis in the industry, sooo this is why I am sort of leery of letting Victoria know just how much of our money that I have actually used to make this happen. We have talked about it over and over, and she's never been on the same page with me about it. The gold market's too volatile is her favorite thing to say, being that she is the "Hedge Guru," she believes that the U.S. dollar will strengthen, because the economy is now turning around, and the interest rates will then increase, which will lead to a drastic decline in gold prices. Yes, she knows the ins and outs better than I do, but this time, I made an executive decision, saying that, I went behind her back, but I feel good about this. Market don't fail me now.

&

After a nice pleasant trip, I'm here. My assistant Myah hooked it up just as I wanted. Rose petals everywhere, candles, two bouquets of orchids, and let's not forget Kem. "Share My Life" gets her every time! Oh, and she really worked it out, she scored these sexy Jimmy Choos in the nick of time, I have to admit, I love buying her shoes, just as much as she loves getting them. Victoria *must* put these on tonight; it's just something about a woman in a $2,000 pair of crystal suede peep-toe pumps. How does the saying go? Happy wife, happy life…

Before I'm done drawing her bath, I hear the door open. She walks in, stunned because she is trying to figure who's invaded her room. She looks around, I see her walk over to the bed, she has some idea, but just not quite, until… she sees the box of shoes on the night stand, with a note that says, "See you in the air later." Suddenly she turns around, her smile, that beautiful wide smile, it melts my heart each time, lets me know that what I do, it's all worth it. She puts down her purse, walks over to me, and gives me the most endearing hug ever.

His Grace, His Blood, His Mercy!

"B-Baby how? When? What are you doing here?"

"Should I leave?" I ask with this little boy look across my face.

"Ahhm no sir, you should not," she says.

I grab her hand and lead her into the bathroom, where there is a lovely bowl of fresh fruit around the tub. I watch her as she stands in the mirror, and pulls her hair up in this cute little bun type thing, then she glides into the tub in front of me. We just relax in the jetted tub together, and then she leans back on my chest, says nothing. Just knowing I'm here makes her world all better. Before long we both are in someplace that only we know.

We talk hours on end about each other's endeavors. I can tell she is beat. I just want to hold her. I am not sure if now is the right time to tell her, but when will it be? She looks me in my eyes, and I'm gone. I can't help myself. I kiss her, and she does it back. I can tell even in her tiredness she wants me. I oblige her. She whispers in my ear, "Would you like to take a flight with me?" I giggle. "Yeah I would." She places on the shoes, and it is on from here. It drives me crazy to see how the moonlit sky that's peeking through the windows illuminates her sultry caramel skin. Her warmth, it pulls me to her, her breast so tender and erect. For this woman here, I will go to the ends of the world and back. Without hesitation, I say it. "Baby, we did it." She continues to kiss me on my neck, and asks in that voice, "Did what?" Between the feelings I have going through me, and the gut-wrenching feeling in the pit of my stomach, not sure if it's the Hen, or I'm just nauseated. "The gold investment; I went through with it. Spoke with Peter, and after long thought, I just went for it." She instantaneously becomes dry as the Sahara Desert! Then... my phone rings. Shht it's 3:00 in the morning.

Chapter Ten

Gabs, what you know about that oooweee...

Sam and I are just leaving Atlantic Station; the girls should be heading to the house in about an hour. To make it seem as though we are really doing it up, I asked Drago to whip us up some cute little non- alcoholic drinks, ahh yeah right. Quinn got us on that. I know she'll at least have some Lime-A-Rita's, that's just how she does. My first time drinking was with Quinn, I remember we were at her cousin Tweety's party about a year ago, and they were trippin' over jello-shots and hand grenades. Still not sure of what's in the mystery mix, but it was all good. At first I was like na'll, but after I tried a couple a shots, I just knew I was a big girl then. As a matter of fact, I just sent a text to Quinn to make sure she gets the hook up from her boy Juelle on the oooweee. Okay, I haven't let you in that part just yet. Yes, my first time trying the oooweee was with Quinn of course last summer, and even though I haven't done it too many times, I don't understand why everyone makes such a big deal out of it. It really isn't all that bad; I just see it as an herb that God created. Everyone has tried it at least once or twice. We all have, even Sarah! I say legalize it, then we will see then how many people are truly against it. Everybody will have cataracts! IJS…

One thing for sure, I know Momma must have gotten to Sam, because Sam has never been on me like this. All the way to the mall she was yapping about how I need to do this and how I need to do that, and mostly how I don't need to do this or that. She used to be so cool. I could pretty much get anything over on her. Now, I don't know. All I do know is that she doesn't need to be trippin' tonight. This thing needs to go off without any problems. So as not to bring any suspicion, the good thing is that there is a nine o'clock showing of "Step Up", at the Fork and Screen. I begged Sam to let us go, she was a bit hesitant at first, but I eventually won her over.,Under one condition; she'll take us and pick us up! Can you say monkey wrench? Thank goodness on the spur of the moment I remembered that Quinn works at the movie theatre, so I convinced Sam Quinn will bring us home, which will work out perfect, because Quinn and I were pretty much thinking around that time anyway. As far as everyone else's parents, they think we're having an all girl's sleepover, in which we are, but what they don't know is that we're going to the hottest club in the city, and we're going to be the best looking crew in the spot. Well, I know I am, and please know it; Gabs don't roll with nobody that is not red carpet worthy! Just never can be hotter than me! Which that is impossible.

His Grace, His Blood, His Mercy!

Last night Rishard and I talked all night. I think ever since I told him I wanted to get with him, he's been straight trippin'trippin'. I believe we've sexted our entire body parts just about, I wasn't cool in the beginning, but it didn't take long for me to go for it, why can't I? Anyway, whose gonna see it? It's just me and him, and I don't think he would put me on blast like that. I'm not Mimi, and he is definitely not Nikko. More importantly, I know if Mommy Dearest had inty idea about it, I already know she'll have Bishop Jakes here live and in living color performing an exorcist on me, might even call in the entire crew of Preachers of L.A., well now that Deitrick Haddon, she can call him anytime. In my Dietrick voice singing, "Sinner's Prayer."

⁊

Dionne is the first to get here; she comes in in full swing! Gucci luggage, Chanel backpack! I can't... I just can't. She looks like a designer's nightmare. First place she wants to go is the kitchen, as usual. Drago already made the joke that he needed to make extra food just for Dee. Just as I'm headed to the door, my phone is ringing off the hook. They will call back. Again the doorbell, I open it, it's Jaz and her older brother Chase. He's home from college this weekend, and even though I know he's my girls' brother and all, I still sneak a peek. Of course, Angel is the last to get here, and as always, her mother has to give us the "do the right thing speech." So to seem as we are so going to do the right thing, we all say together, "May the Lord watch between me and thee…" Ok lady! At some point, the girls head to my room and in between us chopping it up about what's about to happen, and going over our final ensembles for the night, I notice I have 2 messages. I check the voicemail. First one is from Quinn.

"Hey sis," she says. "Right now, everything is all good; Gram thinks I have to work, she knows I'm staying over to your crib after I get off since its closer. So I'll be there at nine, ya'll need to be fly and ready to roll. Oh yeah, I got that too."

The next one is from my Daddy. He sounds a whole lot better than he did last time. I listen to what part I can.

"Hey baby girl, just wanted to call to say hello. I was thinking about you, sitting here trying to figure out a good time to come see you. Maybe for your birthday perhaps, you let me know what you think." Before I know it, I push the end button. Really don't have that kind of time right now.

They're all just about ready; it's me that is taking so long. Go figure. For whatever reason I can't get it together. As hard as I am trying to forget it, the thought that tonight I'll be that close to the man of my dreams, and to know he won't be checking for me, is just a little too much to stomach. He'll have Ms.Thang hanging all over him. How did I let this happen? I should've just given it up that night, then it would've been me stunting with him. Anywho! I do one last pop in the mirror of my Razzler Dazzler lipglass, and take one last look at myself, and if I must say so myself, A girl is looking sho' nuff good. I'm killing this Kaleidoscope Dolce Vita dress, hugging all the curves in the right places, and the Vince Camuto booties are to die for. Just before I turn to walk out of the bathroom, I do a quick boo-tay assessment, and yes, both Drew, and Rishard'll be on this tonight. Just before we head out, Angel reminds us to put on our "special bands" for the night. Which reminds me; tonight I'm feeling kind of Orange. Should be kisses all night long for me.

***

Everything's gone off just right! Considering how she was acting earlier, Sam was so cool about the whole thing. I'm starting to think she has a boo somewhere, but just not letting on; she was so giddy, it's either that or she's had a bag of the oooweee too.

We're here, and Quinn never ceases to amaze me; she's chilling in the cut waiting to pick us up as we planned, and it's so smooth Sam doesn't even notice. I kinda feel like Stoney for a minute in "Set it Off," and Quinn is Cleo, but all we're missing are the hydraulics. Soon as we're in, Quinn lights a blunt, and immediately we go into rotation, puff, puff, pass… Between this and the wine cooler, my nerves are settling down. Wow, as always; Jaz tries to be big girl and goes into a coughing fit. Are we gonna have to do CPR? I think it should be a rule that people with asthma shouldn't be allowed to get in, it just throws the whole sequence off. IJS…

We pull up to the club; my heart is beating something crazy. I hope we have no problem at the door getting in. The fake ID's Quinn made for us need to work this time, because the ones before needed a lil' upgrading, and plus it may not be that easy to just roll in here like that. No telling, Drew may have already blackballed me. Dionne told me her cousin Black says on nights like tonight where it's a younger crowd, they don't card that hard, but Jaz has on enough eye shadow for all of us, so that might help us. I'm laughing to myself because I can't wait to see what that smoky-eye is going to look like by the end of the night. By the time we get a parking spot, the line looks like it's around the corner. Ahhm not! Where is the line to pay more when you don't want to wait? Before we get out, Rishard is already texting me.

8/30/2014 Sat
Rishard: Where u at
9:45PM
    8/30/2014 Sat
    Me: Outside
    9:45PM
8/30/2014 Sat
Rishard: I'm here, at the bar
9:47PM
    8/30/2014 Sat
    Me: K ☺ The line is soo long!
    9:47PM
8/30/2014 Sat
Rishard: Go thru da VIP line. I got u.
9:47PM
8/30/2014 Sat
Me: K.
9:48PM

Thirty minutes later, we are in, they worked! I'm so twisted right now. How about church boy, has texted me twice… Talking about, I hope you have a good time at the party, be safe. C'mon dude really?! He is so blowing my buzz right now.

His Grace, His Blood, His Mercy!

I send him back, Thnxs. Now hopefully he'll go to sleep, or better yet, watch last week's episode of Sunday's Best.

Immediately my eyes began to scan the room. I wish I could say I was looking for Rishard, but in actual reality I'm not. It's the owner I'm somehow afraid I will bump into. Just as I turn to walk towards the bar I look up, and there he is. OMG! He's so fine. I get this cold feeling and feels like my heart skips a beat, and to make it better, he's not with her. What's up with that? He looks at me, and gives me the throw off nod, like yeah, I see ya, but I don't see ya. Dag, I feel three feet tall. As much as I want to go up to him, my first mind warns me not to, so I stay focused on looking for Rishard. After a few minutes, Angel taps me on the shoulder to let me know she sees him. He's sitting at the bar looking so fly, dressed to impress in a grey skinny fit blazer, white graphic Tru Religion t-shirt, and the grey jeans to match. What?!! Plus I look down and this dude is rocking a pair of grey and black Buc's. Ok then. He asks if I want anything to drink, I get a margarita, since I'm already feeling right. I look around and it's like everybody from the school is here. The first person I see on the dance floor is Jordan, as soon as she sees us, it's as though she tries to audition on the spot. She kills me, she is so extra! Alex comes over and asks Dee to dance, it's cool. I can respect that. He's really not my type anyway.

Quinn's been working the room ever since we got here. She is a natural. I look over towards the lounge area, and she has some dude all up on her dancing so close, he looks like he wishes he could just take her home right now, but I don't blame him, my girl is rocking that teal strapless jumpsuit. I peep Jaz getting it in, and can't help laughing; the girl is so fly I bet she regrets wearing what she did, a black and white high neck romper, with pockets. I'm dying laughing so hard because the dude she's dancing with, has her all backed up to him, and the killing part is, he has his hands in her pockets! Where they do that at?

Now that I'm mellowing out, Rishard ask me if I want to dance. Of course I tell him yes, especially since "Magic," by Robin Thicke is on. I love myself some Robin. I wish I was Paula Patton; I'd take him back in a heartbeat. That's what I need, someone to beg for me like he did on the BET awards, beg boo! Come to think about it, I'm about to make Drew so jealous right now. Rishard leads me to the dance floor, and we dance 'til we can't dance any more. He is pulling me so close to him, it's like I can't breathe, but I like it. Whatever is going to get Drew's attention, I'm up for it. Before long, I get so caught up, I find myself imitating this sensual dance I saw on some award show. I can tell it has his full attention, because the only thing on his mind is me.

Apparently my bumping and grinding with Rishard is working. By the way Drew keeps looking over here; I can tell he wishes it was him I was dancing with instead of Rishard, makes me wonder where's his girl toy. No longer than a minute passes, and I'll be–spoke too soon, just when I thought she was M-I-A, in she walks, and not only that, she walks in here like she's the whole thing, like she owns the joint. Why do I feel sick? Not sure if it's because she just got here, or if it's the fact that she is killing those peep-toe red bottom booties! I officially hate her, and yes Angel makes her way over to only remind me that SHE is here.

His Grace, His Blood, His Mercy!

My entire mood has changed, and now Rishard has started to whisper stuff in my ear about him seeing me later. What does he mean later? He even asks can I get out. I'm like excuse me? And then suddenly I remember both Mommy Dearest and my Dad are gone. Umm that's something to think about, but I really can't focus. This is turning into an epic failure.

೧

About an hour and a half later, I have just about danced myself crazy, and the bad part is that ever since Ms. Thang has shown up, Drew has not paid me one lick of attention. I guess it really is over. I'm trying to hide it but my heart is tearing apart on the inside. The more I think about what Rishard asks me earlier, the more I'm beginning to like the idea.

After so long of standing in one spot, I tell Rishard I'll be back, because I haven't seen any of the girls in a minute. Surprisingly, I find them in VIP, WTH? Some BFF's they are, they didn't even come get me. After a few minutes it sinks in, I should've been here all along. I look over and Angel is all hugged up on the couch with this dude that looks every bit of thirty. Looks like, her red band is working. He seems straight, just not my type, reminds me of Pretty Ricky, you know the one that looks better than you, and it's just something about the guys with the diamond pinky rings. He's at least 6'9", with teeth so pretty, looks like he just shot the Ultra Zoom commercial. Again, I laugh to myself, because when he smiled at me, I'm sure I saw the blinng! I am so trippin'trippin', but not as much as Quinn is. I can't believe she's in dudes' lap she was dancing with earlier, and he is actually blowing her a charge! For everybody to see! All-right-then... turn up!

Next thing I hear is J Dilla's, *"Pure Imagination"* bumping over the speakers, and Jaz, comes up behind me, and whispers, "Girl where you been?"

I turn to answer her, "Dancing with Rishard."

She laughs, "I know, you've been locked down with him all night."

I'm thinking the same thing, sorta pissed, because like I said, this is where I needed to be instead of trying to be Beyoncé performing her *"On the Run Tour."* Just thinking about how I've been breaking a sweat to make Drew jealous even makes me laugh, when I know good and well the Rule Book states, "A real woman, never sweats, always keeps it classy."

Quinn beckons for me to come over, "You good?"

I tell her, "Yeah." I can't really say that I am though. The couple of hits I took from the blunt before we came in have pretty much worn off.

Angel says to me, "Girl here taste this." I can tell by listening at her, she is three sheets to the wind right about now, but I can't resist. I need to feel what she's feeling. Instead of what she has, I opt for the oooweee, and this time it feels just right. Now this is the buzz I really need. I look back and Dee is in the corner slow grinding with this man that so resembles Sandino, after he got rid of the homeless man look.

Right when I start to miss him, Rishard comes looking for me. He must be thinking the same way I am. He comes behind me, puts his arms around my waist, and just so happens, a song I've never heard before *"Open Your Eyes,"* is on, and it's just something about the way he looks at me. I'm so feeling him right now, before we can finish the dance, he pulls me by the hand and then we are in our own little spot. He softly pulls my band, and it's on… he kisses me so soft on my lips, for a minute I forget where I am. I just wish he didn't smell so good. I kiss him back. He whispers in my ear, "So you want me huh?" Still caught up in the song, I say, "Yeah." He comes back, "Prove it." I really don't understand him at this moment. Then, he tells me to open mouth open and he places what feels like a piece of candy under my tongue, not wanting to seem so oblivious, I give this ahmm what the– kinda look, and as crazy as this may be, he gently closes my mouth back, and says, "It's all good, after a while you'll like it, just let it dissolve." Okay, is it me, or is it the way he even said that sounds sexy right now? But wait a minute; I'm starting to feel kinda funny, don't know why, but I do know I've never ever felt this way, ever! While we are slow dancing I get a warm feeling all over my body, plus I get this tingling feeling between my legs as if I just want to give it to him right here and right now! For that matter, I want to give it to Drew too! Hell, I might even give it up to church boy! Rishard is feeling some type of way too I guess, because he is not by any means holding back. Hands everywhere, OMG, he is so touching me all over my breast, and right here in the club. This feeling though, I like it; it feels like just me and him, the music is playing, and so are we.

After what seems like a romantic rendezvous, out of nowhere Drew comes up to me and gives me this look as if I have just totally pissed him off all over again. I'm high so right now, all I can do is just stare at him, like really dude. That doesn't faze him in the least, he asks Rishard can he holla at me for a sec, in which of course this is making me feel so special.

"Yo what's up wit u? Why you all over dat cat like that?"

I laugh, thinking he is really joking right now.

He continues, "So you rolling now?"

Not sure of what that means, but I go with it.

Sarcastically I respond, "So what if I am? You don't care."

"That's not even the point; I just thought you were smarter than that."

Now, I'm really confused. I know he's not acting as if he really cares about what, or who I do. I try to switch the subject."

I ask, "What about Ms. Thang? Where is she? Shouldn't you be all up in her business right now?"

He looks at me with total disgusts, and says, "You young azz girls make it so easy for us."

He turns to walk off, and I try to reach for him, and that's when Rishard comes over, and asks is everything okay.

Drew looks back and says, "It's all good partner, it's on you."

I'm standing here looking sorta stupid, but nevertheless, I still feel good. If I don't know anything, I know Drew still cares for me, and you best to believe before long it'll me he's chilling with, but right now Rishard is all over me, and he is the one that is showing me just how much he really cares, and the least I can do is return the favor.

By the time I get a few more dances in, Dee looks at her phone and lets me know its 11:40. Sh–t! It's so time to go. It takes me a minute to pry Quinn away from her boo! He seems a little thrown off we're heading out so soon. Of course our story is we are about to catch another party. Little does he know, we are lucky to not be having to catch the street lights. We're not in the car good, and Jaz is screaming for some Waffle House. Now I think of it, we haven't eaten, and I do have the munchies, but we only have a little time.

☙

Another escapade pulled off. I'm glad I called Sam to let her know traffic was horrible on Peachtree, which this gave us an extra thirty minutes to make it in, which in essence this gave us time to air out, spray the car, and freshen up. That "Romance" Blunt Power air freshner tho! It's so strong; I believe we left the scent in the driveway.

No sooner than we are in and settled, I check my phone and I notice I have missed Rishard's text to let me know he was leaving. Before I can get myself situated to text him back, he beats me to it.

8/31/14 Sun
Rishard: Wyd
1:04AM
    8/31/14 Sun
    Me: Jus gettn in
    1:06AM
8/31/14 Sun
Rishard: So wuz up???
1:06AM
    8/31/14 Sun
    Me: ;-)
    1:06AM
8/31/14 Sun
Rishard: ??

1:07AM
8/31/14 Sun
Rishard: what u gon do
1:07AM
Before I even think about it, I go with my first mind...
> **8/31/14 Sun**
> **Me: K come get me**
> **1:07AM**

8/31/14 Sun
Rishard: cool text me ur address
1:07AM
Without giving it a second thought, I send him the address. I've never snuck out of the house before, but I am tonight. I get another text.
8/31/14 Sun
Rishard: Give me abt 20 min
1:15AM
> **8/31/14 Sun**
> **Me: K, I'll be on the side**
> **1:15AM**

While I'm getting ready I tell Quinn what's up. She looks at me like yeah right. I give her that I'm so serious look, and she immediately hangs up the phone with whomever. As to make sure there are no issues, I need to let the rest of them in on what's about to go down, because the only thing that matters at this point is I can get out of here without Sam knowing I'm gone. I don't even think Angel cares not the least little bit, because she is glued to the phone with Supa Fly. Dee and Jaz deciding to sleep in the basement was a good thing after all, this way it shouldn't be that hard. Sam's upstairs asleep, I hope, so now all I have to do is sneak out of the basement door, which leads to the side car garage. Uumph, he's texting me right now. He's out there, and I can't wait to see him. I am so ready to do this. Quinn does one last check to see if the coast is clear, all clear. I head out the door, but I totally forget about the motion sensor. Not even that is about to stop me, anyway, I'm out dis bit!

I eventually get to the car, and I look back and the trippin' part is that the house is still lit up; sometimes I wish we didn't have all this high-tech security. I hope no one saw me. I remind myself it's almost two o'clock in the morning, and not much is going on in Brookhaven around this time, but for one minute my heart trembles, because I suddenly remember my Mom and my Uncle Lucy saying that there's nothing up after two but legs… And they would be right!

We drive for about twenty minutes, and we wind up in this undeveloped subdivision, you can tell not too much building has been happening, pitch black dark, and the police isn't riding through all heavy. Actually, I haven't seen one yet. We park in the driveway of this house partially built. Really nice. He asks me if I want to walk through, I look at him like, are you kidding me. I think he gets the picture. We sit and talk for about ten minutes going on about much of nothing, and then he leans over to kiss me. I don't stop him. His lips are so soft and wet, a little too wet to be exact. He asks if I liked that feeling from earlier and I have to be honest and tell him I did, but I really need to know what was it that he gave me, so I ask. Without hesitation he tells me it was XTC. For a moment I'm blowed. I don't know what to think, I get scared, but for some reason I'm cool. He notices my reaction, and tells me it's okay. Nothing's going to happen to me. It's harmless he says. I believe him. I can tell he has me. I calm down. He gives me another one, and this time I take it like a champ.

I look up and the windows are all fogged up, the feeling I am getting has me feeling like I am on top of the world. He reaches over to let my seat back, and comes over to me. It's a bit uncomfortable with him being much taller than I am. He eventually makes his way on top of me, and by the way he kisses me feels like I can stay here forever. He takes his shirt off, and I can definitely tell he has been working out. He kisses me again. This feeling tough… He begins to unbutton his jeans, and all I see is the stars twinkling in the sky. Slowly he slides my legs apart and oh yes, there it is, that moistness again, except this time, it feels more like a dripping faucet. I'm ready. He lifts me up to pull down my panties, and help him. I get a glimpse of the Vince Camuto's, thinking both them and me are about to make our debut. Next thing I know my dress is off, and I am lying naked in the passenger side of a Chevy Impala. Before I realize it, he has managed to make his way inside what I call "paradise," and it is now that I can say I am no longer a virgin. He continues to slowly go in and out, in which it doesn't hurt so badly now, but at first it felt as he had ripped my insides totally out, but after a few minutes of breathing through it, now I am finding myself making moves I never thought I had. I squirm even more. We both moan together. He takes a second to let down the windows because between us and the natural energy we have created enough heat to set off an alarm. I catch my breath. I look at my body, my perfect

His Grace, His Blood, His Mercy!

thirteen year old body caught in a woman's body. I wipe the moisture off of my breast, and he comes back for more. As he is making me into the woman that I knew I was, he asks, "Do you love me?" I tell him, "Yes." He kisses me like I'm the only girl on this earth. I'm in love... Drew who?

Chapter Eleven

Victoria, how about a taste of France's history...

It's hard to believe in a few weeks my baby will be another year older, and I just don't know where the time has gone. It seems like yesterday I was holding her in my arms, playing her favorite songs. She really loved Louis Armstrong's "What a Wonderful World", I think played that song so much; I knew it in my sleep. Never would I have thought I would be so blessed to give birth to a child so beautiful, and so brilliant. As much as I try to push that day in the back of my mind, I never can. Every year around this time I get like this. The accident, the accident that caused me to almost lose my life as well as my baby's life, is a day I will never forget. After that I guess God had to bless me with a child smarter than most adults, even me.

    I remember the first time I knew she was different; well I don't like to call her different, I call her "exceptional." At eighteen months old she began reading! I didn't pay too much attention to that in the beginning, but the day she actually floored me was the day we took a trip to the Fernbank Science Center and the question was asked regarding the difference of the gravitational pull on Mars vs. Earth, and my child raises her hand and answers the question. At 4 years old! From then on I knew we had a blessing in our midst. After that my parents encouraged me to get her tested. I fought it for a while, because I have always wanted Gabrielle to be raised as any other child, but the more I watched her excel in so many areas, I had no choice.

She was tested at six years old, and according to the Wechsler Intelligence Scale for Children, she was measured with an IQ of 170. It took me a while to process that, because the average adult measures at 100, and at that time, I remember Lucy and I having a blast. I burst out laughing because I can hear him now, "Well damn, what you mean, my baby is smarter than me?" Lucy always knew… that's why he is her Godfather. Who else? He wouldn't have had it any other way. While I'm thinking about it, I need to call him. He left me a message earlier.

This room of hers is a mess. If I'm not mistaken, I know I told her to clean up this room. Now days what I tell her goes in one ear and out of the other. I know it's all a part of being a teenager, but I didn't sign up for all this. Some days I could just pack her up and send her in a nice little package to her father, priority class, and I'm sure he will send her back, overnight! No I'm just kidding, I'd be a mess. I love her so much, and I couldn't imagine being without her. Maybe that's the reason I refuse for her to go off to any of those colleges. I want my baby here with me; although I do know she has been worrying me to death about joining Mensa. I have discussed with both Malcolm and Marcel, they both are in agreement that Mensa has great benefits, and it will only add to her intellectual abilities. I'm still on the fence.

※

It's ten o'clock already and I am fit to be tied. I have two clients scheduled back to back and one potential client. Demetrius should be here shortly to bring me some file folders. I'm hoping I will be done in time to make it to my meeting. I've missed the last three meetings. It's been so hectic lately.

I spoke with Karla yesterday, and she hasn't been doing that well. Aside of having diabetes, apparently this new guy she's been dating is really not too keen on her status, and she really has been trying to deal with it. She is so in love with him, and actually I'm the one that convinced her to tell him. I feel bad for her because she hasn't had a steady relationship in over eight years because it's so hard for her to share her status with anyone, and it is not that way for me, I was blessed. I will say, having lived this long with the virus hasn't been all peaches and cream for me either. It's like the older I get, the more I have to stay up on my medications, my doctor's visits, etc. Even though I have been positive for fourteen years, every day is still a struggle. It's a wonderful thing that I have Marcel, because some days are way much worse than others. That's why I need to start going back to my meetings, because I miss my ladies so much.

Malcolm keeps calling me. Every time we talk we never can get through an entire conversation. Either I'm busy, he's busy, or he is sick in the hospital. Either way, I really wish he would get himself together. He has never been the one to do what the doctor ordered. When we divorced, he was so trying to do the right thing, but I guess trying to deal with everyday life, and dealing with Aunt Colleen's passing, it was all just so hard on him. I saw him the last time I went home. He looked good, but not like the Malcolm I once knew. He has really lived a hard life. The one thing that has been a constant joy in his life is Gabrielle. He loves that girl. Would practically die for her. I just wished their relationship was better. Since she was old enough to understand what really happened between Malcolm, Noel, and me, she has never really been able to forgive him. After all this time we still haven't told her everything. She still doesn't know that Malcolm, Marcel, and her mother are all HIV positive. I've tried so hard to shield her from that, even though it wasn't easy, we paid a hefty price to have everything negative removed from the internet, that was very hard to pull off, and I'm still not sure if it has all been removed. With all of this high technology today, anything can happen. As far as the case was concerned, we kept all documentation of that.

༄

Another reason to celebrate looks like my potential client is now my new client. I'm very impressed. Her name is Lilliane du Pont, a thirty-eight year old billionaire who just moved here from France a few months ago. I have to give it to her, for a young woman such as herself, she has her thing together. Portfolio is crazy. I'm just excited that her choice to invest in the Diamond Fund was as she said, "her top priority." I can tell she has really done extensive research on the company. By listening to her, it sounded as though she had declined several offers from other funds, but she was particularly sold on us! Demetrius gave me a heads up in regards to Ms. du Pont about a month ago, also I sorta heard about her from one of my "financial friends." So I was already prepared.

Running late as usual, but I'm here. Walking in, my phone is ringing off the hook. I have to take it. It's Lucy. Dammit, Lucy can't this wait? Even though this is his third time calling me. I so need to do better.

"Vic, what ya doing?" he screams.

Trying to be as quiet as I can, "Heading into my support group."

"Chile, you haven't left those lonely, depressed, oh I need a man, women alone yet?"

I can't even laugh at this idiot now. "Let me call you back," I say, hoping he will get the picture, yet and still he keeps talking. I have no choice but to oblige him.

"What's up Lu, with your crazy self?"

"Oh baby, your girl has been promoted to Head Buyer! So you know what that means right?"

Am I really ready for this? I answer anyway. "No Lu, what does that mean?"

Yelling even louder in my ear, "Time to turn up! Now besides my baby's birthday I have another reason to come and shut the 'A' down!"

I somewhat yell back, "For sho."

It's been about six months since I've seen my friend, my other brother shall I say. Every day I miss him so much, and

I can't wait to see him. We've been planning so much for this party, we haven't even had time to catch up.

"Yes suga, it's about to be on and poppin."

Just as I am trying to hurry him off the phone, Tara sees me in the hall and you would think she hasn't seen me in a million years.

Bear hugging me, she belts out, "Mrs. Bouviér, it's so good to see you. We've missed you being here."

I smile and hug her back. "Same here, and you really look good too."

"Thank you, Mrs. Bouviér, coming from you that means a lot. I really have missed you."

Realizing I've been out here way too long already, I tell her I will see her inside, and I also tell Lucy I will talk to him later. Surprisingly, he's cool with it.

Soon as I walk through the door, one of the ladies that I hadn't seen in a while waves at me. As to not make a ruckus, I take a seat by her. She looks worn down, really tired. Bags under her eyes, as if she hasn't slept in days, but by the way she's wearing that navy pantsuit and nude pumps you wouldn't know it.

Karla introduces a new survivor to the group. Her name is Myra, a sixty-nine year old woman who has lived with the virus for well over ten years. She was previously a part of a support group in Macon, but since she now lives in Metro Atlanta she wanted to start coming here. Listening at her story even helps me. I really need this. She tells us she got the virus from her then "twenty-seven year old" lover. Just so happened she had just reached menopause, and because she wasn't getting a period, she felt she could no longer get pregnant, therefore she felt it was okay to have sex with him without a condom, he was her man, and she was his cougar, so what was the big deal. She was good on that, but little did she know her "little man" was positive. Yeah she thought about not being a mother again, but she failed to think that in her retirement she would be faced with this. Even in all of that her story is amazing, because to see her makes me want to go and work out at the gym soon as I leave here. This lady doesn't look a day over 40. She tells us what has been her saving grace besides taking her meds, is that she has begun to take her health more seriously. Before, she had hypertension, high cholesterol, plus she was a chain smoker, but one day she said enough was enough, and that she was taking control of her life. She is no longer on any other medications besides her HIV meds, and she no longer smokes. She just up and one day quit. I am so inspired by her, but with everything I have going on, it's so hard to get out of bed some days, nevertheless go to a gym. I just make it look easy.

Overall it was a great meeting, and I'm glad I decided to come tonight. I met some new people that I will say have given me hope to go on another day. Though I have lived with this for some time, I still need to be around other women such as myself to remind me what it's all for. Case and point, I got the chance to speak with the lady in the pantsuit, and as a matter of fact the reason she is so worn, she lost her job several weeks ago. She has tirelessly been job seeking, three children, one about to start college, one about to be a mother, and one already has two children. Her major is finance… Thank you Lord. She had a copy of her resume in her car. With her qualifications, I just sent an email to Norma, head of our HR department. First thing in the morning she will set her up for an interview.

Chizellé T. Archie

༄

On the way home, I see I missed a text from Lucy. That boy is sick. He sends me a text to tell me he's bringing Broderick! OMG this is going to be more than a notion. Those two together are worse than Times Square on New Year's Eve.

Believe it or not I am starved, I've been going since this morning, and I really haven't had anything to eat. Gabrielle is with Dionne, and I've already given Drago the night off, so I think I'll just stop by Nakato's. I've been dying for the Kaki Rockefeller's. There's nothing like some good ol' grilled oysters topped with mozzarella, bacon, and spinach. Make you wanna hurt yourself. Marcel says he only goes for the sauce; I can't blame him for that, because he's definitely right. It is mouth watering.

Soon as I pull up I notice a Flying Spur, almost identical to mine, the only difference is the color; mine is white, and this one Beluga. Need to drive it more often. I'm guessing Sunday's count, but as far as my Tesla, right now, is what's happening. I'm totally hooked.

As I'm ordering, I notice Ms. du Pont, and a couple of ladies dining in as well. As not to be so noticeable I continue ordering, and before the waiter completes my order Ms. du Pont makes her way over to me. She's beyond ecstatic. She even brings one of the other ladies over to meet me. Not wanting to be disrespectful in any way, I remain cordial, but please know I am so hungry. By the way this lady is talking to me; you would think we were family or something. Ms. du Pont introduces her girlfriend Constance, who is also her best friend, slash assistant. Like Ms. du Pont, she's a very beautiful young lady as well, I'm so loving the black long sleeved shirt dress, and Lord have mercy those Gucci jaguar print calf hair stilettos. Gotta love a woman with style, and judging by the way she hokey-pokied over here, either she's drunk or she needs lessons how to walk in a 5" pair of heels, although I'm sure it's on YouTube "how to walk in heels," but anyway while I'm waiting for my food, I try to get to know a little more about Ms. du Pont.

"It's okay, you can call me Lilliane. To most people I go by Lill, I guess it kinda stuck with me from childhood."

Being nosy, I ask, "What are you ladies up to this evening?"

Constance mumbles with that lovely accent, "Looking for a Buckhead Man."

We all laugh.

Lilliane jumps in, "No actually we just left doing some shopping, so now we are just about to wind down."

"You sound like Debbie Downer," I tell her.

She laughs, "No, it's just been a long day. Still getting things situated. Haven't totally moved yet, so it's just the going back and forth that wears me down."

By this time the other lady walks over, and she is nowhere near as pleasant as the others. A bit older too. Lilliane introduces her as Aimée, her other best friend.

"Are you liking Atlanta Aimée?" I ask.

"Somewhat. It's really not all that. New York's better."

"New York? Where in New York did you live?"

Constance breaks in, "Long Island."

"So… you are from New York as well Constance?" I ask.

"Technically no, I'm from a city outside of Paris, called Le Mans, but I moved there a few years back. I will say, Atlanta is a lot like NY, just on a smaller scale, but the men here are friendlier, now that's a plus."

Aimée adds, "Not all of them. For the most part they seem pretty nice though."

Constance says to me, "You're from New York, correct?"

Smiling so hard I respond, "Yes I am. A true New York girl."

"So is your husband Marcel, correct?" Lilliane asks.

Ahhmmm what the h--, this conversation has just taken a fast turn, but as the gracious woman I am, I say to her, "Well no, he's actually from—"

"Paris." Aimée states.

"You're right Aimée."

"The name Bouviér speaks for itself." Lilliane says.

"Why do you say that?" I ask her.

"Unless you have been sleeping under a rock, if you know anything about diamonds, you have to know "Armand.""

Just when she says this, I feel, impressed, stunned, all at the same time, I feel so wonderful right now. I am so proud of my baby. He has done so well to make a great name for himself.

Be it as it may, I've enjoyed our conversation, and Lilliane and her friends are truly a sweet group of ladies. Once again, Lord I thank you for putting me in a position that I'm able to help others. I know without you I wouldn't be able to do any of this, from day one it has been you.

We end shortly after that, and I'm still hungry.

Chapter Twelve

Quinn, the rules apply to you too...

Traffic is bananas on the way to South Dekalb Mall. I've been sitting here on Candler for at least fifteen minutes, and Gram's would choose today for me to pay her Macy's bill. I am loving my new little ride, thanks to my Sugadaddie Derrick. Before he left, I told him I really needed a whip because between Gram, and work, I need my own. So he took me over to PayLess Car lot and got me this cute little Honda Civic. I just have to pay the insurance. I must say the cookie is as sweet as ever. $15,000 sweet! Rule# 13 – 'Never leave empty handed.'

Right when it seems like I'm stuck, here comes Pee Wee, well Bishop Pee Wee. As usual, he's dressed in full regalia, three piece suits, with the vest, cuff links, and the Now-a-later gators. Today he's rocking the powder blue from head to toe, looking like a sample of paint from Home Depot. He's been out here on this same block for the last couple of years preaching. I went to middle school with Daryl, and he was definitely not the street preacher back then. It makes Gram's sick to pass through here, because her thing is beware of false prophets. I would agree with that, but I'm not that spiritual and all, okay, I'm not spiritual at all, but looks like my boy's game is tight. I know for a fact every weekend he racks up, and to me the only thing he's doing is screaming through some decorated bull horn. Every time I see him I laugh at him, he reminds me of a pimped out version of Jesse Jackson, yelling "keep hope alive!"

Before I catch the green light he has hit me up for a few dollars. He says it's an offering, and it's going towards his ministry, "Give and it Shall Be Given Unto You Ministries, Inc." You can't be mad at him, we all got a hustle, and his blueprint is the Preachers of L.A. He's determined that along with his church, he will have a house with an elevator, and a Bentley, and let's not forget the tag that says BISHOP. The boy is a trip, but just like any other time, he got me. Hashtag… I'm doing it for you Jesus.

Of course, everyone and their mother is in here, and the first person I see is Celeste. She and my Aunt Skyye have been at each other's throats since I moved here. I think it's over Tiger; at least that's what I heard. All I know is when my aunt sees her she goes ballistic. Her nickname is 'Snap Hoe." She's the one on Facebook that when every time you see her she is posing in front of the camera taking selfies and each one of them it's like she intentionally post just for Facebook. Instead of being a model and getting paid, now you being a model and getting likes.

"Hey Quinn," she says.

In the driest tone, I say back to her, "Hey Celeste."

"How's Skyye?"

Really lady. As if she really gives a care how she's doing. Some people are so fake, but I still try to treat her as respectful as I can.

"She's good."

"That's cool."

She walks away as if there's something else she has to tell me, but I'm not stopping her.

☙

Every time I think I'm spared from cleaning the kitchen these little ragamuffins always leave their crap in the sink. Look at this. It would be one thing if I ate here all the time, but I'm hardly ever here. I don't know which place I like to be most, here or over to Grams. At least I don't have to worry about having to share everything with everybody at Grams. It's pretty chill over there, although I do like having the freedom I have over here. Aunt Skyye usually is never home. Tiger and his friends are here more than she is. He's this dude that she has had hanging around here for the longest, if he's not sleep on the couch, then he's on the porch waiting for the post man to bring what he calls it, "his check." If you asks me that's the main reason she has him here, because every month on the 3rd of the month, it's like Christmas around this joint.

Outside of the fact he is two of the girl's father, not really sure why he even lives here anyway. Well, really he doesn't, word on the street he has a spot in Lilburn, but I have yet to see him stay there. I don't even know if they even love each other, because she comes home with so many other dudes, and he never seems to have a problem with it. Things just really get ugly when the money gets low.

The good thing is I get to meet plenty of his sexy friends. That's how I met Juelle, and Rhasan. Juelle and Tiger are real tight, he's his connect. Yeah, I forgot to tell you, Tiger is on that crack rock hard. Sometimes, I think Aunt Skyye is to. I know she is, but she maintains well. She's not that "crackhead" that you can look at and just tell, she's more upscale with hers. She has sponsors that help pay for her habit, and on that note, I guess ain't nothing's for free, but whatever I will say she does it well. Always coming home with a new bag, new shoes, new jewelry, I think she has more than the jewelry store, the only part I hate is that when she puts it all on at one time. Eewww, silver, gold, turquoise, sometimes I'm like okay lady just pick one.

I'm so glad I'm off this evening, I'm supposed to go over to Gram's later, Gabs has lied again to her mom that she is staying with me for the night, in which I don't care, I'm cool with it, but I just don't want her to get caught up. It's like lately she has been trippin' over ol' boy Rishard so hard, she hasn't even had that much time to kick it with me for real. If they are not over Gram's house, they are chilling over here.

Juelle, Rhasan, and Rishard were just riding together a couple hours ago. He told me he was supposed to hook up with my girl tonight. They have been going hard. It was never in the Rule Book to get hooked. Rule #40 – 'Never let them know you love them.' She has so thrown that out the door. At least that what she says.

His Grace, His Blood, His Mercy!

Mr. Man is texting me, and I am so feeling him. This dude has been sweating me for a minute now. At first I wasn't even gon' go there, but a girl gots to keep her playa status going. He says he waited for a minute, but he couldn't wait any more. He thinks I'm so fine; he couldn't keep his hands off me.

> **11/04/14 Sat**
> **Mr. Man: what's up with ya?**
> **3:20PM**
>> 11/04/14 Sat
>> Me: nothn, what's up with you?
>> 3:22PM
>
> **11/04/14 Sat**
> **Mr. Man: I want u!!!!**
> **3:24PM**
>> 11/04/14 Sat
>> Me: really?! Come thru and get me.
>> 3:26PM
>
> **11/04/14 Sat**
> **Mr. Man: over ur way, give me 10**
> **3:28PM**
>> 11/4/14 Sat
>> Me: ;)☺☺
>> 3:30PM

Ooooh, I can't wait! I don't know what it is, but the last time he made every minute I was with him worth it. I'm hoping this time he'll take me to the house, but really I don't have that much time anyways, unless he wants to cool out longer. It's a part of me that feels bad about what I'm doing, but it's not like he's married or anything. So he has a boo, but as Aunt Skyye says, every wo-man for herself, and if I don't look out for me who will.

While I'm rushing to throw on something nice, Gabby calls. Gotta talk fast, I'm on a mission.

In haste, I answer, "Hey you, what you got going on?"

"Not too much, just woke up. Up all night on the phone with Rishard. Girl, he–"

"Gabs, not trying to be funny or anything, but I need to hit you back. Your girl got to make a quick run. Mr. Man is on the way to pick me up."

Laughing she says, "That's what's up! Do you. I know I am later, but don't hurt him, you know how you are."

Laughing back, I say, "And you know it, already got a car, so you already know what time it is."

We laugh and say it together, "Rule #10 – 'No matter what, always put yourself first."

Half an hour later, he picks me up and we waste no time to getting to the spot. I'm starting to think he just may be married because the way he keeps everything on the hush, he must not want her to know. I'm cool with that though. It is what it is. No attachments, just good sex, real good sex.

༄

This man will make you break all the rules, but I can't give in. It's those eyes, the way he looks at you so deep, like he's looking into your whole soul. Makes you just wanna give him your whole paycheck, plus the fact usually everybody else is ready to get up when they are done, but he doesn't. He cuddles, makes you feel special. Uhn-unn Quinn don't even go there… can't be catching no feelings. That's most definitely in the Rule Book, "Never make them think they have the upper hand." Can't be making me all weak.

"What you be doing to a brotha?" he slowly asks, while trying to catch his breath. 'Girl you got that comeback."

Okay so I have been told that what I'm working with is all that, but never have I had it told to me like that.

"Why you say that? I know you have a lot of other females you say that to."

"We not talking about other females, this is about you. And I'm sure you don't care about them, and who said anything about any other females anyway?"

It would really be nice if I can get some idea if he's married or not. Just don't want no drama.

"I give you that. You're right, no reason to be trippin' over anybody else."

Before I can finish he kisses me and says, "Yeah, because who's here with me now?"

Why do I feel like I'm so losing cool points here? Probably because he just laid it down. For a minute I have a brain freeze, but I quickly remember who's in control.

I lean in and kiss him back, but this time it's with much more tension, and passion than before, then I say to him, "I'm here with you."

Looking as though he is ready for round two, he asks again, "What time you need to be back?"

For a minute I forget I have to be over Grams, but ahmm not for real for real. I can do this all night, but I remember too I have a paper due for Monday.

I tell him, "In about an hour."

"Can I have about 15 more minutes, promise you'll be back in time, I need to go by the club anyways."

I don't give it another thought. I give in, and we go at it again. All I can think about is what in the hell was Gabs thinking? She missed out on all this beefcake, but too late, guess is he wanted a real woman this time.

ೂ

I'm convinced Tiger doesn't do anything all day but sit up and get high; the house is still a mess. When I left it was a mess, and you would think I'm the only one that lives here. Mikey left before I did, Tweety is over her friend's house, Tee-Tee and 'nem gone to the game, but I ain't eem' 'bout to trip and clean this whole house by myself.

Soon as Drew drops me off, I can tell Tiger is already looking for a come up. Every time somebody with a nice car comes through he's already thinking it's somebody he can score from, but Drew wasn't even stuttn that foolishness, he let me out and kept it moving.

Dag, Derrick is calling me. What now? I thought he was good. Unless he got something else for me, but on that note I am seriously going to have to call him back, because no matter what I have to turn this paper in, even though I pretty much have a high "B" in English Lit, can't be slipping in the classroom. Playing is cool, but if I wind up not graduating, Grams would straight up have a stroke. She says over her dead body will I become another version of my mother and her sister.

His Grace, His Blood, His Mercy!

I really hate it for Grams sometimes; she's really a cool grandma. She's not responsible for how her daughters decided to live their lives, but as for me, I don't let everybody know it, but that's not even my plan. I do, I want to make something out of myself. Never told anybody this, but I actually want to become a Journalist. I'm even amazed how many articles I have stashed away. My secret girl crush is Oprah. She's my inspiration, but I think everyone just expects me to be Quinn, but the crazy part is that, Bishop Pee Wee was the one that once told me he saw my name written in lights. Either he was looking for a great offering this day, or he knows something I don't. I have dreams like everyone else.

Chapter Thirteen

Gabrielle, the "A" ain't even ready...

My birthday is finally here! Happy birthday to me, happy birthday to me, happy birthday to me, happy birthday to me… Wow, I don't even believe it, but I made it. I'm so excited because my party is tomorrow night. We 'bout to turn all the way up! Then on top of that my Uncle Lucy will be here in a little while, and he's coming with his boo-ski Broderick, and you know they 'bout that life!

As every year I wake an hour earlier to breakfast in bed made by Chef extraordinaire Drago, and like any other year I get a rose with a note attached from who else, Queen Victoria herself, and right when I'm sitting up ready to go for what I know, she comes in smiling as if Christian Louboutin just sent her own private collection of red bottoms.

"Happy birthday my baby girl," she says.

"Thank you Momma," I respond.

"So how does it feel to be fourteen?"

Did she really ask me that? What am I supposed to say, oh it feels so good, or should I tell her, I'm really not the little girl she thinks I am.

"It feels good," I tell her.

"That's good, and I was hoping you would say that, since I have something for you. It's a threefold gift, you get the first today, and tomorrow you'll get the final gift.

Okay so my heart is beating a million miles a minute. Could it be a car? OMG, now you know if it is I am out of here all the time. I won't even need Quinn to pick me anymore, but wait… I can't get a car yet, I'm according to the state of Georgia I still have one more year before I can get a permit, so I'm not banking on that.

"Momma what is it?"

She begins, "I never told you this, but when you were first born, your father wrote you this letter along with a bracelet he gave to you. Of course you wore your bracelet, and yes you were so beautiful.

"I still have it," I say.

"Ahm, yes you do, but the letter, he wanted you to have it when we felt you were mature enough, and minus a few minor adjustments you have proven to be a responsible, and mature young lady. You are so beautiful, and so smart, I can't believe that God loved me enough to give me a gift such as you. So in saying that, we–"

I interrupt her, "Who is we?"

"Your father, the both of us felt like it was time for you to have it. Now you don't have to read it right now, but when you are ready, we just felt like you should have it."

"So why is he not coming for my birthday like he said?"

"Well now that, I don't know, he hasn't mentioned anything to me about that, although I did speak with him recently. So you would really want him here?"

Even I have to think about that for a minute. It's been at least a year since I've seen him. But he has been asking to come see me; I just have never had time. It was that or he was sick. I do really want to see him, and maybe just maybe he has something good for me.

"Well yeah, yes ma'am I would like that, but—"

"But what?"

"Nevermind."

"Ok then, have it your way, you just let me know. But I do have something else for you, also when you were born, your father Marcel gave you a gift as well, not only did he want you to always be happy, he wanted you to always have something of your own. He started a trust fund for you, in which we decided that you should at least be 18 years old to access it. However, we made some calls and we were able to have it so you are allowed to access a certain amount every year until then, so we are giving you your first amount today. $10,000 for you to have, for you to do with it wisely as you choose, with some exceptions, you are not to spend it on anything that God himself would disapprove of."

Really lady, you got to be kidding me. That sounds like everything.

With shear excitement I say to her, "Thank you Momma so much, that means the world to me, and I am so glad that you and Dad trust me enough. I promise I won't do anything wrong with it."

"I know you won't sweetheart. Now it's time for school. Remember I will be there about 11:30 to get you, we have to pick Lucy and Broderick up from the airport at 2:00."

"Yes ma'am."

☙

Before I head to my second period class, I notice I have several missed texts. Three of them are from my Bae, Rishard, and oh my goodness, how did he even know it was my birthday; church boy!

He writes, "Happy Birthday, I pray today is as beautiful as you are, and oh yeah you could have invited me to the party. SMH"

Dude be for real! Just as I am saying this, Jordan walks up behind me, only to thank me for her invite. That was not my choice, blame it on Dionne, it's because of her she will soon become a GEM, but if she keeps wearing those last year's Sperry's I don't know about that.

What a way to start my birthday, another test aced! And considering I didn't even look over it, I should pat myself on the back. This school thing like I always say is overrated. Plus I have $10,000 to work with. Just thinking about it sends chills up my spine. Bae didn't even believe me when I told him. He was like for real?! Can't wait to go shopping, and oh he has to get those new J's.

Heading to my locker, as much as I try to avoid this chick, for some reason I can't. It's like she's everywhere, in the halls, at the lockers, at the club, at the mall, dag, I wish she would just disappear, but anyway I don't even know why I'm trippin' so hard over her. Really I'm not even worried. So what her and Drew are together, a part of me is over him. I'm kicking it with Big Pimpin' now, and I don't care what Drew says, I know he really don't care much for Rishard, and that's why I'm glad we was all booed up at the party.

"So Ms. Lady, you got this hot party tomorrow, and you didn't even give me an invite?" She boldly asks me.

Really right now, I'm sorta lost for words, because why would I invite her. I don't even like her. D'Sharee, whatever, gul please. In the back of my mind, I'm like, Bye Felecia.

She continues, "The word around the school is you really don't care much for me, I'm not sure why, because as far as I know, I have never done anything to you."

It's at this moment I feel like I'm having an out of body experience, as though I am slapping her so hard she doesn't even know which way her head is going. Doesn't she know she's my nemesis? Even before Drew was in the picture, I didn't like her, she just felt like she was all that, and before she started going to this school, it was all about me... well it still is, but—

I add, "I thought the same thing about you, it's not like you have ever said more than two words to me before today."

"Well let me be the first to say, I have no beef with you, but you know how it is, everybody telling you one thing, and then you think another, next thing you know you're not speaking to someone better yet you don't even like a person, and you really don't know why."

Okay where are we going with the lets be friends speech, spit it out. She only wants to come to the party because she knows it's going to be the hottest party in the "A", but nevertheless, we decide to call it a truce, and no biggie to me, like I said, I'm so over ol' boy… Andrew Harrison.

My phone is vibrating off the hook just as I am walking to the office to check out, it's my mentor Ms. Paige updating me on the progress of my experiment we are doing, well I'm doing it, she's just assisting me for the most part. I'm so excited about it.

☙

The airport is packed, we've had to drive around at least four times, but it's not long at all before two of the flyest dudes in the "A" are standing on the curb like they're flagging down a cabbie in New York. With all the comotion they're causing you'd think Obama was coming through Hartsfield-Jackson. Talking about Louis Vuitton luggage for days; looks like a scene from *Coming to America*, and the killing part is Broderick looks just like Semmi, except Broderick is so doggone fine. But the only thing I'm trippin' off of is I dunno whose killing it the most, Brodericks' platinum blonde Mohawk, or that custom purple color my Uncle Lucy is rockin. Suki-suki-ni, and those oversized Gucci aviators are so what's up.

It doesn't take five minutes before they are back at it like fifteen year olds.

"Diva!" They both yell. It seems like they haven't seen each other in forever. When they're together it's all good. I can sense it, she's so happy. I wonder what it would be like if my Uncle lived here. Nope, don't even want to imagine that. Even though at one point I had him wrapped around my finger,

His Grace, His Blood, His Mercy!

I'm not sure if it'll be like having two mothers, and I for sho' don't need that. One is enough!

"Baby girl, what's up with that God forsaken travesty you are wearing?" Uncle Lucy asks me.

I can't stop laughing at him, because he's been on everybody ever since he got in the car, but what do I expect from the Fashionista himself.

Momma laughs too and says, "Lucy, you know that's her uniform, how many times have you seen her with that on?"

He cracks back, "Lawd looks like she is on her way to the nearest monestary."

Broderick gives me that no—you- -don't look, and saves me, "To me, she looks like a well-rounded, smart, educated young lady to me, if I say so myself." He winks at me just so I'll know he's serious.

I tell him, "Thank you." But not before Uncle Lucy says, "Hunti, what you talking about, we didn't wear no mess like that."

I see Momma looking at me in the rearview mirror smiling, as she and Uncle Lucy both say, oh baby, we was too sharp.

Did they just say sharp? OMG, I have to give it to 'em they were pretty fly back in the day, and yeah Momma's still doing her thing. Must admit her shoe-game is something outrageous.

"Before I get started with ya'll crazy people, I'm gonna need something to get me through. " Momma adds. We all know what that is, her Hazelnut Macchiato.

"Chile I need one too, get me an Iced Skinny Mocha, got to have it, and Bae, would you like anything?" he asks Broderick.

"No I'm good, I'll leave that to ya'll two Starbucks followers."

He and I laugh. I'm not sure what that is Broderick has on, but shoot, he smells too good. I'm trying not to scope him out too much just yet, but Uncle Lucy sure knows how to pick 'em. I'm actually a little mad really, his brows are beat, and now that I'm closer up to him, whoever cut his hair, they did that. I know he's a little younger than Uncle Lucy though, but he has his own paper. He models for Tom Ford. Okay, perfect match, fashion buyer, and a model. Maybe he can show me a few more pointers. Never can have enough.

☙

Just about a few hours later, we've shopped so much, I'm even tired. My bed looks like; well you can't even see it. I bought my baby so much stuff; he's going to be like dag. I hope he likes the Burberry shades, and the Gucci high tops. I pretty much guessed his size, but if they don't fit we can take 'em back. I totally forgot the Rule Book, where it states. "Never buy a man a pair of shoes, because next thing you know he will walk right out of your life." Later for that, my boo must look good, plus he'll be at my party too. This will be the first time I'm out with him like this. Haven't quite figured out how to make it not look so obvious that he's my man to Momma and the rest of them, but really who cares, I'm fourteen now, why can't I have a boyfriend. So what he's twenty. I just still can't believe I'm not a virgin anymore. For what it's worth, it feels real good too. Every chance we get we are going at it; I don't even know what took me so long.

My Uncle Lucy knocks on my door, "Can I come in?"
"Yes sir."

His Grace, His Blood, His Mercy!

He takes a look around my room, and all he says is how he remembers designing my first room when I was born. We laugh, because he says Momma had this monstrosity of a bed for me that looked as though it was something Prince George should have had.

"Honey, your room was fit for a princess; Vic wouldn't have had it any other way," he says.

"Yeah I remember, I've seen the pictures, it was really pretty."

"I remember that day like it was just yesterday." He goes on. "You were such a beautiful baby, oh those eyes, I fell in love with you as if you were my own. Never would I have figured that you would be even more beautiful at fourteen. I hope you know how proud I am of you."

"Yes sir, I do."

He looks at me, and says, "Ok now, this is my story honey." I giggle. So does he.

"Anyway, I just want you to know that you are and have been a very blessed young lady. And I have no doubt in my mind that you are going to make us even the more proud. I just want you to remember honey that these little knucklehead boys don't have anything on their minds except getting into those cute little pants of yours. Trust me. I am a boy, contrary to what some may think, yes I love men, but I still know what it's like to be young, and can't wait to get your first little piece of the cookie."

I am so uncomfortable now… really Uncle Lucy, I'm thinking to myself.

He continues, "Look at you, I know it, you're cute, fabulous, smart, all that and a bag of chips, and I am sure those little prep school boys have been checking you out, but please hear me, and hear me good; it can wait. You should wait for that one person that really has your heart; you should wait until you both are mature enough to handle not only the physical side of sex, but the emotional side of sex. It's not all it's cracked up to be. Maybe if I would have waited, maybe things in my life would be different somehow."

I interrupt him, "You don't have to worry about anything Uncle Lucy, I'm okay on that point."

He asks, "So you are telling me you haven't crossed the burning sands as of yet?

I shake my head no, although, I am so lying right now. Little does he know, I have crossed the burning sands, walked them, and laid on them. Stop it Gabby.

He continues, "See I know Vic, she really isn't trying to have this conversation with you because she feels like ok, you are a bright, intelligent young lady, and she knows you have your friends and all. But see sometimes parents can be too close, and they see what they want to see. But Honey Chile, I'm a different type of animal, I come from another side of the tracks. I've done enough, and I have seen enough. Not saying you have, but I know around this time some of you little fast tail girls began to smell yourselves, and you think that the only way to define yourselves is by giving them something they can feel. Well let me tell you once again; Don't!"

I try to keep a straight face as long as I can, but even as he's talking to me, I'm thinking of the first time with Rishard. Mmm, mm, umm. I'm zoning out as I hear him drift into the background. I know my baby is not like that. He loves me. He would never hurt me. He gets me anything I want, and more than anything he is still around. If it was all about hitting and quitting he would have been gone, but I know, he got my back, like I always say.

"Well baby, I trust you if you say you haven't, but remember what I said. Everybody doesn't have your best interest at heart. Ain't nobody gonna love you like we do."

He gives me the biggest hug, and kisses me on my forehead.

"So let me see this fabulous dress you have for tomorrow night. I made sure it would be everything you would like."

I show him my Alexander McQueen party dress, and as I expected, he is so hyped up. He loves it.

"I wanted to give you your gift tonight before all the hoopla tomorrow. I have something for you and so does Broderick, but of course mines is better."

He pulls out the coldest pair of Prada Suede mid-calf, fur-cuff boots. I'm saying to myself Dammmmn! A beast on the runway coming. They are so hot. I give him another big hug, by this time, Broderick is knocking, we both say, "Come in."

"This is a really nice room, of what I can see of it," he says.

We all start laughing. "Yes, I know it's a disaster now, but it'll be clean by tomorrow."

"No worries, what do you expect from a young lady that just shut the department store down. They should have a picture of you at the front entrance with a sign that says, "If you see this young lady, she lives here.'"

"She gets it from you know who." Uncle Lucy screams.

"Yep Momma has been known to shut it down a few times."

"Ahhm excuse me Boo-Boo, I'm talking about me, the one and only, Clothing Extraordinaire, the Fashion Diva, the Best, hated like none other from all the rest!"

Okay, I can't even do this, he is killing me, but it is what it is.

Broderick says, laughing, "Well excuse me André Leon Talley."

We all crack up. "See ya'll some hating something's in here," he says.

"I have this for you birthday girl Broderick says, and hands me a pretty wrapped box. I open it, of course Louis Vuitton. Oh yes, off the charts, my own Eden bag! It's the bomb! I love my Uncle Lucy and now I'm not sure if I love Broderick even more. Na'll just trippin' trippin', but he has come correct. Dionne is going to lose it when she sees this. I know she's going to try so hard to get this one. Not!

"I hope you like it." he says.

"Do I? I love it."

Uncle Lucy jumps in and says. "So what you like his gift better than mine?"

Really I honestly don't even want to hurt his feelings; I love the boots, but baby, this bag tho'. I need to be walking the runway. And oh, Jaz is going to have a fit. She has been begging her mom for the longest for another Louis, but this one is killing it.

I look at my phone I have 5 missed texts. All from Rishard! I reach over to get my phone, and they both say, "That's our cue." They give me a hug. "See you tomorrow."

"I love you guys."

"We love you too."

Uncle Lucy says going out of the door, and "Yes, tomorrow night is going to be epic, we 'bout to show the "A" how to turn up! My baby girl got it like that."

This only makes me even more excited about my party. I read the texts from boo thang, and the first one I get is a selfie! No he didn't, he sent a pic of himself naked standing in the bathroom mirror. Posted up like what! I can't wait to call him. Got me feeling some type of way.

"Hey babe what up with you sending me pics like that and all?"

"Oh so what, I shouldn't have? Can I help it if I was thinking about you?"

"No it's all good, but I just wasn't–"

"You wasn't what?" he asks.

"I wasn't thinking that would be the first thing I see."

"Oh excuse me Ms. Lady, sounds like I offended you."

"Bae, stop it, I didn't say that. Matter of fact I was thinking about you too."

"So what's up then? I know you can get out."

Not tonight I'm thinking. This house is surrounded with the FBI, CIA, KGB, all that. It's a cold chance in hell of me sneaking out of here tonight.

"Don't think tonight is a good night boo, too many people here."

"For what?"

"For what?" I ask him. "My party tomorrow night."

"Oh yeah. I forgot about that, been too busy grinding."

'So you are coming to the party aren't you?"

I know he is not going to flake out on me, and not come, even though my parents don't know I'm with him like that.

"Ion know jus yet. Might not be a good idea for your folks to see me right now, might start trippin' or somethin'. "

"Bae, they don't have to know we together, they can think you are just there with some other people."

"No doubt, if I show, you best believe I'm coming with one of my homeboys."

My heart is racing at the thought of him being there. I am so into this dude. Mainly I want to show him off to the rest of my friends. My girls already know he's my dude, but some of the other chicks at school haven't seen him yet and it's a must that they see the dude Gabs is kicking with.

"I know you say you can't get out, but how 'bout you just tell your moms, you going over to Quinn's Grams' for a lil' bit. I just wanna see you. Well let me say I need to see you. I can pick you up and we can ride for a quick minute. I won't have you out long. Promise."

I think about it, and the idea is not so bad. I can tell her Quinn wants me to come over for a bit.

"If I get out, will you come to the party?"

"For sho. You gon' give me some?"

"Where?"

"Don't worry about all that, I got this."

Now what I need to figure out is how I am going to pull off getting out of here. It's almost nine thirty.

I text Quinn to see if she's at Gram's, she quit her job at the theatre. So she might not be over this way.

Cool. She will be, in about twenty minutes she says. She has to drop something over to Grams.

༄

It wasn't that hard at all getting out. I'm glad Quinn came through for me though. My girl never lets me down. It was smooth sailing when she came over, that was my exit, so now no reason to trip about me being out here so late. If push comes to shove I can always tell Momma I'm staying over.

My baby is so sweet; he picked me up just like he said. We didn't have to wait long at all, he was already there. He stops to get a beer right quick, as well as he gets me some chips and a drink. While I'm waiting for him to come out the store, his phone goes off, I try my best not to look at it, but I can't resist. I pick it up, and it's a text from some girl named India. I'm trying to read it as much as I can before he comes out, all I can make out is her asking him what he's doing, and where is he. I don't want to jump to conclusions or anything, but I know he's not talking to some other girl besides me. I'm not going to trip, that could be anybody.

He comes out the store, and hands me my soda, leans over to give me a kiss, and asks, "You missed me while I was gone?"

In a joking tone, I say, "You know I did."

A part of me wants to asks him who is India, because according to the Rule Book, Rule #18 – 'Always go with your first mind, never second guess yourself.' Really, I just don't want to bring up anything that may not be true. No need to go somewhere I don't have to.

A few minutes later we get to this spot that kinda looks like where a store used to be, but they closed it down for some reason. No one's around of course, so it should be cool we sit here for a while. He lights a blunt and I take a few puffs just to get me going. The more I do it, the more I like it. It mellows me out; relaxes me. It's like when I'm smoking, I'm so chill. We see a few lights one too many times, so much so this spot we are thinking may not be too cool after all. We ride for a little bit more, but by this time, my feelings are starting to rise, and I am so like come on. He heads to his friend's house, over off Dresden. Looks like someone may be home, but he insists its cool for us to park outside.

Before I recognize it we are going at it as if we have not seen each other in a minute. Any other time he comes over to my side, but this time I decide I would switch it up a bit. With my long legs I drape myself on top of him as he slides his seat back, so that I can have more room. I'm so glad this time I'm not as restrained as I was before. No designer shoes, only a cute little denim dress with no panties underneath. He slides himself into me, and while I am trying to adjust myself I procrastinate so that I won't rush anything, I use all my muscles I have inside of me to take every inch of him. I breathe slowly while he pulls my hair just hard enough to give a tug. I eventually pick up a speed as if I have mounted a Clydesdale, and I take it as if I have. He opens my dress to satisfy his view of my breast that are now so full and hard. He kisses my nipples, I moan even louder. I allow my body to go in an up and down stride to the point I picture myself as a yo-yo, my legs are listless. I slow it down, but it is so hard for me to stop, because he pulls me into him, grabs and squeezes my behind and I start all over again. I want him so badly, I'm quivering. He tells me he needs me, he tells me again he loves me. I continue to ride him as if I was a Sheena queen of the jungle. By now I got this thing down. I'm no longer a newbie, I am now a proficient sexual princess. Just as I am about to reach my ultimate climax, both of our phones are going off like crazy. Texts back to back. He tells me to hold up for a minute. I reach over to grab my phone in between the seats, I look at it, 10 texts are from my mother!!! One of them

His Grace, His Blood, His Mercy!

is from my father Malcolm, telling me he's here! I look at it closely, my phone has been on the entire time. 18 minutes and counting! WTF! I have somehow butt dialed my mother. The night I have the best sex ever, is the night my mother overhears everything! The only thing I hear in the background is Uncle Lucy yelling "Oh hell to the na'll!" My whole body goes limp. Right here is where my life will never be the same...

Chapter Fourteen

Gabrielle, so you a big girl now...

I am terrified! Walking through the door I feel weightless. I don't know what to do. They are all staring at me. It feels as though I am about to be crucified. My hair is all over the place, I look a mess. Jacket all screwed up. Eyeliner everywhere from crying so hard before I even get here, I probably look like something out of a horror story. I look up and the first person I see is my father Marcel. His head held down. Uncle Lucy standing with his arms crossed so tightly looks as though he is holding on to himself so that he want knock the hell out of me.

In a tone that I have never heard before, my mother asks, "Where were you?"

I say nothing.

"Where were you is all I'm going to ask you?"

Still nothing.

"Gabrielle Grace Cartiér, for the last time where were you?"

I muster up strength to say, "I was with my friend."

My father Malcolm asks, "What friend? Who is he?"

Uncle Lucy yells from across the kitchen, "And where in the hell does HE live?"

"Calm down Lu," Broderick tells him.

"Sweetie, not trying to get alley, but this ain't even 'bout you right now," he says back to him.

"Shhh yeah I'm aware of that, but–"

"Who in the hell were you with is my question?! Let me guess, Rishard?"

This lady is still asking me that same thing. Her face is blank. It's as though she is trying to be as calm as she possibly can.

My Daddy Marcel jumps in, "So you're having sex now?"

WTH?!! Could he not just embarrass me even more? Just come on out with it will you.

He continues to say, "You're a big girl now, huh? Doing big girl things?"

I'm thinking to myself, how could I be so stupid?

Uncle Lucy blurts out, "You even was bold enough to tell me to my face you had not had sex. Oh, maybe you were trying to say to me, not right then you weren't, but you just wait, I'm about to go in, and I'm about to go in hard, just as soon–"

"Lucy stop it!" Momma says to him. "I got this."

He shrugs his shoulders, and mumbles in a stressed tone, "Apparently NOT, apparently she has it And baby she has it down good. Even got me excited. Hell, I thought I was doing something. Whoever the hell Bro is, best know I'm looking for him. Where he at?! Oooh, where he at?!"

"She asks again with watery eyes, so how long Gabby? Is this what you've been doing while you were having me think you were hanging with Quinn?"

"No Vic, she's the middle man remember?" My Uncle Lucy says. "You know the hook up girl. Third party. Hint, hint, how we used to do."

He won't let it alone.

My Father Marcel asks, "Just so, where were you? Pretty much sounded like you were in a car. Would I be correct?"

"I'll take ten for the win Alex." Uncle Lucy chimes in again!

She says as peaceful and calm as she can, "To your room young lady. You know the one overloaded with all the mess I bought you."

I look back at her, and before I know it, I snap. "You, you bought? I bought that with my own money!"

She begins to walk towards me, and says, "Economics 101, you're smart right, and according to all of the test you've taken, it's been proven, numbers and all, you're smarter than all of us in here."

"Speak for yourself honey; she ain't smarter than me by a long shot." Uncle Lucy jumps in.

Broderick comes in and says, "Well Lu, technically she is."

The look he gives Broderick is one George Zimmerman himself would be afraid of.

Cruella continues, "Let me see if you can pass this one. GENIUS they call you!! I- have-everything, you-have-nothing!"

I look over my room, and yell, "You went through my stuff?!"

Walking towards me she says, in a harsh voice, "Apparently you don't get it do you? So let me help you out," she charges upstairs at me in a rage screaming, "everything in here is mine!

And if you don't like it, you know what you can do! Hit the door! You're grown, you having sex now, you bad."

I continue to go through my things to see just how much damage she's done.

Huffing and puffing like the big bad wolf, she drags on, "Oh by the way, I found the condoms under your mattress if that's what you looking for, plus, looks like you've decided you wanna smoke some weed at that, even got you a couple of Swisher Sweets. Oh you doing it… wanna know how I know? I checked your Facebook, Instagram, you even kicking now, because ya'll so smart, wanna go undercover. And you got the nerve to be sexting??!! You might wanna thank your Uncle Lucy for that. He turned me on to it. So again, you got all the book sense in the world, now's the time for you to put that head of yours to work for more than solving an equation. Can't be too smart if I could guess the password. MENSAGIRL."

Not quite sure where I get the nerve, maybe it's because between all the yelling I'm still buzzing, but I manage to scream back, "I don't have to stay here! I'm smart enough to survive on my own! And I DON'T have to go to school anymore either!!! You know it, and everybody else does too!! I don't need school. They need me!!"

Even my saying all of this, it's that feeling you get when you know you're supposed to meet with your Mentor, because you have an important project that can change your future forever, but right here really can't see how Flavanoid F is going to help me. A blunt maybe.

Out of nowhere my father Malcolm yells, "Gabrielle! Enough!"

"What?!" I ask him. "Like I said who are you to tell me what to do?!"

Right here is where I can see out the side of my eye she raises her hand, and reaches to hit me, but he catches her hand to stop her.

"No Victoria," he says to her as if he's taking his last breath.

The room gets quiet. Suddenly I realize right here is where I have a choice. I can stay here and be subjected to my mother's rules, his rules, everyone's rules, or I can go live with Quinn. I know she's got my back, I can be free to do what I want, when I want, and with who I want. Rule #1 – 'Be you, never try to be anyone else, nobody can be you like you.' So… there it is. I look her in her face, and with all the strength in me I tell both of them I'm leaving. She says nothing, drops her head, then she turns and walks out. Pulls the door shut. Really I expected more.

My father asks, "What do you mean you're leaving?"

"I'm gone; I don't have to deal with this no more." I tell him with tears in my eyes "I'm sick of being treated like a baby. I'm sick of having to answer for everything. I have never given her any problems. I have done everything she asked of me. You don't understand."

"I understand Gab–"

"How?"

Am I really standing here having this conversation with him? I reach for my phone to call Quinn, as hard as I want to be, I'm trembling. My fingertips are tingling. I guess this is what it means when they say buck up, and that's exactly what I'm about to do. Buck up! Just thinking about how she has violated my privacy; I'm fuming. "All my stuff! My journal, everything!" I mumble to myself, "Everything that mattered."

"Excuse me young lady, matter? Gabrielle, what were you thinking?"

For a minute all I remember him as, is the one person who is responsible for us not being a family. So the hatred I have had for him all these years is now at an all-time high, he done bumped his head.

Meanly I say to him, "Who are you to ask me anything? You aren't here. You left us. For another woman as a matter of fact, and you gon'–"

"Hold up, just one minute, you will not stand here and talk to me as if I am not your father."

"My father? My father is downstairs! If I'm not mistaken you have not been to any one of my piano recitals, track meets, debates, anything that involves me. You are always either sick, busy, or something. Now you want to come here and play Daddy. I don't need you or anyone of them downstairs. I have someone that loves me."

I'm so trippin' right now; I don't believe I'm standing here like this. The night before the party of my life, I'm dealing with this. Everything seems so cold. This doesn't even seem real.

He goes on to say, "That's not how everything happened Gabrielle, a lot was going on before you were born. I have tried talking to you several times; you never try to hear me out. I even wrote you that letter in hopes that you would one day read it, and understand just how much I loved you and always will love you."

"That was how many years ago? I am now fourteen. Where have you been all this time? You knew where I lived. I am your only child and the only thing you had to do was be here for me."

"But–"

"But nothing, I don't want to hear any more, you had your chance!"

"I can't reason with you. You have to know I love you. Even though I have not been physically here, I have been a part of your life since day one. Gabrielle I, I–"

"Save it."

Again I reach to call Quinn, this time she answers.

Trying to be as calm as I can, I say, "Hey… can you come and get me?"

She hesitates, "Chick what's wrong? You still out with Pimpin?"

Without trying to let on to everything, I say, 'No. I'm home, but ahmm is it okay if I stay with you for a while?"

I get silence, then she asks' "Where over to Gram's, you know that spot is on lock?"

I reply, "No, with you in the Dec."

Bursting out laughing, "Girl you trippin'trippin', you know good and well it's a jungle over here. You think you can handle that?"

"Really Quinn, you talking about me now. I'm good."

"If you say so, Ion think Aunt Skyye gon' trip, she ain't even here anyway as usual. But if you putting in on the bills, I know they ain't gon' trip. That's right up they alley. So what's up? You ready now? Hold up! Where your Mom's at?! ", she yells.

I know he can hear her through the phone she's talking so loud; the whole block can hear her. It's like the more I continue to talk to her, he's getting this nauseating look all over his face, like he didn't come this far for all this, but what am I supposed to do? I didn't tell him to come anyway.

I give her heads up as much as I can, and she lets me know she's on the way. I immediately start grabbing as much as I can fit into my Coach duffle bag. I'm not even caring right now, all I want to do is get out of this place, see my baby, and then let him know how much of a woman I really am. Now we can really kick it.

He asks once more, "So you are really going to leave? Gabrielle, please don't, I am asking you for the last time, it's not what you think out there. There are people out there waiting to take advantage of you."

WTH? Does he think I was just born yesterday? I'm not stupid. I know how to handle myself. I have my bank account, and I'm not crazy enough to just give it away. Speaking of that, if I don't take anything, I know I need to take my money. At least I know I have that to tie me over until the rest of my money comes through. Man please, I'm going to be good. All I need now is to call Rishard.

Walking downstairs it's like all eyes on me. Uncle Lucy leaning over the counter drinking on what I overheard him ask for earlier, a Mai Tai, right about now. He's speechless, but not long…

"So you mean to tell me, you finna walk your little ass out of this house, and play big girl, huh?"

"Uncle Lucy–"

"No sweetie, you answer me, we came all this way to celebrate YOU, and this is what we get in return? Chile don't you know you are lucky to even still be alive. If your mother would have pulled some sh– like that, oh excuse my French, what the hell, you know that too, quite well I'm sure, so you want have any problems translating this. NO PARTY, it's off!

His Grace, His Blood, His Mercy!

Waisted precious time, and money. Ooooh Chile, I just had a flashback of just how much money, if Madea was here, baby she'd help me, all I need is a calculator."

"It's cool boo," Broderick says, "No loss. It's hers."

Uhnn-uhhn, I know he ain't just put me on blast like that? Come on' dude, really?

"You right about that Boo-Boo, her loss. Hope you got your boots, you gon' need them to keep you warm." Uncle Lucy bursts out and says.

I can tell his head is pretty tight right now. I take a look at my mother, and I'm not sure if it's more anger, disappointment, embarrassment, or all of them, all I know is that this house is too small for two DIVA's one of us must go. I take one last look around what I have known to be home for the past several years, and a rush comes over me. My father Marcel has worked so hard to make this feel like home. It was never my intention to hurt any of them, but… never did I think that when I woke this morning, I would end up here.

She says one last thing to me. "Leave my key, and my money."

Uncle Lucy stands next to her, and says, "Vic, are you really gon' let this chile walk out this door like that? If she was Precious, trust me honey, Mary Jones would be going off! Throwing pots, pans, shoes, crackpipes, I'm just saying. You acting more like sweet little Claire Huxtable. Sweet Jesus where is my friend and what have you done with her?"

She responds, "Lucy believe it or not, I have come to realize some battles are not worth fighting. This one is not mine. It's God's."

He screams like a mad man, "Well take the wheel Je-sus!"

I leave the key. But I take the money. Between that and my account, I should have at least $15,000.

As I turn to head out, all I hear is her saying, "Not sure if I can take too much more."

Chapter Fifteen

Marcel, some things are better left in the past...

I have no second thoughts. No doubt in my mind, I made the right choice. God, I love Victoria so much, I would dare do anything to hurt her, but– this all is a notion. I'm still in disbelief, why did she come here like that? If it was not for Geoff giving me heads up I would've totally been blindsided. We left that alone long ago.

Lilliane was younger than me; her brother and I were best friends. Sébastien and I were real tight, practically grew up together. Even back when I could tell she had a crush on me, he and I used to joke that it was an innocent school age crush, but never did I think she felt the way she did. We went out maybe once or twice. Once things became real intense. We almost went there, but I couldn't. I knew that–Na'll I need to stop, this ain't good. Manhood rising and all just thinking about it. I actually struggled with that for a while, because aside from her I never had feelings for another woman such as her. I tried to make in my head the age difference was only a number, because besides that, she had it all, brains, beauty, and longgg money. Back then I was all about making it. Never the one to toot my own horn, but she was, she was crazy about herself some Marcel. What's up with this? I shouldn't even be thinking like this.

The last time I saw her was in Staten Island, she told me things were good, she had had a son, who was at the time I think was around two years old; she showed me some pictures, handsome little boy. Although I wanted to ask, was there a husband, I didn't, neither did she tell me. I did notice a beautiful brilliant round cut diamond, anywhere in the ball field of I know, seven carats, so someone was around. She said she had moved to the states after they decided to close down the store. Even then I had some bittersweet feelings, because her father; that brother right there knew and did it all. The first black man to own and operate a jewelry house;The House of duPont. I learned so much from him. He and my Pops were then rivals, in a good way though. I owe a lot of my success to him. Got the call last night, she wants to see me. Why now? Why here? Not sure if it's a good idea, being I haven't let on to Diamond we have a history. Wow, come to think of it, she was really excited about her new client too. Don't even want to ponder the idea of…

Speaking of that, everything has gotten so far out of hand. First, Gabrielle has decided now she wants to be grown, move out, "do her" as she says. Then, my baby is trying so hard to keep it together, spite all with the business is going well. Even though this has been one of the best quarters we've had in a while, yet seems like now, there is nothing I can do to make her smile. When we are in church she doesn't even seem happy there.

As far as church is concerned, we've being going most Sundays. When I'm home I make it my business to go. Although it's become way more convenient now, one of thing is that I can stream the service live. It's the next best thing to being there. Really depends where I am though, sometimes the reception leaves much to be desired, but for the most part it allows me to have service wherever I am.

I wish it was something I could do to make it all better, even though she says she's fine, I know better. She fakes it, she fakes it well. That's how she is, always the one to put on the face for everyone. Its' one of the reasons I fell for her. Her heart, has one of the biggest hearts I know of, but she has always been this hard shell on the outside. Plays hard in the workplace, as a matter of fact I get turned on by just watching her do what she does. When it comes to making it happen, no one does it better, but in hindsight, open her up, she's just as tender as a lamb. I'm just hope that all of this with Gabrielle turns around for the better, before it gets worse.

On good note, my investment in the gold market was really a great decision. I have to admit, at first I was like ummm I don't know, especially because Diamond was so dead set against it. I'm just so glad the price has remained somewhat steady. Last I checked, as of yesterday, it closed at $1217.50, which isn't bad being that just the other day it fell all of .30. Some still feel it is well oversold, but the way things are going looks like gold may be around for a minute. Although, again, the US dollar may turn around. Ok here I go second-guessing myself. Maybe I'm just using this as a distraction. I am. But knowing my investment was a half a million, that's reason enough to feel pretty good.

Maybe I'll try and do something nice for Diamond to cheer her up, don't think this is a situation shoes will cure. I have Drago make us something really special, we need a night so that she can forget about work, what's going on with Gabby and anything else that may be bothering her. She mentioned to me that Malcolm is really not doing well. It's hard to believe, because when he was here he looked better than I have ever seen him.

He confided in me, which was a surprise. We've talked before, but never to that extent. After all of that went down with Gabrielle, I felt he needed someone to talk to besides Lucy! Boy boy, boy, that Lucy! But apparently he hasn't been able to come around as much, because he just finished his last course of chemotherapy. With all of the other issues he's had going on health wise, something new pops up. Kaposi Sarcoma. It's the AIDS related cancer that causes you to have purple, brown, maybe even red tumors on your skin, called lesions. He says it's found in the lymph nodes, and the lesions can appear mainly on the face and legs, and this is why he didn't want Gabby or anyone else to see him like that. He was embarrassed. More so, he says he couldn't walk sometimes, because of the swelling in his legs and ankles. It was hard for him to really get around. The bad part is that some of the lesions were found in his lungs. This explains why when he would call, his breathing would sound so badly, but he was so hyped, because all he talked about was getting back on track. So hopefully he'll be fine, maybe just the flight and everything was a bit much. I know it was hard on him though for that to happen the way it did. Last thing we talked about was that he really appreciated me for taking care of Gabrielle. We shook, had some drinks, and that was that. He's a good brother though. I believe he's paid for his mistakes, especially every time when he looks at Gabrielle, I know it reminds him of just how much he wished he could do things over again. It's funny how life goes around. I know I could have made some better choices myself, but it's all a part of this thing we call life.

Just when I reach to get my phone to call Diamond, my phone rings.

"Hi, may I speak with Marcel please?" The soft voice on the other end says.

"Marcel speaking."

I want to ask who it is, but I already know. Just telling myself no harm, no foul in a phone conversation.

She continues, "Bonjour, ceci est Lilli –"

"Oui, je sais qui c'est, Lilliane." I answer.

She laughs, "Yes, you are correct."

Why do I get this feeling in the pit of my stomach? Not so sure if it is a bad feeling either. I find myself smiling.

"How have you been? I haven't seen you in–"

She jumps in, "Almost ten years!"

"Yes that's about right. On Staten Island. Wow, it's been a long time. How have you been?"

"Well me, I've been well. Just getting adjusted to Atlanta life."

"Really, so what do you think thus far?"

She replies, "It's not home."

She would be correct. I have lived several places and there is truly no place like home.

"I agree, but I have found it to be much better than New York."

"Surprised?", she asks. "And why on earth would you say a thing like that? I'm still feeling my way. It's slower, I can say that."

"Well I'm interested to know why Atlanta rather than New York?"

"Let's just say I have unfinished business that's here. Have some loose ends that I need to tie."

Pulling the phone away from my ear, as to not jump the gun or anything, I sure am hoping that business has nothing to do with me.

"Ok, well that sounds cool."

Immediately she asks, "Have you considered my offer?"

Ok, so I know I'm a smart man and all, and here it is this beautiful woman is asking to see me. Well like I said, she was beautiful before, beautiful when I last saw her, so I don't think too much has changed; at least I hope not. This decision should be a no brainer, but… I want to see her too. There is no harm in having dinner with an old friend. At least that's what I'm telling myself. My wife is a very understanding person, but how will she take this? Do I even tell her? Ok, we are talking about Victoria Diamond Bouviér. Hell yes I tell her.

I respond, "Actually I have. What were you thinking?"

"I was thinking more on the line of dinner and drinks, just to catch up. Haven't seen you in a while. It's not a problem is it? I don't wish to cause any confusion or anything."

The rational side of me knows this is not a good idea, and that is what I should say, BUT the other side of me is saying, man are you crazy?! What's wrong with that?

Before I think too long and hard, I tell her, "No; it's not a problem,"

"Wonderful, then it's settled. Is later good for you?"

My plan was to have a nice romantic night with Diamond tonight, but I would prefer to get this over with. I can always do something for my baby, and if I'm not mistaken, she has a meeting this evening herself. Perfect.

"This evening it is. Where would you like to meet?" I ask.

She laughs with a sweet tenderness and says, "You make the call Mr. Bouviér. I'll be there."

"Do you have a specific palate?" I ask hoping she is open.

"No, I'm versatile, but I did want to try this French restaurant I saw the other day. I can't remember the name."

"Bistro Niko, on Peachtree. The food is exquisite."

"Sounds great. What time shall I meet you?"

"Let's say seven-thirty."

"Seven thirty it is. See you then. And you will know who I am."

We both laugh. She's gone. What in the world have I just done? I don't want to read too much into anything. Maybe she is right, this is just a dinner with two friends from the same place. Friends that were very close to making love, friends that–man you trippin'trippin'! The rational side keeps telling me something about this just isn't right. If I know anything, I know I need to let Diamond know I have a meeting tonight with an old friend… ummm nope, let's try I have a meeting with Roberto and some of the other fellas, ahmm nope, that's not good either, how about I just don't t say anything. That's it.

Are you kidding me, I'm sitting at a light on Sidney Marcus Boulevard, staring at a billboard that reads "What Would Jesus

Do?" Even has the nerve to have some man with his elbow propped on his knee, and his hand holding his head up as if he is troubled. If my mother was here she'd ask me, "Son, if Diamond was in this situation, do you think she would handle it as such?" I believe I would somehow find myself reasoning with my own Mother. I miss her so.

⁂

Seven-thirty is here, I don't see her; at least I don't think I see her. I need a glass of wine to ease me. At the moment I'm in the mood for a nice Sauvignon Blanc, therefore, I order a glass of Château De Sancerre, while I wait. Just as he finishes my order, I can't help but recognize her scent. Umph, she didn't. Yes she did. There has been only one woman to embrace the floral-like bouquet of Bulgarian, Ylan-Ylang, Tuberose, Grasse Jasmine, which all make up the timeless fragrance of Jean Patou's Joy .The pure parfume. Good Jesus! She was wearing this when I last saw her. Focus Marcel, focus.

As the waiter moves back, she swerves around him; I can tell he's as much captivated as I am. It's damn near taboo. He waits for her to be seated, but I can't help but stand to get a hug. She looks amazing. Better than amazing. Breathtaking. She's wearing a most gorgeous solid black dress, and I know I'm not the shoe guru, that's Diamond, but I know I saw these black and gold suede crystal and gold leaflet sandals while I was shoe shopping for Diamond. I can't quite remember, but I think they are Guisseppe. Apparently she has the waiter in awe as well. If it was a fly in here it would head straight for his mouth.

He asks, "Bonne soirée Madamoiselle. Aimeriez-vous quelque chose à boire?"

I can tell she already knows what she would like to drink, therefore she waste no time, she tells him, "Oui, je vais avoir un verre de Pommard. Merci."

She looks at me and says, "It's a Pinot Nior kind of day." And the way my stomach is playing hopscotch, I have to agree.

We sit and talk for what seems like an eternity, she laughs, and so do I. Reminiscing on old times has really brought back some great memories. She lets on that Sébastien has been really ill lately, and he has not been able to get around much. After her father passed, he took over the family business, and when she came aboard, things didn't go so well. Eventually, with him and her fighting for power there was a huge feud between both of them. What she thought she was doing was right for the company, apparently he was in total disagreement. She began to bring in new and fresh designers, but Sébastien of course wanted to do things the old way. Business as usual, in which this has caused a long time rift. She hasn't seen or heard from him in over ten years. I this can see the sadness in her eyes.

While we're eating she looks at me so intensely, and out of nowhere she asks, "Do you ever think about the past when it comes to us?"

I choke on my wine, start coughing constantly, because how did we get here?

"Every now and again, I think about those times in France. We had fun, but we were young back then, things have changed a lot."

She looks down at her plate as if I have said the worst thing possible.

"We did have great times together. I think about them a lot. I have always compared everyone to you; maybe that's why I never married."

There it is!! Not married. This most definitely was a bad idea. The feeling in my stomach though. Something just keeps nagging at me. It's like something isn't right. Earlier, I put my phone on vibrate, but I get this weird sensation that I need to call Diamond. Don't ask. I don't know myself, but maybe I just need to hear her voice right now. Earlier I put my phone on vibrate so we won't be interrupted, but now I'm the one that needs to interrupt.

I know I'm fibbing a bit, but I ask, "I have an important call, I need to take this. Do you mind?"

She looks as me with the seduction look, you know the one eyebrow raised look, and says, "No, go ahead, it's okay."

I look at my phone, and it looks like Diamond has sent me a cute text to let me know how much she misses me, and that she will see me when I get home. That settles me, but I still feel the need to call anyway. Goes straight to voicemail. Well maybe she's in her meeting. It could be me, maybe I'm just bugging, it's just the fact I haven't been a situation like this before. I can tell she is clearly coming on to me, and as much of a man that I am, I shouldn't allow this to continue. I do what should have been done in the beginning.

I say to her, "Thanks for letting me take that. You know how business is."

She smiles, "I do." But just when I think I'm about to be free, she asks another question that messes me up.

She asks, "If we had a chance, do you think we could finish what we started?"

Ok maybe I'm on something else, but if I don't feel like Adam right now being tempted by Eve, I don't what this is. And that dress tho'.

"If I wasn't married, who knows, anything is possible." Did I just say that?

She goes in for the jugular. "Marcel, I don't want to beat around the bush, no games, anything like that. I have wanted you since then, I have always wanted you. You are in my dreams, I think about you all the time. I moved here–"

"Wait, hold up, but you are my wife's client, what's that all about?"

"Yes, I know that, why do you think I chose her? She's good, but I wanted to get closer to you. Like I said I moved here because I had unfinished business, YOU!"

Okay, this is where I draw the line...

I tell her, "I think we need to stop here, this is not why I came. I was only hoping we would just talk about some old times, have a few laughs, not this. I am married, happily married, and my wife is too good of a woman to even think about doing anything to hurt her."

Even though the hardcore male in me wants to entertain the idea, I can't.

I continue, "So I think it's best we just call it quits here."

"Are you sure? What about your wife representing me?"

I say to her as kindly as I can, "You are going to need to work that out."

I look at my watch it's almost eight thirty, and I decide we should leave. She agrees. Without hesitation I pay the bill, and we leave. Just as we get to the door, she turns to give me a hug, and the door opens. Here stands Diamond and Demetrius. In the great words of Lucy, "Take the wheel Jesus!"

Chapter Sixteen

Quinn, in Jamaica, it's whatever you like...

If I would have known what I know now, I would have been on that a long time ago. Who would've thought that Drew was trying to holler at me the whole time? Ever since we started kicking it, it's been on and poppin'. Even got Aunt Skyye turning up, although he always cracks the joke how sexy my Aunt is. He has only seen her one time, the time I was taking her to the Food Stamp Office to recertify. That day I stopped by the club because my Boo said he had a little sump'n-sump'n for me. Turned out he did. I told him I needed some money and he came through like he always does. Dropped five hundred dollars just like that.

Things have really been messed up pretty much now that Gabby has been staying here. I'm so used to her being at school, we'd kick it most times on the weekends, I'd do my thing, and that would be it. Now it's like I see her for the most part every day. She either out riding with Pimpin' wilin' out, they shopping, or she hanging with my lil' cousin, Shaun. Since Shaun and Toot turned her on to the spot, we don't spend too much time together, at least not like we used to. For the most part, they hang out at this lil' joint over in downtown Decatur, where they all go to shoot pool and play games. I used to go, but I don't have time for 'em like that too much no more. Not trying to kick 'em to the curb, but I'm on a mission.

Lately, I been noticing 5-0 been riding through deep, I wish she and Pimpin' would find another hangout spot, he's bringing too much heat this way, always hustling. Tiger said the other day some people was riding through here looking for him, asking questions, all kind of stuff. But he gud doe for real, he just got him a new lil' ride, and especially now that Gabs is chilling with him, let's just say, Cha-ching! I know one thing, he better make sure he don't mess around and get too comfortable, Mr. Man don't play the radio. He straight 'bout' that paper.

Of all days we have a substitute. Now that's crazy, if I wouldn't have studied then Mrs. Perryman would've been here, but it's all good. I need to go talk to my counselor anyways. This may just be a good time. I ask permission from Ms. Barwell is it cool. She agrees.

Soon as I walk in into the hallway I overhear these two chicks, Jerrica, and Monay, arguing real loud. Straight RATCHET! From the sound of it, they about to go at it! My first mind is telling me to keep walking, but I stop to hear as much as I can, ok I'm nosey, so what. Anyway, Landrell kinda told me what was up yesterday, plus I saw some bull on Facebook last night. Apparently, both Jerrica and Monay was fooling with this dude named Bryce, over the summer, they call him B-man. Well some kind a way B-Man decides he wants to keep dealing with Monay, and Jerrica somehow found out. She been trippin' on ol'girl ever since. Before she moved over here, Jerrica used to live in Bowen Homes projects before the tore them down, and Monay straight from the Dec, so both of 'em got they own crew so they are always reppin' the hood. Every day it's something, but what I saw on Facebook was Jerrica threatened to stab Monay, so now everybody trippin'trippin', and you know all people wanna do is see a fight.

Oh snap! Jerrica just hit her dead in the face. All I hear now is them knocking into lockers and everything. Somebody just yelled, "Fight!" Now people are everywhere. It's a dude that just bumped right into me not even caring. All he's trying to do is see what's going on. Both the Resource Officer and the Police are in effect. All it takes and they come swarming. It's amazing we don't go through a daily search. We should, with all this going on.

Last, I heard was that the real deal was not so much that Monay found out they were still kickin' it, but the killin' part is Monay put Jerrica on blast. We all know she's a swoop, but Monay had the nerve to pull all of Jerrica's home girls name on the swoop list. Oh I'm sorry let me explain, a swoop is a chick that's sexually active, but the actual Swoop List, is a list of chicks that have been known to go down on a dude. Oh and they ain't even crazy enough to put my name on some list. They ain't that stupid.

After all that looks like they are on the way to the Principal's office. Plus, I know they are going to have to talk with the counselor at some point, but not today. Somebody in this joint is going to the detention center today, all because of some damn social media bull crap. One day somebody gon' get seriously hurt, and its gon' be way too late, that's why if I don't know you, you can hang it up. Delete! Gabby and all of them be accepting anybody. That ain't cool.

I still try to make my way to see the counselor, but so many people are in here, I'll just wait til' later. Too much confusion. I don't know why we always gotta act a fool, all the time. Now a sister can't even get to see the counselor. It's cool though, I can do it later.

Right when the bell rings, I get a call from Rha. Talked to him the other night. He missing himself some Quinn, and plus I shole been wanting some Jerk Chicken anyway. But I don't even know if I got it up to deal with him. Drew got a sistah on loc.

"Ello mi pretty brownin', what yuh doing wit yuh sexy self?"

I let out a sigh, because I don't know what it is, but when he talks to me like that, it messes with me. I love to just hear him talk.

"Just about to finish up here at school, why what's up with you?"

"Nuttin' much, just tinkin' 'bout yuh, missing yuh, mi buddy wanting yuh. Wandering what a pretty gal doing on such a beautiful day."

Oh he needs to stop! This is not good for a girl.

He continues, "No ansah? Mek mi beg no? I have your flava, Plantains, I know yuh love dem, shall I bring dem to yuh?"

As much as I would love to have some hot plantains right now, Ion know. This sounds like a set up. LOL!

I respond, "I could do that. That's what's up." I hate to do this, but I asks, "Can I have some Stew Chicken too?"

He laughs, "Ooh lots betta! Anty-ting for you mi gal. I just haffi a couple of stops to mek. You know Juelle has a breda kinda tied up lately, and on top of running de store, I hardly eba haffi time for yuh. So as dey sey, whatever yuh like, you got it. Now what am I going to get? Hopefully sum-ting ree-aally gud. Slow wine… Perhaps some punany?"

When he asks like that, I'm like hell yeah, you can get it!!!

He adds, "What time is it naw, tree? Ow 'bout five or so we link up?"

"That's fine." I say to him.

"Meet mi at de usual dehso. Wear sum-ting really hot. Plan to get down and dutty. You know, runkus punkus!"

Why do I find myself blushing? Maybe it's just the way he talks to me. Or maybe I have some idea what is in store. Every time I think about it, all I can do is laugh, thinking about Dexter St. Jock! That Eddie Murphy… All I see is him swinging it! In Rhasan's case, over the shoulder!

༄

Just as I thought, Dexter kilt it. After that, I don't need or want to do anything else for a while. I'm good. I saw where Drew was blowing me up. All I know is he has been asking me have I seen Pimpin'. Not today anyway. I know he will be around here before the nights over. Tiger said he heard him and Gabby going in at each other. Probably because he be wanting her to front him the cash so that he can get more product. What he need to not do is slip; because he know Drew don't play, but I think Pimpin' trying to get his own hustle going on. Pretty much him and Juelle got this over here hemmed up.

Dag, WTF, I don't even believe this, I'm trippin' because I know I ain't seeing what I'm seeing. I just saw Gabs getting out of the car with some dude. Don't look like Pimpin' either. She's trippin' now. She looks like she's been drinking, maybe too much.

"Girl what's up with you?" I ask her.

Slurring she says back to me, "Why you care, you ain't never around. You always gone. I guess you and your new boo on some other stuff, but it's cool though."

As bad as this hurts to see my girl like this, I'm not sure myself if a monster has been created.

"Damn Gabs, why you acting like that? Yeah, I got somebody, but you know me, hey–"

"Yeah I know the Rule Book, damn the Rule Book… lately the Rule Book ain't been working for me. I've had to go off of what I know."

"What's that?"

"Trying to survive, I need to open up my own lil' tutoring business, but anyway–and Rishard, oh he got me twisted. He think I'm about to front him for a kilo, he must be crazy."

She pulls out a blunt and begins to light it, and for some reason, something in me snatches it from her. You know, she looks at me like bi-a really? This is crazy. This is most definitely not the Gabby I used to know. Maybe something went wrong. Ok, Quinn, maybe?

"Where is Skyye, I got something for her."

I respond, "I don't know haven't seen her today, what you got some money for her."

"Something like that. She asks me for a favor and I told her I would get it."

"Get what?"

She yells, "Why you wanna know, ain't it somewhere you need to be?"

"Not really, I'm chilling tonight. All of a sudden I don't feel too good." I say.

"What, you think you pregnant?"

A blank look comes over my face. I try another approach.

Hoping this will trigger something, I ask, "Hey, have you talked to your other girls lately, Jaz, Bree, Lorna, you know the GEMS?"

She looks at me like… "Seriously, I ain't seen or heard from them since–"

"Since what?" I ask.

She gets quiet.

I press a little more. "Why haven't you tried talking to them? Maybe you need to call them, See what they're up to."

I don't believe I'm even saying this. Actually I never really cared for them too much anyway. Just can't stand the fake chicks, you know the ones that got everything, and still have nothing. Plus, I thought for a minute a couple of them were on both sides of the streets. But they were her friends so I was like cool.

She pauses, "Don't you think I tried that already?!! Angel's folks want even let her talk to me anymore, and you can forget any of the other ones. I'm willing to bet they ain't even thinking about me, I feel like we have become frenemies."

I rush and ask, "So you have no plans to go back to school?"

"Where is all of this coming from? I thought you was down with me being here, I thought you was going to hold me down."

As much as I don't like this, she's right; this is not one for the Rule Book. I just don't want to see my girl go down like this. Yep me and Drew been kicking tough, but so what, he wanted me from the beginning. So hopefully she will forgive me for that, especially when it comes out that I'm his A-1.

"Listen up, Gabs, I know you're a big girl, you can handle yourself, but all I'm saying is think about it. If I'm in school, everybody should be in school, why do you think the kids around here ask you to help them with their homework, help them with their science projects? If I remember right, didn't you tell me you have a project of your own you need to be doing? What's up with that? I can't even think of the name of it, what is it again? Gel Electro– whatever, you know what I'm talking about."

We both laugh, because we think about that.

She comes back, "Gel Electrophoresis."

"Yeah, that."

Shrugging her shoulders, she blurts out, "I realize this thing out here though, it ain't no game. This is for real and I can't believe Pimpin' out the blue just started trippin' on me, all because he needed some money. I already loaned him $2,000, and he has yet to pay that back. Between us popping tags all the time, my cash flow is getting low."

I want to ask her so badly; does she really think she is going to see those two g's? How about not! My phone is ringing, it's my baby! I need to take this.

Hurriedly I say, "Gabs, this is one of my sponsors, and you know the rule."

His Grace, His Blood, His Mercy!

We both say, "Rule #1, in reverse order, 'Always remember, never to put the 'D' before the 'C.' And if you don't know, dicks before chicks… Always."

"Do you girl, I'm about to go lie down, my head hurts. I need to call Skyye anyway."

Chapter Seventeen

Drew, in the MIA it's always gud doe...

As to bring no heat to myself, I fly into Hollywood International, can't be fooling with MIA. They always have the place surrounded. It's like gate rape. It's rare I ever fly direct for this sound purpose. Kinda pissed tho', because the flight was runnin' behind. I'm still gud doe. Rodriguez knows I'm gud for it; and my car should be waitin' for me, so everythin' should still be on fleek.

Everyone's in place, actually, they left early this morning. Just got a text, all gud. Yet 'n still, Trust NO ONE. This has to happen quick as possible. We don't need no trouble. Only thing I regret about these trips doe is it's always strictly business; no time for play. In an' out.

First class service all the way, Miguel at Prestige Luxury always has me ready. I hand him a fat tip. I waste no time, jump in the Lambo Aventador LP 700, an' ride out. I'm talkin' sweet! Nearly 700 horsepower, an' can't nobody tell me this ain't the life. All I need now is Tasha Mack next to me, hair blowing in the wind talkin' 'bout, "Bae, we 'bout's dat life." I totally agree wit you Tasha all the way. Fo sho', now that's my WCW, but right now I ain't even got time for Tasha, or Malik 2.0… I throw on a little ridin' music, some of that K Camp, "Cut Her Off", Montecristo in hand, adjust the Tones, check my watch, looks like time is on my side. Hittn' the 95, and I'm headed straight to Aventura. If I'm lucky, I'll stop and holla at one my little cutie pies over at Jacque's Ahead of Time.

Damn this traffic is at an all-time stop! I knew better! Even in the Lambo, Ion know if I can get around this. What usually would be a twenty to twenty-five minute trip is lookin' to be almost forty-five. Last time I was here on pleasure I chilled for a minute on Las Olas Boulevard, nice shoppin'! I'm long overdue for some relaxation, and this is definitely the place. Palm trees, pretty white sands, just does somethin' to me. And the honeys all down the strip, make me wanna– but first things first. Paper! Gotta get that paper. As mat a fact, I check in to make sho' my boys are on point. No doubt, let 'em kno; I'm runnin' behind, but not too far away so that we can catch up; meet at the spot, because we 'bout to do this.

About 45 minutes later, I'm here, Aventura Lakes. Push the button, announce myself and voila, we in; me and all three cars behind me. The first is Emilio, my runner; car# 2, is Pedro, backup and #3, my boy Josue riding shotgun. Take no chances. Although I know top of the line security got a brotha scanned heavy. As usual Rodriguez is ready an' waitin'. We head to what he calls the Parlor, then he offers me some Don Julio. I accept the offer. I take a seat on the Plume

His Grace, His Blood, His Mercy!

Blanche diamond encrusted sofa, of course cocaine white, only 50 were made. And he has # 1 and # 50, one for each side of the room. Next, one of his men presents me with the most beautiful kilo of white candy, then he makes just enough of a slit for me to taste. Yes suh. That's it. Numbness to perfection.

"That's what I'm talking about." I say to Rodriguez.

He lets out a laugh, and asks, "Have I ever failed you?"

"Can't say you have." I tell him.

Then I take a whiff of that loud an' I already know. I run it under my nose, an' that's all I need to know its top shelf dank! My man got me set up right. That's why I don't deal wit no one else. At the end, Josue hands him the briefcase with $50,000 in it. Well worth it! I'm 'bout to put dem young boys to work. We load up with Pedro as the transporter. They head out; I should see 'em early in the morn'.

Smooth as a baby's behind, gotta love the MIA. I realize I still have a few hours before my flight back to the "A" might as well enjoy some of this beautiful weather. I can always stop by the Galleria headed back to HIA. What's the harm in pickin' up a few thangs for a couple of my guls, and while I'm there I can get myself a lil' somethin' too.

Been on the grind, so haven't even checked my phone, didn't even realize had it on airplane mode. Scroll through, and I just as I figured, there's a couple of texts from you know who. At first I was thinking it would be a quickie, but I can't seem to shake her. I've been told I'm about as close to a drug as it comes. One hit from me, and you instantly are an addict. Hate I had to let that lil' cutie, what's her name, D'Sharee alone, got tired of doing pretty much nothin'. Come to fine out, she was aight, but not what I'm used to. She played her part tho', arm candy more than anythin', but after I hit that a couple of times, I really didn't even see any other reason to chill with her no more; time served! My motto, the four F's, (Find 'em, Feed 'em, F'ck 'em, Forget about 'em) in that order, and that's pretty much where I'm headed with ol' girl.

I hit up from the party line; everythin' at this point is cool. Steady pace, and the gud thang is, haven't spotted 5-0 like that. Usually they are on the freeway deep, pretty much scoping the 18-wheelers more so, that's why I had my boy Do-Lo hook me up three nice disposable rides, so not to draw more heat. Too much at stake, can't lose the club, that ain't even an option.

On the way here, I was just thinkin', one day a brotha do want to settle down wit a nice honey, maybe een me an ol' Christian gul. Na'll let me stop trippin' trippin', I saw that movie with Ja'Rule, a brotha just got lucky on that tip. They don't make 'em like that for real.

These chicks out here so thirsty, they don't care, they on the club owner, the gas station owner, it don't matter, whoever they think got a lil' somethin', they on 'em like, whoa. Even clockin' the Pastor! I mean these broads these days are scandalous, make Kerry Washington look like an angel.

On the for real, the man can even have a woman on his side, an' I done seen it, they still try an' holla at him. Right there on the front row, wit the transitional clothin' on. You know from the church to the club gear. Not all of it looks like that stuff from Rainbow either. I'm talking about the bougey chicks, the ones rockin' the Gucci, Louis, and what's another one, had a chick ask me for one, oh yeah Tory Burch. Then she had nerve to ask me for some money to put in it! That be the main ones talkin' 'bout preach Pastor, Preach!

His Grace, His Blood, His Mercy!

Plus the part that trips me out, Ion know why a chick thank a dude just gotta have a chick that got it all hangin' out. Not no real dude. Even me as much as I love to get it, to me sometimes, it's even a straight turn off. I need somethin' to thank about, let me at least imagine what you workin' wit'. Straight THOTS! And then they get mad when you call 'em that. Well… what you expect when you act like it, we call it how we see it. That's why Ion have no shame in my game, if that's what you come to me with, that's how Imma treat you. But just so I'm clear, I do like an ol' classy chick, oh I'll take a shake yo booty gul too, but for the most part, like I say, I don't plan to take no anybody home to Momma. I think Steve said it best, A man wants a lady wit some standards. Get Some!

What was I thinkin'; traffic was even worse comin' back, just now pulling up over here at Key Biscayne, but I'm starvin', I can use some paella right 'bout now. It's a must. I have to stop in to one of my favorite spots, Casa Juancho. Take a look at my watch, not too much time left before I need to head back to make sure I'm back at HIA.

Every time I come here, I get the feelin' I have entered a real Spanish experience, from the pretty red brick tiles, to the all the pottery, and the fabrics, just makes me feel like I can stay here forever, but just for a while. Got business at home.

Once I'm seated, I spot the most beautiful specimen made on this side of heaven. I try not to stare too long, but I'm entranced by her beauty. By no means is she anybody's hood rat. Not sho if she's alone, but before I can really tell, the waiter is here to take my drink order, and yes, I have to have it, I get a glass of that Anis del Mono Dulce. I look up, and

I can tell she's peepin' me out too. I give it a minute or two, but I notice she's alone. It's right here I put my A game to work, again.

Her name is Belarmina, Bella for short. She's Cuban. The sweetest thang I've ever seen. Her smile has me lit up like a Christmas tree on the inside, her eyes, look like dancin' stars against a moonlit sky. She's wearin' a gorgeous long golden dress that wraps her waist. Her tiny waist, but I can't help but notice her breast; they are seated so much so they actually seem too perfect. Could be, but who really cares. She tells me, she's lived here in Miami for over fifteen years. Her family moved here to escape everythin' that was going on in Cuba at that time. This is her home.

I invite her to eat with me, she declines because she has another place she has to be, but she does take my number. I explained to her I'm on my way back to Atlanta, and this girl is so damn fine, I even invited her to come sometime. She takes my info and gives me the look it was nice meetin' you, but… I'm stuck. I lost my appetite, everythin'. I finish off what little of my drink I have left. I pay my bill. I ask the waiter, "Does she eat here often?" He says, "Yes, she comes here at least twice a week. She owns a cute little fashion boutique close by." I find myself doing something I have never done before. I go to look for her.

༄

Needless to say, a few hours later, and no sign of her, I know I'll never hear from her again. I board my flight, feelin' some type of way. I have never felt this way before; at least not for some chick. One last look at my phone before it's time to shut it off, no call from her, but a text from the last person I would be getting' a text from. Gabrielle, WTH! What, has she found out I'm doin' her gul?

It's 7:15, and for the next couple of hours all I can do is think 'bout the money I'm 'bout to make, and the honey that coulda been Mrs. Andrew Harrison. But, for some reason I can't stop thinkin' 'bout why is that lil' chick hittin' me up. Last I heard, her and Pimpin' was doin' it, I heard she was cakin' him out. When I last saw him, he was rockin' some tight Alexander McQueen high-tops. When I think of them, I picture him as the ghetto upgrade. Word on the street tho' is he got her out there bad. Just 'bout turnt her out. Puttin' her to work, I heard. I hope that's not the case. For some reason, Ion know why, but I really did like that chick. I was mad as hell when I found out how old she was 'cause she had heart. To me, I think she's just a scared lil' girl, tryin' to walk in some shoes she don't need to. And not only that, don't have to, the gul is paid. Well, she was, 'til she hooked up wit ol' boy. I tried to stop her the night at the club. I could tell then, it wasn't good. Especially when I found out she was on the Mollies.

☙

Your boy done touched down in the "A". Got to admit tired as I don't know what. All I need to know is that my boys still ridin' smooth an' they're on the way. The product needs to make it here safe 'n sound. While I'm thinkin' of it, I need to hit Pimpin' up to let him know it's 'bout to go down. He needs to come through.

Once I'm through security, and all is a go. I text Duece to let him know I'm in and I'm on the curb. It doesn't take long for him to swing through to get a brotha. He tells me everythin' at the club is straight. No problems, all gud. He also lets me know that this lil' chick came through looking for me. Didn't look gud, said she really needed to talk to me. Guessin' Gabrielle. She's sweatin' a dude hard. Nevertheless, I tell him, gud lookin' out.

I text Pimpin', haven't heard back anythin' 'n it's almost an hour, that's not like him, usually he's Johnny on the spot. I even call Quinn to see if she's seen him, really don't feel like dealin' wit her, 'cause Io even have it up for her tonight. My mind is on other thangs, 'n she ain't one of 'em. Yet 'n still she says she hasn't seen or heard from him in the last couple of days, she thinks he's been layin' low. What that means I'm not sure. All I know is that he better have my paper.

Just as I thought, being on the phone with her turns out to be one of those times where you just have to give a phene what a phene wants; a hit. I tell her I'll see her a lil' later. I have Duece stop me by the club, just so I can check out things myself. It was a long time before I felt comfortable leavin' the club wit' anyone. I'd just shut it down first.

As usual, it's jumpin', 'n gud for a Thursday night at that. You know how we roll. Just as we are getting' out, Mr. Walt hits me up for a few dollars to get some cigarettes. While I was gone, I asked him to take out the trash for me, do a couple of jobs 'round here. Some people say he on the smack hard, I haven't seen that. I actually was thinkin' 'bout givin' him a legit job as the maintenance man. Pretty cool dude.

His Grace, His Blood, His Mercy!

Everythin' is straight, just made a call to the chef to give him a heads up that the main ingredient is on the way. He's ready to go. I stop in the office, check the calendar, 'cause if I'm not mistaken, this Saturday is the "Green Light" Party. I know a lot of people will be here, just with my tryin' to get MIA off my list. I ain't been keepin' up wit' my schedule. Honestly, I really do need an assistant. At a quick glance, it is, 'n that's perfect. The new shipment would be in, so that's all gud.

☙

The call I've been waiting for. I'm like a kid in a candy store. They let me know they made the drop, so now it can be cooked up all nice. I'll ne'er forget the first time I saw how it actually goes down in the factory. Naked guls everywhere, I mean naked, can't trust not one body, even the searchers gettin' searched. It was goin' down like a sweat shop in that piece. Look like a chemistry lab! Talking 'bout pyrex glass, bacon soda, and to top it off, the main ingredient. Getting' a rush as I think about it. Accordin' to Chef, I was told it's faster to cook it up it in a microwave, takes about 90 seconds, but he prefers the real deal which may be a full 3 minutes. So I know once it's done, it's made to satisfaction, but the finished product is the best part. All nice, and rocked up.

Once I'm back at the crib, pick up the mail and throw it on the counter, in no mood for goin' through no bills tonight. That's what I have an accountant for. I do come across a letter from this lil' jump off I messed with about a year or so ago.

Chizellé T. Archie

I call her my lil' Twitter bang. Believe it or not, I don't even feel like readin' it, but what I do feel like is givin' Quinn what I bought her back. Me. I call her over. She obliges. Trick loves the kids!

Chapter Eighteen

Gabby, Green means go, red means NO...

My head has been killing me lately. Could be that I've been hitting the oooweee a whole lot more. It's like every day Skyye and Tiger wanna smoke. Seems like that's all we do now. I must say after a while, it becomes real expensive. I'm still waiting to get my money back from Rishard. I'm starting to think that may never happen.

I've called Drew several times. No response. I really need to talk to him. I'm sure I'm the last person he wants to hear from, but I need him. Today makes the fourth day I have not talked to Rishard. After the fight we had, I have not heard from him since. I hope it has nothing to do with him losing Drew's product. Lately, I've been thinking I might need to get a job to help out around here more.

Right now, I'm on the way to go talk to this dude named Owen that Skyye hooked me up with to make some extra money. Sounds pretty cool. All I gotta do is look cute. That's a no brainer. The way she puts it, he runs this company where you may have big time men like politicians, stockbrokers, even Fortune 500 execs looking for a pretty girl such as myself to make certain appearances, like for a business dinner, something like that. Even though we know I'm younger than the average, it's a good thing because my body is most definitely not young or average. I can easily pass for 18, even 19. Plus, I still have my ID Quinn made for us if anything jumps off.

With what feels like a cross-country drive, we make it to Loganville. I thought when we rode the other day to Tigers spot, I thought that was wicked, but out here, these are really the sticks. Yeah we passed a couple of McDonald's and all, but don't look anything like what I'm used to.

Now Owen, is this nice looking white man, I have to give it to him, kinda looks like a mix between Chris Hemsworth, and Channing Tatum. Pretty blue eyes, blonde hair, with a rough neck twist. He seems very happy to see Skyye, it's sorta like an old reunion. He asks me to do a couple of walks as if I'm ripping the runway, maybe to make sure I have no gunshot wounds anything like that. He asks are these my eyes or are they contacts. I'm like really dude? Who does that? He even asks if this is all of my hair. What are they used to? He says he's asking because they, the clients like a little versatility. I need to be able to switch it up if need be. I can do that. I can wrap it, curl it, even braid it up, and throw on a wig if I have to. If Taraji can, so can I.

Looks like I passed the test. I'm supposed to start tomorrow evening. What I want to know is how do I get paid, and when? Owen tells me that naturally I will work for him, and he will get a part of the money that I will make from my assignments. I ask how much of the money he will get; he tells me 20 percent of what I make. Next he ensures me that all of the clients have been screened and checked. Apparently the company has a security check in place. The one drawback is that I may be asked to stay longer, and if so the client will have to pay extra. Doesn't sound like a drawback to me. I only hear, Cha-ching! I ask what my hours are, and he tells me I would need to be prepared whenever a client requests me, so that could be anytime, but never any later than 1:00. Finally I ask since I don't have a car, will the client pick me up. He says yes, and it will always be from a secure location. I'm wondering why they can't just pick me up from Decatur, but oh well.

While we're riding back to the house, Tiger calls and just as always they're going off on each other. Well let's say he's going off on her, and I'm willing to bet it's over money. She hangs up the phone and says to me his check didn't come yet, I'm thinking to myself, "again!" and the gas and light bills are behind. I know I gave them money last week. What's up with that? I so know they are going to hit me up for something else. Between them and Rishard I feel like a walking Wells Fargo.

Believe it or not, my girl Angel called me. She wanted to let me know about the party at Etcetera tomorrow night. We talked for a minute. We caught up on old times, and she had me cracking up about Dionne. She's being herself as usual. Seemingly some chick wanted to jump her because she was bragging about her new bag. If they only knew, Designer Knockoff! Angel also told me she needed to talk to me about something, but because things are the way they are, it's no big deal, it's not even that important. She says after everything went down, and her parents found out I had been lying to use her as an escape goat, pretty much all of them have kinda fell back a little. She did say worry wart has been asking about me a lot! Church Boy! As soon as she told me that I was like really? Only because he's been texting me so much lately, but I haven't responded. Just not in the mood to hear no preachy speech.

As far as the party goes, I really wanna go, and I know it's going to be off the hook, but my funds are kinda tight, but ahmm I could, no don't even think about it Gabby. Last I checked I had at least $3,500. I should be able to swing it. I hope Quinn's going because if she doesn't I'm SOL. She's my ride. Unless, Rishard and I go together, at least I hope so.

༄

Finally, Drew calls me back! I was starting to think he couldn't stand me. AND on top of him calling he actually sounded like he wanted to talk to me. I let on to what's been going on, and for the most part he tried to get in my stuff about how I need to go back to the crib and all, but that ain't even happening. I am determined I am going to show them I'm not only just brains, but, I can handle myself.

I told him about my new job I'm supposed to start, and he went off on me! Not sure if it's because I didn't hit him up first, but nevertheless, we worked out something. I know Skyye gon' be something pissed, but I got to do what I gotta do, and it sounds like this will make me way more money than dealing with Owen. So not only will I be at the "Green Light Party," Drew's paying me to work at Etcetera! All I have to do is be a

His Grace, His Blood, His Mercy!

hostess, pass out drinks, and assist the ballers in the VIP. All tips belong to me! Oh yes, it's about to be off the rector scale!

※

I'm so excited! My first job! I must admit, I'm ripping it! I'm just saying, the hottest green and white baby tee with "LehGo" printed across the top, pair of green short-shorts. I also pulled my hair into a cute bun on the side, and let's not leave out the crystal platforms, 4 inch mind you. Not being bragadocious or anything, one thing about me, I make my own style, so instead of looking all plain Jane like everyone else, I tie my shirt into a back knot! Pow! Gotta show off the tat I just got. Don't think anyone else is rockin' a serotonin molecule, b.k.a. "the dopamine tattoo." Regardless of what's going on in my life, I'm happy with me, and spite what my mother calls "The Tramp Stamp" I just thought it would be cool to show my inner happiness. So as the song say's "ready to go right now…" party starts in fifteen minutes. Bracelets on deck! I'm feeling kinda red…

A couple of hours in and I've made over $400 in tips already. This is turning out to be even better than I thought. VIP is jumping, and I can tell its so much money to be made that even I can't handle it all by myself, Drew sends China up, this other girl that also started working tonight. At first glance she's got it going on, the way she's working this dude makes me look like I might need to audition for amateur night at Pin Ups first, not feeling Magic City ready just yet, but in the meantime, I plan to step my game up.

I've been so busy I didn't even notice my girls were here. Truly everybody who is anybody is here tonight. D'Sharee made her presence known I see. From what I heard she and Drew are done! I knew that wasn't going to last long at all. She wasn't even his type, and I can't believe now she's kicking it with Alex, that figures.

Heading to the bar I peep Angel out, she's all over Drew! Pretty much throwing herself at him, and for a minute I'm stuck, checking out how she's grinding all up on him, and the trippin' part is, he doesn't move. Where they do that at? First of all, when did they get so tight? It's like a girl been in the Dec only a hot minute, but from what I can tell either she's been coming to the club more than she tells me, or tonight she's Casper the friendly ghost, but I can't stress that.

Not too sure on how she looks at me now, but Quinn's here, and for the most part she gave me my props, although I could tell she had this look like, what's really up with me working here in the club. She's really hard to read these days. One minute she acts like the Quinn whose taught and shown me everything I know, and then there are other times where she's this Ms. Goody two shoes, trying to act all brand new. I admit, I'm not the same person anymore, but what am I to do? Rule #6 – 'The game doesn't change, only the players.' And now I'm in the game for real, it's like her protégé has grown up and she can't handle it. She'll be alright once she sees I can do this.

Just as I get my orders put in, Rishard comes up to me; it's about time. I haven't seen him since he left from over Skyye's. This boy is a trip, I can't believe he's trying to be all up in my face as if he owns me or something, straight sweating me, talking about, what I'm wearing? What dude? I'm about to say to him "you're not either one of my daddies." Oops, no he didn't, this boy! Oh, uhn, uhn, he's in here pulling me by my arm just because I won't leave the club with him. From across the room, I see Drew looking over here. By the look on his face, he senses some drama, and I can tell he's about to get all in Rishard stuff.

"Yo bro, wassup? Is it a problem or what?" he asks Rishard.

Rishard looks away like some lil' punk, I knew it!

Drew continues, "Man wassup, where you been hidin'? I hope you got my paper. I know you ain't stupid enough to show up here without it."

All Rishard can do is put his head down as to say, "Naw, I ain't got it." I don't want to seem stupid or anything, but, I'm not sure how the whole game goes, but… looks like while Rishard's been acting like he's the man, evidently Drew's the man. And maybe that's why I fell for him in the first place, well I guess you can say I'm still there. I know I act as if I don't care anymore, but it's something about him. I love him! Drew that is… and at some point I'm still going to make it up to him.

Looking like a black John Gotti, Drew tells him, "Walk to the office wit me right quick."

I take one look at Rishard, and I'm wondering what is it that I have seen in him this long, makes me nauseated seeing him follow behind Drew like some lil' puppy. It registers to me this is my cue to keep it moving, but I want to ask him so bad where is my money.

Back in the VIP, I see first-hand what it means to make it rain. This one guy I know has at least 10 stacks, and he's setting it out. Cristal, Dom, Moët, you name it, he spending! He gestures for me to come over, and a part of me is like… "who me?" I look towards him, and my heart sorta flutters because I'm guessing this is my time to show what I'm made of. Thanks to my sneaking some moves from China, I got this!

Before I realize it, I've given him a lap dance to remember. This is like a high. I can do this all the time, plus the money is bananas. I'm not even thinking about the money Rishard owes me. I've been so caught up, I haven't even noticed some people have left. I look for Angel and Dionne; I guess they are gone. No goodbye, nothing. Quinn told me she'll be back to get me, but since she saw Rishard she may think he's taking me home.

Looks like it's all good. I guess he was able to cough up Drew's money, so huh, odds are I won't be getting mine anytime soon. He comes over to me and ask if he can come by later tonight, because we need to talk. He needs to tell me something important, but I'm not even trying to hear anything he has to say to me. First you take my money, then you push up on me as if you are going to try to jump me, and then come to find out you really are just some peon, do boy, ugggh. Talking all that crap like he's the one running things. Whatever.

☙

Two o'clock in the morning and we are still kickin' it like it's alright. I guess that's why it's called Etcetera; it goes on, and on, and on… Drew said earlier he was going to be shutting it down soon, but these dudes are something serious, I mean for real ballers. Turn down for what?! They're still buying the bar out, and still tipping. Last I counted, it was almost $2,000; I'm like we need to party like this every weekend. I'm thinking, going like this, I'll have enough for my own spot. Umm that's a thought. Maybe I can sweet talk Drew; he'll get it for me.

I know one thing though, I'm so tired, all I want to do is go straight to sleep. I get a minute to check my phone, 2 missed calls, looks like one is from Ms. Paige, and another call from a private number. I try to listen to the voicemail, but it's hard to hear with Crystal Caines blasting in the background. I try and make out enough, seems like she said this is India! India? What?! And it never fails, that boy has sent me I know four messages tonight alone! I need to stop being so hard on him, maybe go out with the boy at least one time, just then maybe he will leave me alone! He sends these messages at the craziest of times, for instance at 8:00, he sent his favorite line; "Just thinking of you, hope you are safe, and hour later, he sends this heartfelt message, "God has you here for a reason, you have something left to do. There's strength for the stage you're in right now." Awwwe; how sweet. Moving right along! No serious. I have to admit, he does have a way of saying the sweetest things to me. Who knows, maybe next lifetime.

Even though a few people are still here, I start to wind things down. Drew calls me into the office, and for some reason he has this look on his face. Not sure how to take him.

"So I see you have grown up a whole lot since our last encounter," he says.

Perplexed I say, "Well yeah, a lot has happened since we were last toget–"

He stops me from talking, and puts his finger over my lips. With a hushed silence I look at him just as I did when I first fell for him. He looks just as good as he did that day.

He doesn't hesitate, he jumps right at it, "Tonight you showed me just how big girl you really are. You held your own; I was checking you out, handling them boys like a pro."

I giggle. Thinking to myself, so true, I did, didn't I?

He reaches out his hand, pulls me over to him behind the desk, and the next thing I know here he is, massaging my shoulders, rubbing my back, and as much as I want to pull away from him, I can't. I stand here and allow him to caress me in places that I have only allowed Rishard to go.

Softly he whispers in my ear, "How does it feel?"

I'm speechless. I keep playing back in my head the last time we were in the hotel, and all I can think of is when Quinn kept telling me he was going to think I was a tease. I can't let him believe that. Here is my time to make it up to him. Show him.

I take a deep breath, and I say to him, "It feels nice."

"Should I stop?"

I have most definitely grown up because the last time I was shaking, scared to death, but now, I'm ready.

In my big girl voice I say, "No, don't stop."

Before I know it, he positions me over the desk as I face the door; he's standing behind me like a soldier at attention. Every touch from him sends a feeling of warmth through me. My spine even feels as though it's aligned just right. He's unbuttoned my bra, and hmm hmm, my breast, he's holding them as if they were the key to the city. My shorts have been pulled down to just the right point, where he has open access to what feels to me right now as the Atlantic ocean. He kisses my neck, puts his hands on my hips as to tell me to bend over. I do, and oh my! I hold my breath, because out of all the times I have been with Rishard, I have never had this feeling. My knees are trembling, my heart is racing, it's like it's just us two going from mountain to mountain. I forget there are still people here. I don't care. Neither does he. We stay this way for what seems like a lifetime. As I continue to squirm, and gyrate my hips in such a way that even turns me on he continues at a pace slow enough, that he may get a ticket for driving too slow in the fast lane.

He asks, "Have you thought about me?"

It's right here I realize I'm crying, not because I'm afraid, but because for the first time, I realize I could be making love. Even with my squeals and moans, all I hear is the music continuing to play over the loud speakers. I can't concentrate, because he pulls me over to his chair while he sits down, and gestures for me to straddle him, I follow his lead. He looks deep into my eyes, and just as he puts his arms around my waist, I gasp for breath again while I inhale the man I have waited for. Just as I fix my mouth to say those words, the door pushes open, and it's Quinn! She burst in right as I'm resting on top of Drew, and to my dismay, she says to him, "You muthafu"– He doesn't flinch. Here I am shirt pulled over my head, breast open to the world, as naked as Eve and Adam were in the garden of Eden, only thing missing is the tree.

I get myself together as she storms out. I've somewhat zoned out because I'm so blowed I don't know who to be mad at right now. As if nothing has happened, he stands up, pulls his pants up, fixes himself, and looks at me as if to say, what's wrong with you? I'm numb. Everything I had in me is now dead. I head to the bathroom in his office, and right before I get totally dressed, I hear a knock at the door. I overhear Deuce tell Drew there's a problem outside. I immediately figure its Quinn trippin', but I couldn't be more wrong. From what I can see from the bathroom, it's about five or six men waiting to see Drew. One turns his back and on his jacket it reads FBI and another reads DEA. Dag, where is my phone, I wish I could talk to my Daddy Malcolm right now.

Chapter Nineteen

Victoria, home is where the heart is, well was...

Okay God what's next? You said you wouldn't put any more on me than I can bear; my child is out there, only you know where, as if she has lost her mind. I haven't seen or heard from her, I called Skyye just to check on her in which Gabby isn't aware of that. I asked her to say nothing. She promised me she wouldn't. It just makes me feel a little better knowing that she's with Skyye. We didn't hit off to well when I first met her, but she has seemed to be a pretty nice woman. For that reason I have been able to sleep some at night; not much.

    I am so frustrated with this whole Marcel and Lilliane ordeal, I need a trip, but I don't know if I would be a horrible mother to leave Atlanta while my child is not home. I have all but canceled so many of my engagements. I have actually dropped my client load a bit. I've let Demetrius run things for a minute. I have had to step back, regroup, try and get myself together. Last time I went to the doctor, I was informed that my viral load had gone up, and I'm sure why. I did, I stopped taking my meds. I stopped everything. I haven't slept with Marcel since that day at the restaurant. He hurt me. He hurt me to my core. He says he didn't lie, but he didn't tell the truth either. I'm wondering how many more of his past suitors I have come in contact with. He's been trying so hard to make it up to me, I feel that he's being honest about the whole thing, but it's so hard to feel like if he wouldn't have gotten caught, just how far would we have gone.

My head is hurting so badly, not sure which is hurting worse, my head or my heart. Lord, why does this keep happening to me? I've read my bible from front to back more than once, I've given time, my tithes, I just don't know anymore. I'm sitting here thinking back to when Gabrielle was a baby. Everything as hard as it was on me then, was still so simple. Never in my dreams did I ever imagine my baby would one day grow up, and turn into this little talking back, neck rolling, defiant person I know I didn't raise. You gave her to me because you trusted me to teach her, show her, nurture her, to love her. Lord I'm tired. There are days when I just feel like giving up. I'm fighting this disease even though the doctors say it is under control, but my body is just so tired. I have done my best, the best I know how and here I am, too ashamed to let the people at church know that me, Victoria Diamond Bouviér has a child that is doing drugs, having sex, and so much so, she has left my home, and the worst part I allowed her too. I didn't even stop her. What does that say about me?

Just as I prepare to run my bath water the phone rings, and its Lucy, haven't really talked with him since all of this has happened. I'm always the one to have everything under control. He looks to me to be the one in control. Everyone does, but I'm not sure how to handle all of this. Lord I need your help.

"Hello Bernadine!" he yells on the other end of the phone. "I know you aren't still over the having a pity party; you know how I feel about that. I ain't coming!"

"Hey Lucy, how are you? I'm fine, aren't I always fine?" I answer him. "And as far as a pity party, no, I'm not, I am just trying to process everything. It just all seems like a lot right now."

He butts in, "And what is this I hear about your client and Marcel? You know he's called me because he feels like I'm the only one that can talk some sense into you. Girl don't you know that man loves you, what are you thinking. Every man is not like Malcolm. I know he hurt he you, but he's not Malcolm. He made a mistake that he is trying to correct, but you want let him."

I sit here listening at him, knowing that for the most part he is right, I think I just need a reason to be upset with someone besides Gabby. I feel as if I take it out on him, then I won't have to deal with what's going on with Gabby.

"Has he ever lied to you? Has he ever given you a reason to think has now or ever been untrue to you? I don't think so, so what would make you think he would now. Okay, I'm a man, hush Victoria! Anyway, like I said, I am a man, even though I am a gay man, it doesn't mean I don't feel. You know I have been battling with that for a while now, but that does not change the fact that I know what it's like to love someone so much that their happiness is what gives you a reason to smile. I love Marcel, he's a great man, has always been. I'm not saying that because I know I can get free jewelry for the rest of my life. No I'm just kidding. On a serious note. You need to stop feeling sorry for yourself, you have raised Gabrielle the best you could. You've done your best as a mother. Sometimes these children have to learn the hard way, even my God-daughter, she has to learn that there are consequences to every action."

"But Lucy, I've told her that before."

"I'm sure you have, but this is my time to shine honey, will you let me please? All I'm saying is that I'm not sure how the story goes in the bible, but you know the one about the boy that left home, and wanted to do all this stuff on his own, got out there, start partying, spending money on the guls, doing God knows what, but after a while that got old–"

I stop him, "You're talking about the Prodigal Son."

"Okay then Mrs. Bible Trivia, so you know what I'm talking about, but the moral of the story is, just like he came home, my baby is going to come home too. I know she is."

Tears began to fall down my face, because no one knows how much I want that to be, but she hasn't called, or anything. All I've done is pray that she is alright. I think I have burned the Potter's House prayer line up.

He continues, "But until then, you need to come see your parents. They miss you, and I know you miss them too. You need them. Marcel has paid for your ticket. It's all taken care of."

Is he crazy, does he think I'm about to leave my baby, and my man with some woman that is waiting for me to leave. No sir. Although the idea does sound like a good one, I still don't know. I haven't seen my family in a while, maybe I need to.

His Grace, His Blood, His Mercy!

We end the conversation on that note. I love him so much; he always knows how to get me in a better mood. I hang up feeling in much better spirits. Brooklyn here I come.

※

Three days later, I'm on my way to see my parents. Have some quality time with my mother, and my father. Actually, I haven't seen Jules in a minute either. He and Reese just got back from the Dominican celebrating her birthday. At first I thought it was so crazy how all of that went down, but she has turned out to be a wonderful sister- in- law. I guess he needed to see what was out there, and he did, but in the end he found a woman that loved him beyond that and they have been happy ever since. Plus, I admit I would have chosen anybody over that snake in the grass Trenton.

Who else would be here to pick me up besides my father? Still fresh and so clean. No one but my daddy would pull up in his Bentley, stepping out in a pair of Diesel jeans, a green and blue plaid button down with the cardigan wrapped around his neck looking like a teenager, and to top it off, no he didn't pull out the suede penny loafers. And if I know my daddy, Brooks Brothers all the way; not bad for a seventy-eight year old man. Not being partial or anything, but Momma knew what she was doing when she fell in love with my daddy.

"Bonjour, mon sweet Diamond!"

"Hé Papa." I say to him.

"Hows' my baby girl? Why is she not here?"

This is one time I wish I could just turn around and go back to Atlanta. I don't like lying to my parents, especially

Daddy. I've never been good at it, and at forty-six years old, it still doesn't feel good.

"She's at home Daddy, you know she has school and all, working on this big experiment, so you know–"

"Yes, I know, she's just a young lady that has grown up. And now has no time for her Grandparents, even if we are the best in the entire world."

He's so right. She has grown up, and he has no clue of just how much. I feel horrible, nauseated as a matter of fact. I just want to break down in this car, but I can't. I just can't help but think of the last time we were here; she was such a sweet girl. She had such a great time with them.

"How's that son-in-law of mine? I spoke with him last week; he said he was preparing to open another store. I am so proud of him, proud of both of you. You both have managed to do your thing and still find a way to keep the love candle lit. I like that about him; it drives me insane to see how much he loves and adores you."

I smile, because in spite of everything going on I get a tingly feeling inside, because when I think of how long my parents have been together, although it all hasn't been peaches and cream, they have stayed together.

"Have you spoken with Malcolm since he was there for Gabrielle's party? I was really glad that he made it. I know Gabs was too."

Saved by the bell. We're here. It never fails, when I'm here at this place, it's at that moment that little girl with the four long ponytails, cute dress, handmade by my mother, and can't leave out the fabulous pair of shoes, even if they were Buster Brown. It's then she comes back. I take a deep breath because this is why I'm here, to spend moments with my parents in hopes that it'll help me balance the chaos in my life.

Momma hugs me as if she hasn't seen me in ten years. It hasn't been long at all. I guess that's what it's like when you're a mother. When your children grow up, and move out, you cherish every moment they are home with you. First thing she asks is "Where is Gabby?" Okay so what am I? I know they're glad to see me, but I'm beginning to realize it's not really about me anymore. It's the grandchildren. Later for me.

It's not an hour that I'm here, and the doorbell rings. I hear Momma singing "Jules, my Jules." I'm so excited to see him. I head to the door, and give both him and Reese a hug. I hear Daddy mumbling under his breath, "Don't see him unless Diamond's here."

"That's not true Pops," he says. "I'm by here all the time; guess not enough for you, huh?"

Oh Lord, here it goes, it has always been this way, these two can't be in a room longer than fifteen minutes with each other before it goes to hell in a hand-basket. Last time I talked to Julian, he told me Daddy still hadn't gotten over the whole Trenton situation; and that's been how long ago. He and Reese have even had a child, my sweet nephew Daniel. He's nine now, and he's already talking about being a judge. You would think daddy would be ecstatic with that, finally then he'll get his Supreme Court Judge. My beautiful niece Melanie is now in school getting her Doctorate in Philosophy. I'm so proud of both of them.

I sit and shoot the breeze with Julian for what feels like all night. Reese decided to go ahead home, had to help Daniel with homework. Meanwhile, we stay up just like old times reminiscing on when everything was as good as it gets. He and I have never had any secrets, and it's funny that he out of the blue asks me, "Vic, what's really up? Why are you here and both Marcel and Gabby are back in Atlanta? Is everything okay?"

I take one look at him, and I all but lose it. "No it's not, it's not okay, but it will be."

"What's going on sis? You can talk to me. What is Marcel–"

"Nooo, nothing like that, it's just, it's just–"

"What?" He asks.

I gain my composure and I tell him. "It's Gabrielle. About a month ago, actually the night before her party, she left out to meet some boy, and apparently wound up with him and didn't realize her phone was on. And I overheard her having sex in a car."

He seems unmoved. Or maybe it's just me.

I continue, "On top of all that, I found all kind of stuff in her room, condoms, blunt paper, all kinds of stuff. She's been smoking weed, and doing who knows what for a while. You should have seen her, and heard her, she was out of control."

He looks at me and says, "Welcome to the Jean-Pierre life. Been there done that. Mel tried that after I sat her down and explained to her some things, she began acting out too. Started staying hanging out late with her friends, lying about where she was; we went through it. Just didn't want to say anything, because Pops already had so much going on and we didn't want to bring anymore on anyone else. But, I will tell you, this too shall pass. I know you feel that it easier said than done, but I know what I'm talking about. Even me, I did it. You didn't know, but yeah I used to smoke weed too. Who wouldn't with Winston Jean –Pierre as your father? How you think I made it through college?"

We both laugh so, it helps me. Though the thought of Julian smoking weed is too funny, that's like Carleton getting high, minus him dancing and singing to Tom Jones. Just knowing this gives me hope. I don't feel so alone. Especially knowing that Noëlle and I had was the Queens of High, but I was in college. And let's not even go there about her, makes me mad all over again.

So glad we talked. That's why I miss him so much. He knows just what to say. Life was hard on him though. Daddy didn't play the radio with him, when I think about it, I'm glad that's all he did. Well… that's not all, but…

❦

Eight o'clock Saturday morning, and Lord have mercy, I am in heaven. Momma wakes me to a breakfast cooked for the entire neighborhood, but let her tell it, it's for us. Momma, please tell me you didn't. She did. By the time I'm dressed I walk into the kitchen and lo' and behold sits Bishop Michaels. Leave it up to Daddy, he's not phased one bit, he's still in his pajamas, drinking a cup of coffee, talking about "Morning Pastor, I take it you're here to collect early, I suppose. What you think since Diamond's here we may skip out on service tomorrow, and skip out on the tithes?"

He responds, "Good morning to you too Brother Jean-Pierre, and no I'm not collecting, but if you wish to give, there's no better time than now."

Daddy burst out laughing, "I bet it ain't." he says.

Momma jumps in, "Winston, there you go with that word."

Still mumbling, but loud enough for us to hear, "Woman when you gon' realize that I ain't neva planning on not using the word ain't. I keep telling you Merriam and Webster had me in mind when they added it the dictionary. So ain't you got some breakfast to finish?"

You have to love him. She pays him no attention. They are magic like that. Even Bishop Michaels knows him by now.

After we eat, I'm so hoping and praying that he only came to break bread, but I'm not that lucky. He asks if he can talk to me before he heads out. How can I deny him that?

"So how have you been Sis. Bouviér? You're looking well as always."

"I'm good Bishop, just been working, being a Mom and a wife."

"Is that it? How's your spiritual life? You still connected to a local church?"

What is this? It's wayyy tooo early in the morning.

"Yes, sir I am. We have a great church we're members of, and our Pastor is just as wonderful, a great teacher. He's been very instrumental in my life, just as you have."

He comes back with, "So then you know that little girl of yours has a place to come home to. And if you stay on your knees, keep reading your bible, trust and believe that all things work together for them that love Him, then you will have no need to hold your head down, no need to feel that people in the church will shun you. God's has already paid the price for that. He gave you a charge as a mother. Take that charge. Go and get your child. She doesn't belong to the streets. For she is a child of God, 1 Peter 2:9, she's chosen, she's a royal priest hood, a Holy nation, she's God's special possession, that He may declare the praises of Him, who has called her out of darkness into His marvelous light!"

At this moment my face soak and wet, because Momma has done it again, I thought she didn't know, but she's always praying for me, but daddy on the other hand is still tripping, because he belts out, "Now after that Bishop you mean to tell me we don't need to pull out the collection plate? Ushers, will you come?" Even Bishop laughs. He gives me a hug, and whispers in my ear he loves me.

The house is quiet, no words to be said. I feel so, not really sure how I feel. Momma never ceases to amaze me.

"Momma how did you know?" I ask.

Daddy yells from the living room, "You know that Lucy can't keep nothing!"

I shake my head, walk to my room, to call Marcel, because I need to let him know I love him, and I am sorry for how I've acted. Just as I look at my phone, I have a message, it's from Malcolm.

He sounds frail, "Victoria, I really need to talk to you." He's coughing uncontrollably. I can hear the bells going off in the background. Nate gets on the phone apparently and says, "Vic, it's me, if you get this message, Malcolm is not doing well, he's here in Mount Sinai, ICU."

I drop everything, put my clothes on, and tell Momma and Daddy I have to go, because I'm headed to the hospital to see Malcolm. Without thinking I forget my cell phone, I run back in to get it. I jump in the car, and head to Harlem. As I'm driving so many things are going through my head. Good, bad, everything! The whole Noëlle thing, the Sidney thing, I'm remembering it all, but the one thing I'm really remembering is that first and foremost this is my child's father, and out of all of that, she was the best thing to ever come from Malcolm and me. I immediately reach for my phone, and I call her, she doesn't answer. I call back straight to voicemail. I will try again later.

I'm glad I decided to take FDR, because the bridge is shut down, so this is so much better. I don't remember the last time I've driven this fast in NY, it's like God has opened the streets for me to get through. Even though we are no longer married, I would be lying if I didn't say I'm scared. I would hate for anything to happen to him as I always pray for it not to. My phone rings, it's Lucy. I put him on speaker.

"Hey you, Daddy told me you were headed to East Manhattan? How is he?"

"Not really sure, all I know is that Nate said he's not good. I just need to see him for myself."

"I feel you. How far away are you now?"

I tell him, "Pulling up now."

"Okay."

"I'll keep you posted."

I approach the nurses' station, ask the nurse for Malcolm Cartiér's room, she looks at me like who in the hell are you? Gul Bye! I don't have time for this, not this morning. Thank goodness I see Nate coming out of the room, and it's like he's seen a ghost. He hasn't seen me in well over fifteen years. It's been a long time. First thing he says to me is "Victoria, I'm sorry." My heart drops, "Is he?" I ask.

He replies, "No, he's holding on. He's waiting for Gabby, for you. He was waiting for your call. What–how did you get here so–"

"I was here when I got the message. How is he doing?"

"Doesn't look too good. The doctor said his heart just isn't strong enough anymore, and I think with everything going on with Gabby has taken a toll on him."

I reach for my phone to call her again, no signal.

"May I see him?"

"Yeah that'll be good."

I walk in, and it all these feelings take me over. It's one thing to talk to him on the phone, but it's another to actually see him.

I can tell he is in and out of sleep. I say quietly, "Malcolm, it's me Victoria." He struggles to wake. He opens his eyes long enough to see if it's me.

"Hey you, what you doing? I thought we talked about this. You promised me you were doing the right thing."

He tries to sit up. I ease him. "Shhh, no talking. Your body is weak."

He still tries to sit up, steadily saying he has to talk to me. My God whatever it is it must be very important. He's been trying to talk to me forever.

"We can do that some other time Malcolm, now is not the time."

He insists, it's as if he doesn't say it now he never will. His voice trembling and he is sounding so weak. His breathing is shallow.

"Victoria, I'm dying. I know I am, but it's something you should know, something Gabrielle should know before I pass. Where is she?"

Please tell me he didn't asks that now. There is no way I can tell him she still is not home. I don't think his heart could take it.

"She's in Atlanta with Marcel. You know, school."

"Did she ever get that project started? What about Mensa?"

"Malcolm all of that is too much right now, you need to get better. We can worry about that once you are out of this place."

He coughs again, and again. I can hardly tell what he's saying. Each time he coughs another bell goes off. Lord this is too much. I began to pray. I touch him, his skin feels so rough. He grabs my hand while I am praying.

"Victoria, I love you."

I keep praying.

"Victoria, I am sorry, I know I always say that, but this is not for you. It's for me."

I keep praying.

"Please hand me my bag, I have something to show you." he says as if he is afraid we will run out of time.

Once I'm done praying I reach for his bag. He musters strength to hold his head up. He pushes the button for the nurse to come in. She comes immediately. He points toward his mouth. She gets this machine to suction his mouth.

"You can lie back down now."

He presses, "I can't. I have to do this."

He pulls out a soiled manila envelope that looks a mess. It's been folded so it's tearing at the crease. He hands it to me. Really you want me to open this?

"You should read this."

His Grace, His Blood, His Mercy!

I open the envelope in which there is a letter along with what looks like some type of certificate. From what I can read it says.

January 5, 2001
Malcolm,
Now that I am lying on my death bed, I only think it is fair to let you know that you have made sure that even after I am long gone I shall forever live on. Think back to the day when I came to your office. I was so scared even then, but I was sick, and no I didn't understand why at the time, but we all know why I was sick don't we? What you did say was that I had better hope I wasn't pregnant, but what you didn't know I had already been pregnant.

When we took the first break from each other, and you didn't see me for a while, it was because my mother had me come live with her until I got myself together, until I recovered, from the cesarean I had. Yes Malcolm we had a baby, I had just started my career, and it didn't look like you and I would ever be together. You kept telling me we would, and somewhere in my mind I was stupid enough to believe you. I should have known you were never going to leave her!

My mother had me stay with her and my twin sister Skyye. They helped me with her. Yes we have a little girl named Quinn Mercí. (She's named after my grandmother, and because I knew if she lived it would be because of God's mercy, and she did, so I wanted to tell Him Thank you!) She's beautiful. I never had planned to tell you because for some reason I still loved you, and I didn't want to make your life any harder than what it already was, but when I realized that I will never see her grow up, I will never attend any of her games, never meet any of her boyfriends, because of you I will never see anything. My daughter will be motherless!

I hope you are somewhere pandering this, and if you have any doubts I have enclosed a copy of her birth certificate, in which your name is not listed as Father because we were not married, you were married to someone else, but if you are the man I know you are, you know this not to be untrue. For once man up, and do the right thing. You know how to reach my mother, she will be expecting you. Oh and please know if Skyye ever cared anything for you; please know you are now the bane to her existence. In other words, she hates you, and any and everything that's connected to you.

Lastly, I am not sure what God has in store for you, but I hope you will love her just as much as you love the baby you now have. Isn't it funny, now you have a Merci and a Grace.

Sydney

Jesus!!!!!! No this is not happening !! This cannot be. As much as I want this to be lie, as a woman, I have to know there is a possibility. For one second I pause, hell yeah it's true, my daughter is now with Quinn, and not to mention that, uugghh, Skyye! What?!!! All I can do is look at Malcolm with a disdain I have never felt before. All of these feelings have come back all over again, and all I feel is rage!!

I try again, and again to reach Gabrielle because now my baby is in danger more than ever all because of her father's selfishness, his indiscretions, his downright lying, cheating, behind! I am fuming! I can't believe this. One would think that it really wouldn't mater too much, but my child, my baby girl is involved in this foolishness. She and Quinn have been friends since we moved to Atlanta! I recall the conversations with her Grandmother about how they moved to Atlanta after her mother died, but as far her father went, he had died a while back. My God! How many lies can one person tell! If I have ever felt horrible, it's now. As a mother I didn't protect her, I didn't pay enough attention, all I was focused on was being successful enough so that she would never have to want for anything. I just wanted to be a good mother. This HIV is still haunting us! Even from the grave!

After a few moments, I hear the nurse call STAT!! Malcolm reaches for me with all the strength he has, but I can't reach back, I don't know why, this doesn't even seem real. My entire life has been a lie, and this man is dying right in front of me. Nurses, doctors, everyone is running in to try to save him! A nurse pushes me out of the way, because really I feel as if I weigh a ton. I look over and Nate is crying. It's his brother, they've been a pair for a long time, and I'm sure he has been here with him the entire time. A minute later I hear a long beeeeeeeeep. The sound goes forever in my head. I have no breath to scream!! In my head I'm yelling Malcom!!!!! I look up and here is Lucy. He holds me, I feel nothing.

Tonight has been one of the worse nights of my life! I can't even begin to process this day. I promise if I didn't know any better I would think I have been cursed! I have sat up all night talking to my mother, she has said so much without saying anything. I still have not reached Gabrielle. Lord please let her be okay. I have prayed until I can't pray anymore.

It's 2:00 am. I check my phone; nothing. I immediately pick up the phone call my Marcel. I need him. I need to have him here with me. I don't think my bed at my parents' home has ever felt this cold.

"Hey baby? How are you?" he asks.

I just hold the phone. He says nothing either.

A few minutes pass, "I need you," I say softly.

"Would you like me to come? I'm sure I can charter a jet–"

As much as I would love that, I tell him, "No that's okay. I'll be home tomorrow. I have to find Gabrielle."

Before I can continue, he says, "Already on it. I need you to try and rest as much as you can. Trust me; it's all going to work out fine. I know it doesn't seem like it right now, but God is protecting her, just as he is protecting you right now."

I respond, "But baby, I feel like she is in harm's way, I feel as if she is somewhere where she needs me, but she want let me know."

"Do you trust Him?"

"With everything I have. I'm just beginning to asks, where is He? Is He not hearing my prayers?"

"Remember what it says, when you are going through a test, you should know the teacher is always quiet during that test. Right now, this is your test."

"Why do I always have to be tested so?"

"Baby, I've come to realize that God doesn't operate the way we do. He does things not so that when we come out of the storm we have a testimony. He makes sure that when he brings us out, He ultimately will get the glory."

"But Malcolm, what about that? He's gone and I can't even find her to tell her."

"Do you trust Him?"

"I do."

"I know this is easier said than done, but I need you to rest that pretty little head of yours. In the morning I will have everything waiting for you, and just know this, we are going to always have storms, but they don't last always, and the same God that brought you out the first time, He'll do it again. Hakuna Matata."

"Hakuna Matata."

☙

Preparing to board the jet, I look over the New York sky, and so many memories of this place flood my heart, I'm sickened, I'm heartbroken, but I hear a voice that says, "Oh wait honey! All of this fabulosity can't take off without me!" Here he is, my brother, my friend, my Lucy right by my side.

"Lucy, you came."

"Chile shut the front door! I know you didn't think I was going to let you go back alone. Sweetness, we 'bouts to do us a couple of drive-by's, now you didn't let me get that Noëlle, but Boo Boo Ms. Sydney don't even know what's about to go down, but Ms. Skyye is about to find out Brooklyn style. I got my gloves, my Vaseline, and my combat boots! We about to spray some gasoline all over Decatur, ain't that the place where they say it's greater?!"

I find a laugh in me. "Yes you road lizard, that's what they say."

"Well how about this, not until Brooklyn Finest rolls through. Power up the Tesla, because we 'bouts to ride…"

Chapter Twenty

Quinn, they say what's done in the dark...

Things have been crazy since the other night; Drew won't take any of my calls. I have called him so many times. I'm still trippin' how he flipped the script like that. Every time I think about it I get sick. After all that crap he was spittin' to me, he wound up gettin' with Gabs anyhow. And that–, naw, I can't even be mad at her, she didn't even have a clue, but she ain't have to do it like that. I haven't seen or talked to her since then. I don't know where she went. Her Mom's is going to kill me!

 This isn't like me; I haven't had any desire to kick it with any of my other dudes. Since I started fooling with Drew, I admit it, I got caught up, all I was thinking about was how and what he could provide. The hurting part is I really thought he felt something for me. I talked all that to Gabs about the Rule Book, and look at me. My all-time favorite rule, 'You can't play the game with the game show host.' Now that's funny, the game show host got played!

Word on the street is Etcetera was shut down. The Feds busted in right after I left. I thought something looked a little strange. I just hope Gabby didn't get caught up in all that. I couldn't believe how she was up in the club going at it like that. They probably going to get him for having minors working in there, not to mention, they were doing all kinds of stuff, XTC, Mollies, oh and what's the kicker is half the VIP was doing lines! I didn't even have an idea it was going down like that. All I got to say is Juelle, Pimpin', all of 'em they going down. Ah man, my Boo Rhasan might get caught too. I bet Pimpin' finna sing like Jennifer Hudson.

༄

I see my cell has been blowing up, from what I can tell its Mrs. Bouviér. From the messages, she ain't playing. She sounds pissed. She keeps asking to please tell Gabs to call her, she has called her several times, and she won't answer. Same here. I can't get her either, even though I know she don't want to hear anything from me, but I really do want to know where she is. Tiger says she came by and picked up her things, she left in Black Land Rover; that could be anybody.

We have a couple more weeks before we are out for Christmas break. I swear it doesn't even seem like Christmas. We don't even have any decorations up this year. I know the kids might not have a big to do because Tiger and Aunt Skyye have pretty much blown the money we had. I will say this; it was a blessing to have Gabs around. I know she would at least make sure the kitchen was cleaned. It was like we had our own little Cinderella. I miss her. Dag, Gabs where are you?

I get home and it's a note on the dresser from Aunt Skyye. I'll be home around five this evening, we need to talk. Humph, I wonder what this is about. I look at my cell, it's already 4:45. I go in the den and here sits Tiger. Looks like he just woke up. That could be true. The day in the life of Tiger, sleep, eat, smoke, sleep, and pretty much in that order.

"You know where Aunt Skyye went?" I ask him.

"Naw, last I saw her she was heading downtown, she said something about going to the courthouse." he replies.

"Courthouse? What for?" I ask.

"Probably about this house. You know they trying to take it right. It's in Foreclosure, has been for a minute now."

I'm like Foreclosure, that means we need to either get the money up or they will put us out of here. I will not be one of those people you see their stuff all out on the curb and all.

"How much does she owe?"

"Let's just say this; they ain't trying to take no money from her at this point."

"What does that mean? We can't pay them the money?"

Out of nowhere he just goes ham on me, and starts cussing and everything!

"Not you too… now what you want to blame me. Everyone else does. Talking 'bout I don't give anything on the bills. Hell, I'm paying just like she is. Maybe if she wouldn't keep tooting up, we might have something, but she been so messed up ever since your Moms passed she ain't been right since, that's why–"

"That's why what?"

"Nothing man, she gon' talk to you, she need to, she shoulda talked to you a long time ago instead of lying to you. It's a shame how she played that lil' gul. She shoulda never let her live here in the first place. Pretty much had her turning tricks for her, it's was just that wasn't nobody going for that. That's a baby. Ain't nobody trying to go to jail over no babies. I know I ain't."

I'm still not understanding him. He's just saying a bunch of nothing. I hear a car outside, and I look out of the window, it's Skyye. Looks like she got a lot on her mind as usual. I plop back down on the sofa, and as soon as she walks in, she looks over at Tiger and says to him, "You need to leave." From there they go at it.

"I ain't going nowhere!" he yells.

She yells back, "Leave my house now!"

"Your house? You know damned well who house this is."

She gets quiet. I feel like I am in the middle of something I do not need to be in. I get up to walk to the back. She stops me.

"Quinn where is your friend, has she been back here yet?"

"As far as I know of no."

"She don't need to, you done made a fool out of her long enough don't you think?' Tiger mumbles in the background.

She continues, "I need to talk to you, it's very important."

"Okay, so what's going on?" I ask.

Tiger shouts, "This here is your house!"

A look comes over my face as to say, WTH is he talking about? She tries to sit me down, but she has a look of disgust, a look of anger, I don't know what it is. She hands me a huge envelope and in it is all these legal documents. One of them is my birth certificate. Others are documents about the house; others are about her guardianship of me, well looks like Gram is my guardian. But there is a letter from my mother to Skyye. It reads:

> January 5, 2001
> Skyye,
> As I spend these last few days with my daughter, I wanted to take this time to say some things to you that I have never said before. When we were younger, I always wanted to be so much like you, you were my girl. I saw how you were top of the class at everything, I actually envied you. Especially when you started dating Darrell Thomas. Oh I loved myself some Darrell, but it was you he wanted, and I didn't realize then that you loved me so much that when he broke my heart, you wanted to break his, so you decided to act as though you were so in love with him just to break up with him. All because of me.
> You were always the stronger one when it came to men. You just knew how to play it. I was the one that fell so hard for them. Just like I did with Malcolm. You told me all along to leave him alone, but I wouldn't listen. You hated him for hurting me, and when I got pregnant with Quinn that only made it worse. I wanted to give her up, but neither you nor Mom would let me. This is why I never told Malcolm of her, I didn't want to disrupt his life. She was such a beautiful little baby. I am going to miss her so much.
> When I was able to come to you to share with you about how I had gotten HIV from Malcolm, I didn't

know how you would take it, I didn't know how to take it! You knew about his wife, how he wasn't planning to ever leave, you knew about his new baby that was on the way, you knew it all, but you didn't falter, you still loved me. The great thing is that Quinn was spared this horrible disease. This is why I am asking you this favor. As my twin sister, no one knows me like you do, and no one will ever love my child as you will. I need you to protect her. Show her what you showed me.

Last I heard Malcolm and his wife Victoria have divorced, and they have a baby named Gabrielle, so now my Quinn has a little sister, and I hope and pray they one day they will meet, love each other as sisters, just like you and me. I need you to make sure that happens. I am signing guardianship over to you, as I know you already have two children of your own. My sweet nieces, oh I love them as if they were mine, but I know you can do it. You are Skyye!

To this day Malcolm has not known anything of Quinn, once I am done sending this to you, I plan to send him a certified letter letting him know. I am not sure how he will respond, but I ask if he does wish to be a part of her life, allow him. He is her father, and I do not wish this on anyone. Even with his status he deserves to know. He may not have too much time with her.

Please know I love you, and I always have. I know I have not always told you, but I do. You are the best sister a girl could ever wish for.

Sydney

His Grace, His Blood, His Mercy!

My heart drops. I am so conflicted right now. Could this be? Is Gabby my sister? Oh my goodness. How? How could this be? She looks at me still with more anger and rage than ever before.

"I'm sorry I didn't tell you. I couldn't." she explains.

I am not hearing her. This whole room is moving. My stomach is burning on the inside. I immediately throw up. I soon find myself purging over the toilet. I'm sick.

ಌ

A little while later, I get myself together. I pick up the phone, I look at all the pictures Gabby and I have taken, do we look alike? And this man… I've seen him several times. My father is still alive. I've been looking for him all this time! I need to find him. I need to see him. My daddy, I need to get to him! I immediately run into Skyye's room, she's sitting on the bed reading the letter again.

"I just want to know, why did you tell me my father was dead?" I ask her.

"To me he was. He killed my sister, and he killed a part of me too."

I scream at her, "But what about me? I deserved to know he was alive. You said he was dead."

She looks up at me, and says, "He is. He just died this past week."

I heard her, but for one minute I recall the 3 letters my mother said. HIV! Oh it just got real…

Chapter Twenty-One

Victoria and Lucy, Charlie's angels minus one...

"*She won't answer me either,* now I know she done lost her mind," Lucy says.

I still haven't talked with Gabrielle. All of my calls are going straight to voicemail. I don't know where or what could be going on with her.

"What did Ms. Skyye say when you talked to her? You know I've been fuming ever since we left BK. You know it ain't nothing for me to slide on those throwbacks and ba-be go in on 'em! I might be a Puerto Rican beauty, but I still can get down low!"

This thang is so crazy. Always keeping me laughing, trying to keep me focused; even though I am so agreeing with him. I don't even believe that this heifer had the nerve to allow my baby to live with her knowing she and Quinn were sisters. This has all been too much to handle. Then to know I haven't reached Gabrielle to tell her about her father. I can't do this. I just can't.

Her mentor called, and I even gave her the number to reach her at Skyye's, not sure if she did or not. I haven't heard anything back as of yet.

"So… what's up Vic for real? What are we planning to do just sit here and wait by the phone? I need to go find our baby, and I'm sure you feel the same way. I know Marcel says he has it taken care of, but this is something that cannot wait. Especially because she is out there, and has no clue that her father just died."

I just thought again about that… Lord have mercy, I'm not sure how she is even going to handle all of this. Lord I am leaning and depending on you right now to fix this. Please she's just a baby! Once again my face is filled with tears. Not sure if I am crying because Malcolm is gone, or if it's because Gabby is unaware that he is gone! I know one thing is for sure, Lucy is right. I just can't sit here and do nothing. McAfee Road here we come.

☙

Every time I have somewhere to go, 85 is shut down! Looks like I may have to take 155. The traffic this way isn't looking too good either. Druid Hills is backed up, and what should be a quick ride is now turning into a road trip!

"Have you talked back with Nate at all?" Lucy asks.

"Not since I last talked with him."

"Arrangements, what is he thinking?"

"As far as that goes, I'm not sure either, but I do know Malcolm had always expressed to me his wish to be cremated, but I don't know. Things could have changed."

"I think I remember this area, isn't this where they thread eyebrows right? I have never been able to find anyone to get mine just right, and plus honey the price was he just right. $5.00 baby and they want to charge $11.00 over in Cobble Hill. So you know how they doing it in the East Village."

"Yeah you're right. That's one thing I have noticed things are cheaper here. At least some things are. Depending on what you're trying to get."

"You know me, I'm always down for a shopping spree.," he says.

Giggling, I asks. "You're not looking for any knock offs are you? If so I got the perfect spot for you."

As soon as I can say it, he burst out, "Oh uhnn uhnn sweetnesss, I know you not talking about the place that one of Gabby's lil' friends was telling us about, what is it?" He laughs.

"What, Greenbriar??!!" I ask.

"No that doesn't sound like it, some kinda market." He adds.

"Oh, you talking about Old National Flea Market."

He cracks up, "That's it. Honey I saw one of them bags that child had, I felt so sorry for her, I wanted to give her mine. She talking about that's a Jimmy Choo, I wanted to ask her Jimmy Whoo? No sweetness, Jimmy didn't sign off on none of that foolishness! Some of that mess you see, the stitching is coming a loose before you even wear it."

Just as he's going off, I feel my phone vibrate. Didn't realize I had a missed call from a private number. That doesn't make me feel any better. It's taking forever to get to McAfee, people are everywhere! Apparently it's an accident ahead. What is this the winter version of the Glenwood Festival?

"So what is this, buy one get two free sale day today? Chile if I wasn't on a mission to find Gabby, I would have you pull over and I'd just feel compelled to show these these children a few things bout dressing honey, cause this here is a just a catastrophe! If I see one more person with a pair of leggings on with the overpriced house shoes I am going to scream!"

As bad as my heart is hurting right now, I look over at Lucy and all I can do is laugh. He is so right, neither one of us is UGG fans. Just as we come to the light at Glenwood and Candler, we pass a bus stop. Out of the corner of my eye I catch it, hoping Lucy somehow misses it, but why would I think he would, the fashionista of all fashionistas.

He screams, "My people my people! Now look at this. Please tell me why is this woman carrying the "Peoples Version" black and orange Petite Malle Epi standing at a bus stop, with 2 children hanging on her ankles, and one on her hip, and all of them look like they need their hair combed. I know this bag is a $5,000 bag! I saw it debuted at the 2014 show. SMDH! Now, she is casket sharp with her black faux leather leggings, even rocking the thigh-high boots, and gots the nerve to try and pull off the faux fur vest. If I had to guess I would say H&M all day long!"

I can't even laugh at this fool; he is on some other stuff. I'm trying to get to my baby! But Lord knows he's right.

He continues, maybe this is his way of keeping his mind off what's about to go down. "You know I don't have a problem with no one and the way they decide to dress, and do their thing. I wasn't always the Head Buyer for Bergdorf's. So I had to learn as I went along, but my problem is this here, like Madea says, "know your fabrics, know your fabrics, I'm like, know your designers, know your designers! Know what your designer will and will not make. Better yet what was ever made by the designer, e.g. the Multicolor bag was never made in a backpack!!! Know what bags the average person working a regular 9-5 is going to carry. Please know the average person that can afford a Louis Vuitton is NOT going to carry a runway bag with all the embellishments, brass, crocodile, all the bells and whistles. Oh yes I've had to fake it 'til I made it too, but I knew enough to start out with the basic Speedy bag! But nooo… we gots to have the top of the line. I bet some people don't even realize that the an authentic Louis Vuitton will NEVER have that little white circle tag with the LV hanging on a string attached to the handle, a real one will always have the tags tucked inside the pocket! And to add those little authenticity cards, Really! They are fake too; Louis didn't do that! There will be two tags; one with the name Louis Vuitton telling you what type bag it is, and the other will have the model number, and possibly a care booklet, along with your receipt of purchase. Oh and speaking of that, they need to know if your bag has a D-ring, the "production code" is located under that, not inside the pocket, and this code has two letters followed by four numbers, indicating where the bag was made, the year, and the month! Lastly, I wish I could just tell 'em, if it has plastic wrapped around the handle he didn't do that either. I remember overhearing two women arguing on Canal Street, one swore up and down that her bag was real because the LV's on the back were all going the same way. If I had time, I would have stopped and turned around to tell her, "lady, lady... with a true Louis Vuitton Monogrammed bag you should always see that the LV's on the back of the bag will be upside down. Because the designer uses ONE continuous piece of leather to create that bag, therefore if all of the design is going one way, this is what you should see!"

He finally takes a breath, and I say to him, "Somebody done made my Boo mad, but you hit it on the nail. But the sad part is with all that said, they carry the fake $5,000 bag, but don't have the 10% $500.00 for tithes! Sad, just sad."

He looks back at me, and says, "So true, but no Boo, Skyye done made me mad."

I turn my head away as to not show the tears.

About 15 minutes later we pull up to this house on McAfee. I'm kinda mad that I have never been here before. Going by GPS this is not what I expected. I'm not surprised though. Didn't really think Quinn would be living in a shack. Grams wouldn't have it that way. Just as we pull up, I see this man about 5'10" or so that comes to the door. We don't get out right away. Not sure what we could be walking up to.

"Girl, I got my Glock."

As bad as I don't' want to, but this boy right here... straight crazy. He leans forward as if he is about to really pull out something. Oh God, he does! I look at him with the look you get when your friend is cool and laid back, but when it comes down to the ish they turn into Keisha in New Jack City.

He turns to look at me, and says, "Rock-a-bye baby! I told you the real Puerto Rican Princess ain't no joke. Later for Joseline Hernandez. Let's do this."

I say nothing. He puts it behind his back. He even has a holster and all.

His Grace, His Blood, His Mercy!

Before we make it to the door this young man comes up to us asking what we looking for, cause he got the loud, the purp, even that skunk weed. He tells Lucy he can get a bag of loud for $10.00. This child even tells me I look like the boogie kind, maybe I want that smack, being I'm driving this high ass car he says. WTH? Lucy does this get back jump, and that's all he wrote. Lord, is this what my child has been around all this time?

This creepy looking guy says, "Hey, can I help you?"

"Hi, I'm Victoria, Gabrielle's mother, is she here?" I ask him.

He responds, "Who, Gabrielle, naw, I ain't seen her in a few days."

My heart beats faster. Lord where is my baby? I see Lucy beginning to squirm.

"Is Skyye here?" I ask.

Hesitating he replies, "Yeah she's back there."

"Well could I speak with her please?"

"Well, she ahmm, she—"

"Please sir, will you tell her we're here?" Lucy says to him.

He takes a look at Lucy, and dressed in all of his fabulosity, this boy is standing here with some retro Jordans on with the tongue pulled out, and a pair of Seven jeans, help us Jesus. Who is he supposed to be, a hardcore Fashion Critic?

Next, here she is. I have come face to face with the woman that has had all intention to harm my child. Okay Vic, think about what Marcel has said, we don't know all of the facts yet, so do not jump to any conclusions. Anyway he would have a fit if he knew Lucy and I were over here in Decatur impersonating Bonnie and Clyde.

In a dry tone she asks, "Hey, what can I do for you? If you looking for your child, she ain't here."

OHN! No she didn't.

"Ahmm, Skyye I am here to get my daughter and her things and leave."

She belts out, "I SAID–"

"Ooohhh don't do it, don't do it!" Lucy sings.

She clears her throat, and still with a condescending tone she says, "As I was about to say, your precious daughter is not here. I have not seen her, since she and Pimpin' got into it."

Who in the hell is Pimpin'? I'm thinking to myself. Some drug dealer, I hope and pray not.

I ask anyway, "Who is Pimpin'?"

"I guess he's her Boo or whatever. You should know who your child is hanging out with."

Loordddd, give me strength! I see Lucy's hands going towards his back. I softly press my hand on his arm.

"I am not here to go there with you. I need to find my daughter, and you will be dealt with another time."

At this time I see Quinn coming towards the door. She doesn't look at all grown up like she usually looks, today she looks like a normal seventeen year old girl. Hair pulled back in a ponytail, eyeglasses, and regular clothes. None of that over the top stuff.

"Hello, Mrs. Bouviér," she says to me.

I tell her, "Hello baby."

The ugly side of me wants to be so angry with her, but I realize it's not her fault; she is just as innocent in this whole thing as Gabby is. All I want to do is hug her. A baby trying to find her way.

"Gabs isn't here. I'm not sure where she is. I've tried calling her, she will not answer me. She's not talking to me right now."

"Why? Does she know about?"

The look on her face says it all. Tears fall down her face, she is speechless.

She continues, "I'm not sure if she knows or not."

"So you have no clue where she could be?" Lucy asks her.

She says, "No, maybe she's with Drew, but probably not 'cause he's in jail I think."

What is this, jail, people I have never heard of?

All of a sudden Skyye says, "I hope she knows that bastard of a daddy of hers is long gone."

A chill goes through me. The only feeling I have now is fury, and before I know it, I charge at her, but somehow Lucy stops me."

"Vic, I'm angry too right now, but this is not the answer, not from you."

He looks at her, and in a seething undertone he mumbles, "But most definitely from me. Vic she's not worth the time of the day."

I need to be on the same page with him now, but to think.

She goes in, "I know this is not what any of you wanted to hear, but everyone is tripping because Malcolm is gone, what about my sister? Has anyone thought about that? He took her from all of us. Because of his insatiable desire to have as many women as he could, he sacrificed my sister, who had a child. And not to mention who loved him so much so, that she was willing to never let him know of Quinn. But you, I respect the fact you were caught up in the whole ordeal, okay, I'll give that to you Mrs. Victoria Diamond Cartiér, or whatever your name is now, so you did not know either, but he did, and he caused all of this! So yes, I hated his ass, I despised him, and everything that was connected to him. He took her away from us, her child, my mother, and from me! She was the other half of me and now she'll never see her child—"

As I stand here listening to her vent, this so called hard woman that has probably spent the last 15 years or more relentlessly hating me, my child, grieving her sister. I look at her, and with all the tears she's shedding, all I can do is feel for her too. Malcolm did, he caused all of this.

I tell her in the most sincere voice I can, "Skyye, we do not know each other, but we have been brought together for whatever reason it is, but I am sorry. I am sorry for the loss of your sister. I have asked God to help me to forgive a long time ago when I had to come to terms of how to deal with it, not only that, every day I am reminded of what was left behind. Me and my own health status, each day I wake, I have to thank God for allowing me another day to live to fight this! There are days I am not sure if I can get out of bed, but somehow He gives me the strength. Then I look at my baby, and I pray so hard that she is spared of it, and she never has to face the real reality of knowing what it's like to live with HIV. It's not easy! I still have to take medicine every day of my life just to survive, and yes I know this in no way helps you, because your sister is not coming back, and neither is Malcolm, but what- we- can do, is try to make it right."

I hear Lucy grumbling something.

I continue, "We can make sure that these girls grow up and know their father loved them, because however God fixed it, He made sure they were able to be together to this point. So my being angry with you, your hating me, it will not solve anything. I do know I have a child that needs me, and I need to find her. So if you choose to continue to hate me, go ahead, I can't give you that, because my bible tells me, I have to love you as He loves me. In saying this, I thank you for at least not physically hurting her, and for whatever it's worth, thank you for bringing Quinn here. She was Gabby's first friend, and now they are sisters, so I thank you."

I look at her, and then I take a look over at her guy, and I realize again, just how blessed I am. I have a man that loves me, and who has always protected me, so I know now it's time to go. Just as we turn around to head to the car, I hear Quinn asks, "Mrs. Bouviér, can I go with you to find her?" I turn to say to her, "Yes baby, yes, you can."

Lucy looks back and gives her a look as to say, you ain't want none of this. While walking to the car, my phone vibrates again, and I look down not realizing I've had it in my hand all this time, and the phone says, "Gabby" I hurry to answer it.

"Baby, where are you?" I ask her. There is a silence. I ask again, "Gabby can you hear me? Where are you?"

All I hear is the baby I once knew, and she says to me, "Momma I want to come home."

Chapter Twenty-Two

Marcel, sometimes the woman knows best...

It's been a few months in, and I should have listened to her! I'm on my way to the store early this morning, and I get a call from Geoffrey! He sounds like if he could, he would just turn in the towel right about now.

"You got to be kidding me! What?! Victoria is going to kill me!"

"Man, are you watching CNBC? They are talking about it now," he says.

Of all days, when I am preparing to make this the happiest time of my baby's life, I get the news that my investment has turned out or the worst! From what I hear, it's not as bad as September 29, 2008, the day the House of Representatives rejected the government's $700 billion bailout plan. That day the Dow obliterated, if I'm not mistaken 1.2 trillion in market value. Now today, I am getting a call that I have, because of my own manly thing gone and lost us a mere $1.5 million, just in the gold investments alone! I'm dead. She is going to leave me.

"Marcel, you hear me? Man, what's up? Are you there?"

I hear him, but I am somewhere else, all I can focus on is how am I going to tell her, because of our own investments this just isn't a good day, for either of us. I see I have another call coming through, and I have no doubt who it is.

"Hey baby, how are you?' She asks, with that sweet sultry voice.

I pause, "Hello my love, I didn't bother you this morning because you were sleeping so peacefully. Just didn't want to disturb you."

She doesn't prolong, "Sooo… have you heard this morning's forecast?"

I try so hard to listen for some sound that she is not totally in a foul mood, believe it or not, she sounds at such a peace, it even scares me.

"Yes I have, and I'm on the phone now talking with Geoff, we are trying to come up with some type of strategy. I'm sure your phone has been going off all morning?"

"It has, and I am trying so desperately to remain calm. You know we haven't had anything like this in a while, but as you tell me, I'm to trust in God, and believe that it is all going to work out in our favor. He has already answered my prayer regarding Gabby, and I believe He is going to do it again. I have just come to say to myself, that this is the day the Lord has made."

Okayyy then, so now here I am the one that is freaking out, but I can't let her know about it, because she expects me to be the strong one, hold her up, give her the encouraging words she needs. But, I can't help but think about all that gold

I have tucked away in the safe. I am feeling like I just need to have a gold party. No, just a little humor.

"You are right my love, I, myself, am believing and trusting in Him that He will do all that He said He will do. I am just so blessed and so grateful to have you in my life. You have truly been the joy of my life. When I look back, and I think over just how much you and I have shared. I must say if it comes to it, and we wind up losing everything, I must say, I still will have it all. Because I know that as long as we have each other we have everything."

Now you did that boy! I have to give myself a pat on the back for that one. I will say, a brotha surely has a way with words.

She softly says, "I have two questions; one, so how much did you lose in your gold investments, and two, by any chance have you spoken with Ms. Lilliane DuPont?"

I choke, but at the same time I man up, and say it, "Not sure of how much exactly, but I have a rough figure around $1.5 mil."

Silence.

Next, I say, "And as far as Lilliane, no I haven't. Last I heard, she called to tell me she apologized for putting me in such a compromising situation. But she did ask would I be willing to see her once more. Even tried to make a very irrefusable offer, but I declined.

I wait for a minute for her response. She says, "See you tonight. I will have your bags packed."

She hangs up.

I click over and realize Geoffrey is gone. Guess he got tired of holding on.

Chizellé T. Archie

❧

Later on, I try to wrap my head around the idea of heading to Malcolm's funeral. This has really been a very hard struggle, because I have seen this man basically disintegrate in front of me, while at the same time here it is, Vic and myself have been struggling to battle this thing every day. Yet, I have been more than blessed to be an elite controller, but I still have the day to day battles that every man has. My body is aging; I still have to make sure I keep myself healthy and fit. Even though I am on no meds, I have been considered for various studies, but I will cross that bridge later. For now, I plan to continue to live my life, love my wife, if I still have one, trust my God, and continue to love Gabrielle as much as I did the day I first laid eyes on her. I plan to continue to raise her; be that father figure in her life, especially now. I also plan to help Quinn as much as I can. Malcolm would want that. Lastly, I plan to make sure I use my head first, in spite of what the love of my life tells me. I hate to say it, but it's a reason why that serpent tempted Eve, but you know Adam was the man, and it was up to him to make sure she didn't eat of that tree, but see Satan knew if he could just get through the woman…

Just as I am putting together what I plan to wear, I ask myself, what Victoria would want to see me in. Okay I'm kissing up, I see she has my bags packed, but remember I'm the man, LMBO. So I choose what, of course, who else but Lucy picked out for me; the Black Armani Collezioni Core Gio Two-Button suit, Diamond loves, with a solid black Armani dress shirt. Diamond loves me in Armani. Well she loves me in anything, no just kidding, no I'm serious, she does. Anyway,

His Grace, His Blood, His Mercy!

to top it off I pull out the black Christian Louboutin Viking Flats, might as well, because I know if I don't have stock in anything else, knowing who my wife is, this pair should be on Christian!

Malcolm, this one is for you man.

Chapter Twenty-Three

Drew, what goes around comes around...

Trafficking, Possession with the Intent to Distribute, Sexual Exploitation of a Minor, Statutory Rape, Prostitution, man these folks must be out their minds. They say they got videos, reports, plus a full witness list.

For the last couple of weeks, all I find myself doing is passin' by the club. I even found myself just sittin' in the parkin' lot. I remember when I first decided to open the club; I was like it had to be located in Midtown on Peachtree at that. Now, I have to ride by 'n see the bars on the doors where everything I'd ever hoped for held inside.

I know it's too late to be talkin' 'bout what I coulda, woulda, shoulda done 'cause I have messed up so bad. Ion even think I can ever fix it. The Feds are tryin' to work wit me, but the deal is I have to give Rodriguez up, and man I ain't sure if

I'm ready for the consequences behind that. But when I look at what I'm facin', I gotta do what I gotta do.

I still can't believe that, lil' dude, Pimpin' was the one who helped the Feds. Not only that, I don't believe I was stupid enough to slip 'n let Mr. Walt, well Mr. Davenporte, gank me like that. That dude was workin' wit the Feds all along, a real BAN! I shoulda known betta, but I let myself get caught up. Got greedy, didn't even realize that they were talkin' every time Pimpin' came through, but that explains it. Apparently, when Pimpin' went missin' for a while, they caught him. From what I heard, he threw the product out the window, but they caught up wit him. So, I guess in turn he became the informant! A muthaf– but that's how it works. I always say trust NO ONE.

The good thing is my boys been loyal as far as I know, but they still got 'em for conspiracy, all of 'em, 'cause they got 'em on tape, but they still won't talk doe. My boy José, we been down for a minute, Ion think he gon' snitch on me like that, but these days who knows.

Even talked to Deuce yesterday, he says he's gonna to try to hold it down for me. He even told me that this beautiful woman who looked to be Cuban was asking about me, but he told her I was actually out of the country. I can't believe she really came to see me. I wish I could ahmm, na'll I don't even need to entertain that now, got too much on my plate.

Right when I pull up to the house, I get a text from Quinn, didn't expect to hear from her, especially after what went down. As hard as I am, I didn't even expect that to happen like that, I thought she was gone. Didn't think she would double back, but I guess she did. I'm sure by now she's heard 'bout everythin'. As a matter of fact, I'm sure she has, that sexy ass Aunt of hers probably told her everythin'. I shoulda just left it wit her, but after that dude Tiger kept running up his tab, I had to take something to hold as collateral. I had his check card at first, but that wasn't working, so I had to get the next best thing, his woman. I have to admit, now that is one MILF I am going to miss.

My phone keeps going off, finally I check it.

12/11/14 Wed
Q: I need to talk to u
5:35PM
    12/11/14 Wed
    Me: Wuz up
    5:54PM
12/11/14 Wed
Q: I went to the doctor today
5:55PM
    12/11/14
    Me: And??!!
    6:24PM
12/11/14 Wed
Q: I'M PREGNANT!!!!
6:25PM
    12/11/14 Wed
    Me: Gul Bye!!!
    6:26PM

That chick must be on sumthin'. I know she trippin'trippin'. There is no way she could be pregnant. Now everybody is tryin' to come at a brotha. It ain't even happenin'. Next that lil' Gabby chick gon' be coming at me with sumthin'. If I ain't know any better I would have to say the saying is right karma is a bi-A! I can't even sweat that right now. I grew up with an absent father, and I always promised myself I would never do that to my child, but I can't even trust her. She's been wit some of everybody! She probably don't know whose baby it is.

※

Today has been one of those days, and if neva before, I need to try 'n enjoy my crib while I can. According to the Feds if I don't cooperate all of this is going to be gone. I'm so glad I didn't have anything here at the house. All my cars except the BMW have been seized. I feel like I'm in a twilight zone.

I kick back 'n get comfortable, turn the ringer off; really not in a mood for too much of nothin' tonight. I guess I need to go through my mail, at least see who else is trying to catch up with me. I come across this letter I thought I threw away. As I am opening it up I began reading, and this lil' honey that is sending me this; I know I ain't messed with her in a minute. I know it's been over a year now. I know what I'm seeing, but I'm not believin' this. She claiming she has tested positive for the luggage, and I know good 'n well she ain't telling me I need to be tested too. What? HIV? Man, GTFOH! My mind draws a blank. This can't be happening.

Around 7:45, I can see my phone light up, everything in me tells me not to look at it, but it's my attorney, I have to get this. I answer it. I know I'm bein' punked. This dude is callin' to tell me that there has been a break out at Benneton

His Grace, His Blood, His Mercy!

Prep Academy, there are several female students claiming to have slept with me, and at least three of them have tested positive for HIV!

Chapter Twenty-Four

Victoria and Gabrielle, it's hard to say goodbye...

As I sit here staring at someone I thought I would spend the rest of my life with, I feel like an outsider, yet I feel as though all eyes are on me. Malcolm and I have been apart for a while and even though we've lived separate lives, it's still so hard to believe we are here. But the one thing that gives me peace is that when I look to the left of me, I know that God doesn't make any mistakes. Even in all of this, He sent me someone that has never hurt me; He sent me a love of my own.

    Seems like it took Gabrielle forever to get dressed, and she's only been back now a few days, but I look at her and she is so much stronger than I was. Still today, I haven't told her the complete story, and I am leaving that up to her as to when and how she wishes to deal with it. But I can't stop thanking God for bringing my baby back home to me. Not sure if it has registered to her yet about she and Quinn, because from what I gather there are some things that they both need to work out, but I am sure it will all take care of itself.

Without trying to look so noticeable, I scan the congregation, and I hate to say it, but after all of these years I still get an uneasy feeling. It's as though I take a look at every woman, and I try to ask myself, without asking myself, because really at this point it shouldn't matter, but, I can't help wondering how many of these women are here to pay their final respects as one of the women he laid with while he was with me. I know I have asked God several times to help me to forgive, but some things are just so hard to forget.

After the services, I find myself just standing around hugging and greeting people I vaguely remember. Of course, my love is ever near, as always he makes sure that I know he is here for me. There is this one lady though that comes up to me, I think she is Malcolm's cousin from Chicago. You would think this lady and I talk every day. I have never been the touchy feely type of girl, but honey this lady is gripping me so hard my insides are flipping. She tells me how much she loved Malcolm and what a good boy he was when he was little, what happened when he became a man is the question, but that's neither here nor there. She tells me how sorry she was to hear that he had passed from cancer, because the last time she saw him he looked so good. It's so hard because I know the truth, yes he did, he developed cancer later on, but I know firsthand what contributed to Malcolm's demise. Guilt!

If there is one thing I hate about these repasts, whatever you wish to call it, is how everyone has to take a plate out. You know that's my pet peeve. I catch a glimpse of Lucy over there gulping up another handful of the macaroni and cheese, and even him, I'm willing to bet my life on it, he is going to try to walk out of here with a plate with some aluminum foil over it. Ughh, can't stand it! Just tre' tacke'.

I notice Gabrielle has a lot of her friends she's made over the summers here. I see a lot of them have come to support her. That's very nice of them. I'm not sure what this thing is with she and Quinn though. Gabrielle is trying to be very sweet about it, maybe because she realizes that Quinn has never had the chance to know her father. And even though Malcolm was absent for a great deal of Gabby's life, some by choice, I know this is very hard on the both of them. The hardest part was seeing them standing over the gravesite saying goodbye; goodbye to a man that has brought them together in more ways than one.

By the time we've said our final goodbyes, I look back and in the midst of it all Gabs and Quinn are hugging each other. I know this is not a laughing moment, but as Momma says, sometimes you have to laugh to keep from crying. I don't want to laugh, but it kinda reminds me of Celie and Nettie, just these two don't have that hair; Good Jesus, that hair! But if someone didn't know, they would think they are over there playing the game they played, it's on the tip of my tongue, oh yes, in my Celie and Nettie voice, "Ain't no ocean, ain't no sea, Makidada, keep my sista' way from me, Makidada"… before I know it, I'm crying, again.

☙

Chizellé T. Archie

The next morning, before we are getting our things together to head home, Nate calls me because he says there are some things he needs to discuss with me. Not sure what at this point is there for him to tell me. Lord did Malcolm leave me some money?!!! Oh, okay, on a for real note, really I'm wondering what this could be about. We are scheduled to leave in the next couple of hours, so I ask him if he can swing by my parents. I would like to spend as much time with them as I can. He agrees.

Naturally, it doesn't take long for my parents to take to Quinn, especially Daddy, he keeps saying she looks like a modern day Lena Horne. I think that's pushing it a bit, but she does favor her a little. Momma of course has done nothing but treated her as she would do anyone else, like family, and that she is. She is our family, and Malcolm I thank you for that.

Though this is not her first time being here with the family, this is the first time she can say she is truly a part of it. I know some people may feel like I shouldn't give this child a minute or a second of my time, but I was never raised like that. When I look at that woman we call Mrs. "D", I can only think of how she taught me how to love. Even when it feels like you are not getting any love in return; she taught me to continue to love. Then Daddy, he's always wanted a big family, so one more is nothing. Yes, I know she's not my biological child, but somehow I feel responsible for her. Before we left Atlanta she mentioned she needed to ask me something, I'm guessing it's to live with us. Gabby has been asking me for the longest. I guess we will just have to see about that.

Twenty minutes later, Nate is here, and he seems a little rushed, but that's cool with me because so am I.

"Hey Vic, glad I was able to catch you, don't want to hold you up anymore. Can we talk outside?"

That would be cool, but it is the middle of December so I'm thinking not, a girl is used to Atlanta's weather now.

I ask him, "How about on the back porch, it's closed in."

"That's fine with me," he answers.

We sit down and he begins to tell me how much he knew Malcolm loved me and Gabrielle. I have heard this song before, but he says he just really needed to let me know because towards Malcolm's last days he had a chance to reflect on a lot of things, of how many people he hurt along the way. He says his heart had become so heavy with sadness because he was never able to be there for Gabs. He even shared with me that he knew all along of Quinn, but he felt it was not his place to tell me that. Malcolm insisted that he be the one to tell me.

He continues, "Just the other day I was going through some of my brother's things, and I didn't know he kept so many things to himself. I guess he felt he had hurt enough people."

"I can see where he would be like that. He did his share of making a mess of things for sure." I respond.

He keeps on, "As I was looking through all of his things, I guess in the times where he would be by himself, I can tell he would make a lot of notes to himself. I'm guessing this way his way of preparing himself for this time, but while I was cleaning out his trunk, I came across something that totally blew me."

"And what was that?" Somewhat unconcerned, I asks in a hurried tone.

"Malcolm had a list of names of people he wanted to somehow make amends with, and I came across, yes, your name, amongst a few others, but I also came across a name I did not recognize."

He shows me this balled up piece of yellow paper where you can tell he had been scratching through. I see where he has three names under the heading "Children". First, there is Gabrielle's name with several hearts next to it, then there is Quinn, and beside her name reads, "please God let me find her," then there is a name Rishard, out beside this name it reads, **my only son, please forgive me, ** as well as it has another name next to it in parenthesis, (Amina McCants.) At this point, I have this uhh-uhh look on my face, because I don't even have the energy to deal with Malcolm and his drama from the grave. I just can't… Suddenly, my memory goes back to the night I came across Gabby's diary, and I strongly remember her writing the name Rishard, Rishard, Rishard, even had the initials "RMM" and "GGC." NO!; this is just too far off base. There is no way Malcolm can have *another* outside child that just so happens to live in Atlanta. This is just way too much! This man is not six-feet under yet and he is haunting me still!

Finally, there may be some light at the end of this tunnel, Nate tells me that Malcolm did not make a formal will, but he was in the process of completing one. Therefore, even though there's no legal documentation giving him Power of Attorney, one good thing is Malcolm did add him to the account as an authorized user. So in saying this, he tells me that with his bank account alone, he had over $500 thousand dollars sitting in savings. He tells me he would like to give Gabby half, Quinn half, but this other child, is well, let' just say we aren't sure yet, but in the meanwhile we will have to deal with this as we go.

His Grace, His Blood, His Mercy!

☙

A week later… I have been thinking so much about my conversation with Nate. Therefore, we are doing the best we can to celebrate Christmas, and of course the house is as beautiful as ever! I have even called on my one and only Event Planner Extraordinaire, Preston Bailey! Who else can make it look like Christmas at the Bouviér's home?

When I began to put this whole thing together, I had no idea my baby would be home, now was I hoping and praying she would, no doubt. So when I returned home I immediately knew I needed to do just what that father in the bible did who had the son who went off, but eventually came back. I needed to welcome her home properly!

Just as Marcel said to me on the flight back, no better time than to give her the party she missed. He loves her so much, and when I think of how he has always been there with me as a father figure in Gabrielle's life it amazes me. Sometimes we take people for granted, because we just get to a place where we just know that they are going to always be here with and for us, but that's not the case. I never thought about how God orchestrated that thing in such a way that, who would have thought, all these years later a man that I was chosen to represent is now the man chosen to represent me.

I believe I kinda gave him a scare too. For a minute a brotha was looking a little sideways, I guess he thought I was going to go left where it concerns our little "situation", but Daddy has to know it's going to take way more than some little Diamond Heiress to make me walk away from the Angel of my life! Laughing to myself, and if anyone knows me,

Chizellé T. Archie

Diamond Bouviér wasn't born yesterday. Since Ms. duPont was so adamant that she was meant to be with Marcel, she and I came to a little wager. How about when we went over all the fine details outlined in the contract, there was a clause which states, if for any reason the investor wishes to renege on his investment there would be a substantial penalty. It looks like Ms. duPont was really over her head trying to manage her families estate, so let's just say on behalf of Diamond Investment Fund, we are now 75% share holders of her company. This, in turn, means Ms. Lilliane duPont works for me! So, I was never worried about Marcel's little $1.5 million blip; I always had my eye on the bigger prize.

And, oh yes, got a call today from my girl Zoe! She's on her way to the ATL and she'll be here for the next couple of weeks, which that will work out perfectly, and she'll be here to celebrate with us. She's still doing her thing; she now has 4 buildings here in Atlanta. She is in the process of bidding on a contract for a building in or near Midtown, as well. So I can't wait for her to get here, she says she has some news for me. Could she be getting married, likely not, I can't even see that. That girl is way too busy to have anytime to settle down, but anything is possible. Demetrius is available! Now that would be a weird combination.

I can't believe it; World AIDS Day has come and gone. We didn't even participate in the Aids Walk this year, although we did donate, it's not the same as being there. It has just been so much, since everything with Gabrielle, it has been so chaotic, I'm glad I decided to let Demetrius handle things for a while. I could not have asked for a better assistant. The best! Recently I've been thinking of taking things in a new direction, but haven't quite worked out all the details of that just yet. But you can bet it will include Demetrius. His loyalty has been like nothing I could ever imagine, just in the last couple of months; we have over 20 new investors! Marcel has mentioned I need to think of the idea of taking Diamond Investments global. I love his saying… can't stop, won't stop!

Now that Gabrielle is home it's as if she and Sam have become bosom buddies. I hear them in there laughing about this and that. Sam had me laughing though; apparently, Gabrielle has become the reigning champ of pool. Now I guess she will be able to school Marcel on a couple of things, not hardly, that man has that down packed. I love to see him when he beats his guy friends, they can't stand it! But me, it drives me insane, its' those times where he is just able to kick back, relax, and enjoy himself; there is nothing better.

As for Sam, evidently she felt I no longer needed her around anymore, and I reassured her she is family; she will always be needed. We both laugh, maybe now more than ever. I'm no fool now, that little girl has been gone for a minute, lived and survived in Decatur Georgia. I'm sure she learned a few things over there in Decatur, where it's greater. The thought of that, I don't even want to think about it…

I know one thing since I've been around Gabs and Quinn more these days, between those two, my head has been spinning. I thought I was up to par on my text messaging codes, but some of this mess these children have invented is ridiculous. I can't even keep up, she sends me a text with 303, 143; who would think that means Mom, I love you? Then, she says I promise I am going to DTRT, "Do the right thing" Really?!! Who has time to sit and decipher all of this foolishness? Do people not just speak intelligently anymore? Even Lucy had nerve to text me some crap JOML, "Jesus on the mainline," What?!! Are you kidding me? I bet it's one for that too; RUKM.

I forgot to do this earlier today, things have been so hectic lately I haven't even had the chance to stop and slow down. I need to take a look at my chart before I get busy and forget once again. It's amazing how things have become so advanced these days. I think it's so beneficial that I can now look at things in my medical record that helps me understand things better, as far as my diagnosis. It helps me keep up with upcoming appointments, any referrals I may have in the future. I even have the opportunity to request refills, so that now I don't depend on my nurse to do it all for me. It's been over a week now therefore my lab results should be back from my last visit With everything happening, I was so stressed, I knew I shouldn't have stopped taking my medications, if anything I should have learned after all of this time, there is no room for error.

Thank you Lord! The new regimen I've just started Stribild is working! My t-cells are up at 688, and once again my viral load is undetectable. Whew! What a relief, I can't wait to share this with Marcel; he is going to feel so much better. Of course he is my biggest cheerleader, and he has never made me feel bad, he reminds me that it's' one day at a time. Ultimately we know Who has control.

༄

My goodness how time flies, it's almost 4:30 already. Supposedly, I am to meet the ladies for our Annual Christmas party, so I'm hoping I can make it on time, but before I began to get myself prepared I get a knock at the door, and it's Gabrielle. She is in a talkative mood. It's been a while since she wanted to crawl in my bed just as she did when she was a little girl.

As much as I don't want her to move, I ask her, "And to what do I owe this visit?"

She grins and looks up at me with those eyes, those eyes that makes my heart melt, she says to me, "Momma, I don't know how to really tell you."

"Tell me what darling?" I ask.

"I know I hurt you, and I know I said some things I never should have said. I really did a lot of things I never should have done, but I'm sorry. I'm sorry for—"

"Shhh, you don't have to say anything, I know baby. Believe it or not you are so much like me, and so much like your father. You have my determined spirit, while at the same time you get that stubbornness from your father."

We both laugh.

I continue on, "No serious, I will never know why you acted out as you did. And, trust me I questioned God many nights. I called out to Him, even told Him I didn't sign up for any of this. In my heart, yes, I was afraid, I was afraid that you were out there with people that could never love you the way I do. I had to trust and believe that He would keep you safe, and He did. Now, I am not going to say I am okay with the fact you went out and got your little "Tramp Stamp".

She jumps in, "You saw that?"

"Girl, look it is not too much I miss. Well, I can't say that either, because I admit, Momma has had a lot going on. And I realize that like I always say to you, I put a lot into my career, and you don't know this but Momma is getting older."

She looks at me as to say really lady, are you just now realizing that.

Still talking I tell her, "Gabby no matter what, I am going to love you through everything, I am going to be here for you. You are the air I breathe, and you are the reason I get up every day and go when my body is tired, when I just don't feel like it, it's because of you."

"So have you talked to Quinn yet?"

"Not yet. Why, what is it?" I ask.

"I think you should talk to her, if you talk to her the way you are talking to me, I believe it all is going to be okay." She replies.

Out of nowhere she asks, "Momma where is that letter you had for me from Daddy?"

I look at her, and ask, "Are you ready now?"

"Yes ma'am, I'm ready."

I feel like all is good in the world, I haven't felt this good in so long. I tell her once she left; I realized she had it on the side of the bed. I wasn't sure if she had planned to take it with her, but I lean over and reach inside my nightstand, and just a I pull out the letter, I hear the doorbell ring.

Here stands a neatly dressed man who actually looks to be anywhere around 28 or so, and he has along with him a young lady who is rocking the cutest pair of black Kate Spade Peso loafers, that she can most definitely leave with me, but on another note, I greet them.

"Hello, Mrs. Bouviér, Victoria Bouviér?" he says.

"Yes I'm Mrs. Bouviér, how may I help you?" I ask.

He goes on to say, "We're with the local Health Department, and we're here to inform you that there have been cases reported recently where several students at Benneton Academy have been exposed to HIV, and your child, Gabrielle, has been anonymously named as being one of those exposed."

I'm not sure if I am hearing him correctly, but I think all the blood in my body just shot to my head.

He continues, "And because her name has been given, it is advisable that you have her come either to the Health Department to get her tested, or you are free to take her to your Family physician."

He hands me a card with this number printed on it. I feel as though I want to pass completely out right now, but I'm afraid if I do I just may not make it back, because my worst nightmare has finally become a reality!

❧

Its nine thirty and I'm sitting on the side of the bed still in disbelief. I've done everything to rationalize this in my head, and I simply can't do it. This is unbelievable! My baby, Lord, please tell me no! For the last hour or so I believe I've paced this room back and forth hundreds of times. I don't know whether to cry or scream, but the main thing is I don't want to freak Gabby out. I'm so confused, so nervous, it's tearing me to pieces to even fathom that I'm going to have to finally tell her the truth, the truth of my status, and , her father's: OMG, Malcolm, damn you! In all of this it dawns on me not only is she is going to have to learn the truth of all of this, she will have to learn Marcel's truth too. Either which way, I'm not ready. Lord, I stretch my hands to thee!

Sunday we will all be in church, front row that is. Don't know what was I thinking, the Mother's got that entire row taken up!

Chapter Twenty-Five

Gabrielle, the best lessons learned, are in the lab...

Walking these halls it feels like a total different place, a lot has happened since I last graced BPA with my presence. Not really sure if things will ever be the same. I am still getting some really ugly looks from classmates, and I can't say this for sure, but even some of the teachers are looking at me strange.

It's lonely walking to class by myself, I'm so used to having this big entourage with me. Now it seems like I am the new girl on campus, and we know how that goes. It's cool; I was able to keep my locker. Although, no one has stopped by, no one has made any funny jokes, or invited me to any special parties. I did talk with Bree on the way in this morning; we sat and ate breakfast before she headed to her class. Even she has changed.

Now that the new year is in, I guess the school is on a new thing too, looks like there are new rules regarding cell phones.

Chizellé T. Archie

The way Mr. Cromwell makes it sound, you are going to have to go to the moon and back to use your phone. We are pretty much on a search basis around this joint. I'm serious; I'm talking about body scanners as soon as you come in.

Didn't realize so many of the kids were using; well, let me say; selling drugs as much as they were, and now that Etcetera is shut down everyone is looking crazy. Everyone is trying to find another club to hang out. After the police figured out what all was going on in that place they had no choice but to shut it down.

The bell rings and on my way to lunch, I run into guess who, Church Boy! Well, Albert. He wore me down. It's partly due to him I'm back in school today. The night the club got shut down, I thought to myself, who else can I call that will be willing to help me. He's fifteen now, so he has his permit, but he still couldn't drive. Mmm, mmm, mmm, so he sent his cousin to pick me up. Just so happens his God-Father is part owner of the "W", so I was blessed to stay there for a couple of days until I got myself together, and I'm glad I did. Since then Albert and I have become a lot closer, I never realized we had so much in common; maybe because I never paid him any attention. Quinn even thinks he's a hottie! Go figure. For the most part, after I told him I had been helping the kids out in the neighborhood tutoring them, helping with their homework, he was like c'mon, you know where you really need to be. I was more ashamed than anything. I didn't want my parents to know that I messed up royally. Actually, this Sunday he will be speaking to the teenagers. So looking forward to that, with the way my life has turned out, I need to be there. As my Grandfather Winston can say, 'I need to be slain in the spirit!'

While we are sitting here having lunch, he leans over to let me know he has now started chewing Doublemint. I crack up laughing.

"Gabrielle, I'm so glad you decided to come back," he says, with a smile about as big as Andre on Victorious.

Okay, I admit, yes, even the girl who was big enough to move out, still has a love for Teen Nick. Shoot, Ariana Grande', that girl is a beast!

"Thanks for helping to convince me I needed to come back. I really did miss it. You know that's all I really know. I will say this, I thought I could just use the knowledge I was born with, go out there, and make it, but I was–"

Just thinking about how I allowed myself to become so biggity with my Mother and fathers, disrespect them, and mainly myself, a tear swells in my eye.

I keep talking, "But I really thought I could handle it all. And Rishard, uugggh, he never loved me. I found out he was just making a fool out of me all along. I haven't seen him in a while, haven't talked with him either. He's tried to call me, because he keeps saying he has something to tell me, but I'm too angry right now, really don't want to hear from him."

He looks at me and says, "Gabrielle, I can't even imagine what you endured while you were gone, but I do know God had his hands over you the entire time. And as far as you being ashamed, that is just a trick of the enemy. I'm a friend on FB of T.D.Jakes Ministries, and I was looking at this video, I think it was called, *Living with Uncertainty*, and I thought of you. It said, 'Don't be so aware of your guilt, that you are unaware of your own freedom! Sometimes we become so riddled with guilt that we lose all sense of ourselves.' Gabrielle, you have to forgive yourself, and let it go! Forgiveness is the key that will set us free. Once you repent, God forgives you, and so should you. Remember there is liberty that Christ has made us free, and be not entangled again with the yoke of bondage."

Okay now shouldn't he be in a pulpit somewhere preaching? If my Granddaddy Winston was here, he would say, 'Now ushers, will you come.' I've never had a friend in my life to speak to me, to encourage me so. It's like when I talk to him, it's like talking to Steve Jobs, may he rest in peace, but after this I feel as though I can go out and create the next Apple Product. Before I realize it time is up, and I have to get ready for my next class. On the way, I see I have a text from Ms. Paige. She says she has some new information for me.

༄

While waiting on Drago to finish dinner, I jump on the computer to gather more research on our project. I am so excited because even though I now know everything about my mother, my father Malcolm, and my bonus father Marcel, I am still trying to adjust. In light of everything else that is going on with me, I think I took it better than my mother was expecting. When she explained everything to me, you would have thought we needed an ambulance. Lady! Really, I do know things. I just regret that it had to happen to us. But, as my father Marcel always tells me, no matter what, trust God with all my heart and lean not to my own understanding, know that He is going to work this thing out.

At the last minute, I was able to persuade Ms. Paige to go another way with the project. In light of all the devastation that this monster called HIV has caused me and my family, it has made me want to do something about it! I was lying down the other night reading a POZ magazine, and I began to see all the people that have been diagnosed. And when I saw how many of us, more so teenagers, I began to cry all over again. Then I came across an article about The Berlin Patient, a man in Berlin that was diagnosed with HIV, who had lived with the virus for 11 years. He was diagnosed with another illness, myeloid leukemia, a type of cancer that attacks your bone marrow, in which he had to end up getting a bone marrow transplant. It said, that today after the transplant, this man is the only person on Earth to be functionally cured of HIV. Some researchers believe it to be because he wanted to participate in an experiment that would see how the transplant works. So he intentionally chose a donor that carries the CCR5-Δ32 mutation, in which this mutation is what makes you immune to HIV. From my research, this particular homozygous gene blocks the T-cell surface as to where the virus can't get in. Wow, only 1% of the population has this, and apparently this is not normal. So, after the transplant, the T-cells that grew back had this mutation. Looks like he was taken off all his HIV meds, and therefore the virus was not able to replicate itself. This is the bomb!

After reading all of this, I find it to be crazy because Ms. Paige and I had already talked about how I wanted my Duke Project to be something of importance; something that would have a lasting effect. And in light of my current situation, what would more important than for me to help find a cure for HIV!

The best thing to happen to me, besides the club being raided, was while I was on what we are going to call a hiatus,

Ms. Paige was busy doing most of the homework. Somehow she was able to retrieve DNA samples of the Berlin patient!! So, it looks as though we have some serious work to do. This weekend its' going to be epic. It's about to go down in the lab!

※

It feels much later, but it's just now eight o'clock, and while I am in research beast mode, Quinn comes in wanting to talk. This sister thing is more than a notion. I'm not used to really having one of those to really call my own, but because our father was a rolling stone here we are united. Don't get me wrong, I haven't just gotten over it all willy-nilly, but I am trying to realize she was just like me; looking for love in the wrong place. She just told Momma and my father Marcel about the baby. The sad part is being that she is now positive too. So from here on out she has to be especially cautious with this pregnancy! No more of the oooweee, or anything else for that matter.

Momma, a Grandmother, now that's hilarious. Well, you can say she will be the flyest Glam-Ma Brookhaven has ever seen! Me an aunt already, man I'm still a baby… really Gabby did you just say that? Humph, guess I did. Yes, I still have a lot of growing up to do, but for now, I believe I have learned so much in these past few months. BTW, maybe we do need the patter of baby feet around here. That way Momma can have another focus besides-, na'll let me stop that, that's wishful thinking. That lady will never stop, it's not in her, that's why she is Diamond Bouviér! The hardest working and baddest chick on the block! My mother!

His Grace, His Blood, His Mercy!

Quinn tells me that Skyye has tested positive as well. They say generational curses are something else! Here she was, hating me and my mother so, until she put herself, and yeah of course that lazy Tiger, in harm's way fooling with Drew! Drew, I can only take a deep breath, because when I think of how much I thought I loved that man. It turns my stomach to think of all the damage he has caused all of us. I would have done anything for him, but he hurt me so badly. I trusted him, I don't know why I did, but I just thought he cared.

Furthermore, as far as Drew is concerned, looks like he is going to be sitting really pretty for a long time. With all the drugs they found, sounds like he was going to have the streets hemmed up. As much as I cared for him, I can in a way say I'm glad they got him! It's too many of our people losing their lives to drugs.

Wow, just thinking about that, I saw so much while I was away. Girls my age, already crack heads, doing things for money. Okay, here is where it turns personal again. That so could have been me; it was me. Just not to that extent, but like I said if that night would have never happened, who knows where, ahmm, no Gabrielle you cannot think like that. In spite of all the things that have recently happened to me in my life, I refuse to let the devil place any type of defeat in my spirit. I just keep telling myself, I am more than a conqueror.

Before I wind it down, I get a call from my Grandmother. I know that whenever she calls I may as well buckle my seatbelt, because she is probably going to lay it down. I'm talking about pull out your bibles, an turn to Genesis type of lay it down. But these days hearing from her really makes me feel good.

"Hello my sweet darling." The sweet voice on the other end says.

"Hey Granny, how are you?" I respond.

"Well baby, Granny is good, just trying to make sure your Granddaddy is taken care of."

I laugh out loud, because we all know that is no easy job.

"How is Granddaddy?" I ask.

"You know your Granddaddy, honey, he's about the same. Still won't let anyone sit in that chair you all bought him all that time back."

Yeah I know, he is a mess about that chair, I mean he won't let anyone, not even me sit in it. He even goes so far as to say we have to pay him because he's retired now, so we need to give up the money.

"Well, tell him hello, and I love him."

"I sure will baby, and you know he loves you too, just as I do. You do know that don't you?"

"Yes ma'am I do. I really do."

"You were on my mind, and–"

Here it comes, I already know she is about to get crunk. Let me get comfortable.

She continues, "So I thought I would give you a call and see how things are coming with you; see how school is coming? I know a lot has happened in this short time, and I wanted you to know that no matter what you can always talk to Granny. I love you so much, and I don't ever want you to think there is anything you can't talk to me about, and that includes sex."

Really lady?! I want to say to her so bad. Where they do that at? Who talks to their Granny about doing it, and I shole don't want her talking to me about her and Granddaddy; can you say ewww?

I reply as nice as I can, "Yes ma'am."

"You know Gabrielle, I hope you know that your mother gave me and your Granddaddy fits too. She tries to act as if she was such a good little girl, but you should know there were many days I had to put something on her fanny. Now her father was a different story. There was nothing she could do wrong, the sun rose and set on Victoria when it came to Winston. As far as I was concerned, she was going to do what I said and as long as she lived in my house, she was going to abide by my rules, and there was to be no exceptions.

That's what's wrong nowadays with you children, you think the world owes you something. You all have no desire to get out and just get it. You feel like it is supposed to just happen overnight. That if you can't have it the way you want it, then so be it. You all are just going to rebel until someone listens. But as for me and my house, that was not happening. There were curfews, there was restriction, Granny didn't play that. Now you could have tried to pull one or even maybe two over on me, but you best to believe after that it was over.

Now your Uncle Julian, that was a horse of another color. Now yes he still had to abide by all the rules, but he was trying to, bless his heart, he was trying to go so far out of his way to please your Granddaddy. Now Winston didn't play with Julian, he was very firm with Julian. There were days I felt a little sorry for him, but nevertheless my point is this here, what you are going through is called growing pangs. And you should also know that God will never bring you to anything to not bring you through it. Yes, there is a penalty we must pay for each and every sin we commit, but remember if we ask Him to forgive us; He is just to forgive! He is a forgiving God, because He loves us. He knows we are going to mess up, but He also has laid it out for us that if we just ask Him, he will do it. Now know this, there are sometimes God tells us no for a reason, because He knows that if He gives us what we ask for, we may not to be able to handle it at that time. So, he pulls back, and allows us time to get it right.

Not sure if you know this or not, but there are things even at this age that has happened to you; where you should tell God thank you for not giving certain things to you. For instance, when I think back at a time in my life, and oooh honey, Granny was in love with this man, and I thought he was the icing on the cake. We were going to get married, have children, do all of those things. But baby, that man turned out to be the worst thing ever. SO YOU KNOW I had to tell God thank you for not letting me be with him. And see, He sent me your Granddaddy. Even now I'm a little skeptical about that; no, just kidding. God couldn't have made a better choice for me. I hope you understand where Granny is coming from. Didn't mean to be so long, but I– "Hello, Gabrielle, are you there?"

I immediately jump up because I realize I have dozed off to sleep. I mean I really didn't try to, but I got the gist of the story.

As not to appear sleepy, I sit straight up and say, "Yes ma'am, I'm here."

"Okay darling, well like I said Granny just wanted to hear your voice, tell you I love you, and let you know it's going to be alright. If we just trust Him!"

His Grace, His Blood, His Mercy!

OMG is this about to be round two. Where is Granddaddy, I know He would say 'Now 'D', it's time for the benediction', let that baby go to sleep.

I reply, "Thank you Granny, I love you too."

I pause, because I'm waiting for her to start back up, but she doesn't. So we hang up. It's a huge part of me that misses my Granny so. There are a lot of times I wish we lived in Brooklyn so I can see my grandparents more often. They are riots, especially my Granddaddy. I think he missed his calling. He would have been a great comedian.

Before long, I drift off to sleep, and all I can think of is how much I pray one day that we can one day be able to say there is now a cure for HIV.

Chapter Twenty-Six

Gabrielle Cartiér, college here I come!

A year later... It's the most beautiful Saturday I've seen in a long time! Here we are, Momma, my dad Marcel, Granny, and, of course, Uncle Lucy! We're here tugging my things into my dorm, yes my dorm. And if these people knew who really was about to take Washington D.C. by storm they would have been a bit more prepared! As we say back in the ATL, "the struggle is real." This can't be my dorm! Really people?

Of all the choices I had, MIT, Harvard, Yale, Columbia, Spelman, Georgia Tech, even the Fashion Institute of Technology, yes, I'm here, Howard University. I'm about to embark on the greatest adventure of my entire life. Its official, I'm the only fourteen-year old to grace these halls, and oh am I ready! I've already enrolled in all of my classes. Of course my major is Biology. So yes I'm Pre-Med with a focus on

Epidemiology. Later I plan to go on to complete the Medical Scientist Training Program, to work on my MD and PhD in molecular genetics and cell biology. Whew! that's a lot…

Momma finally gave in, but we had a little help. You remember that Duke Project? Turns out Ms. Paige and I blew it out the window. Come to find out we did so well that while in the midst of testing those DNA samples, I stumbled upon the greatest thing ever. At the final hour, it became clear we had done something no one else had ever done. We discovered a vaccine for prevention for HIV! So you can say your girl Gabs is paid! After the CDC got word of my experiment, it went viral, and I couldn't believe it, neither could Momma; they wanted to buy it! So… let's just say I am now $2 billion dollars richer, as well as they offered me a Summer Internship!

After I came down from all the excitement, I began to focus on what I really wanted to do. More than anything, I wanted to be in school, I wanted to be around people that I could relate to. Well, okay, we are all aware that I'm the youngest here, but I needed to be in a place where I could sit in a classroom setting. I wanted to participate in lectures, have a Professor. I wanted to experience college life, and let's be real, I wanted to go to the parties too. One thing was for sure, I wanted to attend THE University, where it all began! $\Delta\Sigma\Theta$, and anyway Momma wouldn't have had it any other way! You know the crimson and cream has been embedded in me since birth.

I take a look over this room, and then I turn to look at everything I have with me. It's way over the top, they may just put me out of here, but I'm going to have to manage. First thing is I'm going to have to get used to this bed. OMG, look at the mattress, it doesn't quite ring Ritz Carleton, but I'll make do. If I can live with Quinn and the rest of them, I'm sure I can make it work.

Haven't met my roommate yet, but I know she's from Birmingham, Alabama. I know at least I will have someone that can hook it up southern style. You know what they say about the girls that can cook, but hey I'm not too bad myself. Even though we had Drago, Momma ain't no joke in the kitchen. Oh, she taught me a few things along the way, just thinking about the deviled eggs she makes for the events at the church, and oh, the White Chili Taco Salad, not to mention the rotel dip (breathing hard) will make you hurt yourself. Keeping my fingers crossed; maybe she made me a surprise dish?

It's at this moment it hit me, I'm about to really be away from home, miles away from home to be exact. Tears begin to form in my eyes, because now it's time to really show and prove. Everyone is depending on me now, and my mother, I look over at her with that big beautiful smile, how she's standing in the corner observing everything, taking it in, making sure if she has to at any given moment come through, and let Howard know whose really in charge, there is no shame in her game. She's scoping out the scene. All at the same time, I can see how much she is going to miss me. She doesn't want to show it, but I know it, this is killing her, but she knew she had to let me go, in order for me be what God had for me to be. I still can't believe she had been placing all of the offer letters in a trunk since I was eleven years old. It wasn't until I was accepted into Mensa that she spilled the beans; that too was on her. Apparently, she found my application and sent it off. When I think of how much she has sacrificed for me to be here, I get an overwhelming feeling in my heart. Her own needs, her health, even sometimes going behind my dad's back to give me things she said she wouldn't. Like this last shopping spree we took before coming here. I now realize that it's nothing she wouldn't do for me.

By the time we get everything situated, and we take a tour of the campus, it doesn't take long to see who is really going to miss me. Even though I don't get the chance to see her that often, I am so grateful for this summer that I was able to spend with my grandparents. They have been such an instrumental part of my entire life. They have helped shape me in ways no one knows. Sometimes I thought Granny was a little too hard, but I realize that it was only because she loved me. And Granddaddy, he's so funny, I'm just going to miss listening at him tell me all the stories of his growing up as a man. I bet he really was a mess back then; a whippersnapper, as he calls it!

The day is just about over, it's been a long one though; we've had so much fun. I hate to see them go. I think Uncle Lucy has everyone on campus' number saved in his phone. Well let's say; any guy that he thinks may try to have any dealings with me, so I guess it's safe to say, that's everyone. Now how embarrassing is that. I'm already going to be looked at as the weird girl on campus, now I have to contend with this. If I know Uncle Lucy, all of those numbers aren't to check up on me.

Well, it's that time, and I have to say goodbye. My father Marcel tells me how much he loves me, and how proud of me he is. Uncle Lucy jumps in the truck, and yells, "Don't make me come back no sooner than I have to!" I laugh, because I know he means it. Granny, trying so hard to fight her tears, she gives me the sweetest hug, and, tells me she loves me, along with this long list of do's and don'ts. Ok, Granny I got ya. It's Momma that causes me to lose it. Her hug is one that a child will never forget. No matter what I've done to hurt her, no matter how proud she says she is of me, it's something about knowing that I was with this lady for nine months before I came into this world. I shared the closest moments ever with her. It's a hug that lets me know, she is here, and she will always be here. She turns her face away so that I can't see her tears, but I know they are there. I love you too Momma. I watch them drive away.

༺༻

First day of class, wow, I'm here in Washington D.C. living on my own. It's hard to believe that a year ago this time my life was so much different. Who would have thought that I would've been so crazy and in love with someone that turned out to be the worst thing that ever could have happened to me, but at the same time, turned out to be the best thing to ever happen to me.

We found out that the other three girls that slept with Drew was none other than my ex-girls, Angel, Dionne, and yep, you guessed it, Jordan, he even got to her too. They say it's the ones closest to you that you have to be aware of. I learned that with Quinn. The sad part is, now they have a disease that they have to live with the rest of their lives. Thank goodness, there's medicine, and if they do what they are supposed to they will be just fine. If anybody knows that, I do. I just pray this teaches them a lesson.

Chizellé T. Archie

Last I heard, I don't think Mr. Andrew Harrison will be carelessly sleeping around anymore. On top of all the other charges he had, after they found out about the girls, Angel's Dad pressed the issue, and because of that he was also charged with HIV Criminalization! About a few months after it all happened, he called apologizing and all of that; I was like Boy, Bye! Although, he did insist he didn't know he was positive. So from what I understand, he may just get off on that charge. It's going to take a lot to prove he intentionally transmitted it.

As far as Rishard, I finally found out what he was trying to tell me. India, she wasn't his "other girl", she's his Aunt, his mom's sister. He moved here with her after his mother died of AIDS which she contracted it from his dad, Malcolm Cartiér!!! He found out all of this when he was in jail. Apparently, India and Skyye had an all-out hatred for my father, and somehow they hooked up to make our lives a living hell! The crazy part is India hated Skyye just as much, so she went as far as to get with Drew, so that he can play Skyye, so that they all can play me. In actual reality, they all got played! Dag, this thing is no playing matter! Oh, but I forgot to tell you, I was spared the HIV virus, thank God! We found out I am a carrier of the CCR5-Δ32 gene! But, I didn't get off that easy. I did contract Syphilis from Rishard, so that was a shot of Penicillin, a big shot of Penicillin! Enough to let me know that sex is the last thing I am thinking about…

So you ask, what's my next step? I know I have a lot of homework ahead of me. You know your girl Gabs, I'm so ready for it. Who knows, I just may run into President Obama, and he and I can sit down and discuss this Healthcare Reform. I'm doing research now, remember. So as far as this HIV and

His Grace, His Blood, His Mercy!

AIDS virus, as long as I have a mouth, I'm going to shout it to the world, instead of turning up for any and everything, it's time to Turn up Against HIV! IJS…

Sincerely,
Gabrielle Grace Cartiér, M.D.

P.S. I now understand the meaning of Grace and Mercy! It's me, look at me, wouldn't you think so?

Glossary

WARNING it is strongly advised, that those over the age of 25 study this PRIOR to reading! If any questions please refer to urbandictionary.com!!! Or a teenager in your house…

#	Hashtag
123	I Love You
ABC Sex	Anniversary, Birthday, Christmas
ARFKM	Are You Freakin Kiddin Me
BAE	Before Anyone Else
BAN	Bit** Ass N****
BFF	Best Friend Forever
BTW	By The Way
Bye Felecia	When someone is leaving, and you could really care less, Felecia, a name of a girl no one is sad to see go
Dey	They
Doe	Though
Fleek	On point
Friend Zone	What you attain after you fail to impress a woman you're attracted to.
Gate Rape	TSA airport screening procedure

Chizellé T. Archie

GTFOH	Get The F*** Outta here
Gud	Good
IJS	I'm Just Saying!
Ion	I Don't
IDK	I Don't Know
IKR	I Know Right
KMSL	Killing Myself Laughing
LMB/AO	Laughing My Butt/A** Off
MILF	Mom I'd Like to F***
MOS	Mom Over Shoulder
OHN	Oh Heck No!!
OMG	Oh My God (Goodness)
Playing	both sides of the street Bisexual
Ratchet	Ghetto
ROTFL	Rolling On The Floor Laughing
RTO	Registered Text Offender: Someone who is known for sending back to back text without a response in between.
SMH	Shaking My Head
Snap H**	Someone who constantly snaps pics posing for Facebook
Twitter Bang	Hooking up with someone who you've spoken less than 140 words to.
TTYL	Talk to You Later
Turn Up	Getting loose, wild, partying, have a good time
WTH/F	What the Hell/F***
WYD	What you doing?
X	Ectasy
Yada yada yada	Conversation Glosser-Over, similar to Blah blah blah

His Grace, His Blood, His Mercy!

FYI... the 411 on sex/snap bands and their meanings.

Please know if your child comes home wearing a colored bracelet, in some instances along with their friends, they could be playing a game called the Sex Bracelet game. In game, either a girl or a boy, at any time can go up to them and pull or snap their band, whichever color they are wearing.

Parents!!! Just know this DOES NOT imply that every child that has on a colored band is, or has, played this game. My intention is to bring awareness to the things we have no clue about. Therefore, I hope you read this carefully... Please be aware some are quite interesting!

Color Code for Middle School persons:

Clear	Whatever you want
Black:	sex, coital or oral
Orange:	kissing
Yellow:	hug
Blue:	oral sex, or lap dance
Red:	Body contact, lap dance, french kissing
Red & Black:	69
White:	Friendship
Green:	give a flower, or touch me or hug
Pink:	flash your stuff
Purple:	holding hands
Gold Glitter:	make out

Afterword

My beloved, finally! We are here. It has been a minute but God has allowed me to once again do the very one thing I love. Write! Yes, there were some challenges along the way, even times I didn't think this would come to pass, but those were the times I realized more than ever I had to. I owed it to all of you, the ones that waited for Victoria to return, the ones that truly believed in me. Most of all I owed it to HIM!

First let me say, I am tired! I never thought it would be this hard to be a teenager in today's world. How do you all do it? I have to give it to you; you all are some of the smartest, resourceful, talented group of young people I have ever come across. My mother has always told me everything tends to repeat itself, fashion, dance craves, hairstyles, cars, etc. They just come back in a different form. So yes, please know in a world where you have children struggling to read, barely knowing how to put a complete thought together, NOW we have another version of talking; it's called texting! It has officially gone to a new level.

Before I penned this book, I had an idea of what I wanted to portray, but I had no idea of what it all entailed. I have learned so much, I have learned an entire new language, a foreign language so to speak. I recall taking Spanish for the first time, I had to learn how to first break down the words, read them, write them, nevertheless understand them, and over twenty years later, I still can't hold a conversation. But as of today, one thang fa sho, I can honestly say I'm gud wit it doe, so all ya'll outz der tryn ta read dis her, plz kno, it juh got real!!

Really!! Why???!! No disrespect to my Facebookers, Twitterians, Instagrammers, all that, I get it, we want to be unique, create our own little thing. But it just wouldn't be me, if I didn't say, at some point we have to be held accountable!! We have innocent babies just beginning to form their words, learning the difference between a noun and a pronoun. Now they have to decipher another language all together. Like I said, it's all good, while talking amongst others that really understand. The sad part is when the ones you are sending the messages out to DO NOT know the difference, and I am not talking about children. I am speaking now to my adults!

I have been criticized on several occasions for receiving a text message from another adult where I honestly had to tell them, if you can't text me so as I can understand it, and not kill myself trying to figure it out, DON'T! I can't and I won't! By no means am I knocking shorthand, but where does it end? It's a difference between shorthand, and laziness. So in saying that again, I get it, but please know, if you are that brilliant to come up with it, be brilliant enough to do something with it. Who do you think came up with the Urban Dictionary? In the great words of all of you, Leh Go!

Now, I got that out of the way, I can breathe. Now, on to my parents, this book was not only for my young crew, it was for you too! I have spoken with many of you that have said you are aware of what your children are doing; "you know your son or daughter will come to you and talk to you, regardless," "Oh not my child, we have a great relationship, he/she we talk like friends." Ahhm, newsflash! Yes, your child too…

I have been on this parenting journey now for six years. I never thought I would see or hear some of the things at this time. Many days I have asked Jesus to take the wheel, because well, you know, LOL! Seriously, we as parents must be aware of any and everything our children are doing. The most I had was sneaking in the closet to talk on a phone that was attached to a cord, where my mother would follow the cord, and I was caught! Not these days, we have so much to contend with, social media, Facetime, Skype, Tango, Snapchat, everything is instant!

I included the glossary for you to learn some of the terms your child may be speaking right in front of you. You can never be too careful. Do what you have to do, not telling you not give them their space, but really parents let's be real. We were young too. I pray that some of the things you have read will somehow help you, teach you, so that you can always be two steps ahead, so that you can learn about topics to talk to them about. The same for you parents that have older children. I realize that times have changed, everyone is kicking it, oh excuse me, turning up. But, I ask you to please, please realize YOU are their parents, not their friends. Yes, it's great for them to know they can come to you, but there is a line… a thin one!

In the last book, I stated for our men to stand up and take your rightful place! We need you! Our children need you, we as women need you! I need you to protect me! You know my pet peeve, what's up with your pants hanging so low to the point if anything was to ever break out, how can you run to protect me or any other woman for that matter? Men, and I say that strongly, it's time to get it right. It's time to Man UP! There is a generation of young men to come behind you, and they are looking at you; everything you do and say!

Finally, to my mother's, we have to be role models to our daughters. Not by showing them what to wear, but showing them what **not to** wear! As I always say, it's nothing better than showing some CL along with the ass! Whoever came up with less is more got it wrong! At the end of the day, and this is said with love, a real man will ALWAYS choose the one he has to imagine about!! When it comes down to it, being a Queen is better than being a Bad Ass Bit** any day, and a smart one on top of that, is Priceless!

Love,
Chizelle'

Acknowledgements

Well, here we go... First let me say thank you this time may be slight of an understatement and maybe a bit overstated to some; nevertheless, there are some people that have been a true blessing to me. First person first, my Mother, Mrs. Catherine Williams Packer; Mommy, thank you for listening as usual, especially when Judge Judy was on, and you really didn't want to. LOL! I think, well I know, you are the only person that has read my book so much, you can just about tell it to me. I am so blessed to have you here with me again to see this thing happen! After all we've endured. I love you. James Packer, Dad, thanks for the new memories! I love you! Hattie Mae Williams, my 88 year old Grandmother! Lord have Mercy, I thank you for her. Gran thank you for the laughs, the encouragement, and yes understanding that this time, I had to go a little harder, and being okay with it. I admit you were the one I was afraid of; hope I made you proud! I love you.

My Pastor, Dr. Craig L. Oliver, Sr., thank you again for allowing me to be a student in your class. You have no idea of how much you've inspired me and helped me in some of the best and worst times on this road, but hey, that's why I know it was divinely orchestrated that you would be my conductor!

Chizellé T. Archie

My First Lady Chi'Ira Oliver, thank you for your smile, your spirit, for being here for me more than you will ever know! My Elizabeth...

My editor, Renee Crutcher, I'm laughing as I type. No one knows what we've been through. I thank you so much for helping me, even in the lowest part of your life! Love you girl. You have been such a blessing, hope we got 'em all... if not we'll blame Gabby! KMSL!

Nate Dyer, cover extraordinaire, we did it again! Never doubted you, not one minute, even with the emerald green! Thanks, you rock.

Tyora Moody, Ty!! Okay, now you have been with me from day one of this project, and you have truly been a gem. Thank you so much for helping me, and realizing how lost I was without Dee... but you showed up, and showed out! Love ya! Can't wait for the tour. Mr. Reginald Walker, thanks for all of your help. Truly a blessing in disguise. Ms. Mia, thanks for everything, you are a lifesaver! Dr. Albert Anderson and Ashley D. Boylan, PA, words can never express how the both of you helped with the research. It came together so well, I really wish I was Gabby getting paid from the CDC now. Thanks! To Mr. Peter Grant, USA Gold man, thank you for schooling me, when I get some money I'm coming looking for you, so hold those bars for me!

Now to my soldiers in this thing, S.R. there is no way I could have written this book without you. My street guru, my teacher, got me even questioning some things, LOL! Can't wait until you read it. Also the Dun Dada, Ra! Thanks for helping your girl; you helped bring Drew to life!! To my sweet, my friend, Charles ChuckE Wilcox!! What it do?!! Thanks babe for telling it like it is, no matter how much I didn't want to hear it, your advice was the bomb.com, see I did it! Thank you and I love you for it.

To my family, my other mother, Momma Mae! Thanks for loving me, and always encouraging me, as well as give Daddy a hug for me, I'm still ready for his project! I hope you like the tribute… it was rough!

To my sister girls, all of you, now, I am trying to be good here, must I go there. Dee, thanks for looking out on the hip-hop tip! Had no idea you knew so many rappers… IJS! I love you, the sister I really thought you were! Stacey, just reminiscing…"He who walks, walks alone" never thought after all of these years I'd write those words in a book! **#thechevette**. Tina, now you have chapters two plus some more, now stop harassing me… I love you girls. Ta'Marra, now you know, thank you will never be enough. Finally! You have been on me for five years, and I pray I make you smile through everything!! Love you. Jada, Honey, thanks for saving me on so many levels! I love you girlie for being here for me. Godmommie tales!! My Godsister, Tencie Leigh, like I always tell you, I love you, and there is nothing you can do about it! So proud of you, you have no idea! My sister Ophelia, I hope you are happy now! Here it is. I love you lady. Tish, sisters 4 life! Thank you for being here, I will always love you! Ronnie, my new found sister thanks baby for being the strength you are, you have held me up at our lowest, and I love you so much, and so does Ms. Celie!! Chimmy! Thank you, girl the Master's paid off! You did it… Hope you like how I hooked it up. Love you baby.

Whew! Okay, so to my babies Johnna, Noel, (hope I made you proud) Caitlin, Sheridan, Mikhaela, and the rest of my Diamonds in training I love you girls, and I am sooo proud of you!

Trying to wrap this thing up, said I wasn't going to do this, Carl Buckethead Jackson, man, we on it again like Bonnie and Clyde! I love you baby, thanks, you always say what I need to hear!

Finally, to my family and other friends I have forgotten, all of you, Chizzie loves you from the bottom of my heart! Now Madea is putting up the sign telling me to get somewhere and sa-down. Catch all of you next time!

#ILOVEYOU

Resources

Where to get tested
If you or someone you may know would like to be tested for HIV and not sure where to go, please call the National AIDS Hotline 1-800-342-2437

How to Prevent the Spread of HIV
Specializing in a wealth of information as far as prevention The U.S. Centers for Disease and Control National Prevention Network is a great outlet. They can be reached at 1-800-458-5231, or you can access their website at www.cdc.npin.org

Overview of HIV
The Body is a commercial website run by the Body Health Resources Corporation; it has easy to understand terminology which provides a wealth of information of HIV/AIDS by having question and answer forums with HIV physicians. Access their website at www.thebody.com

Also the Center for Disease Control provides information by gathering statistics about the spread of HIV in different populations by listing a numerous amount of articles, newsletters, brochures, along with providing question and answer sections. You can reach them at 1-800-342-AIDS, or by accessing their website at www.cdc.gov/hiv

Information about Young People ages 13-29

HIV stands for **h**uman **i**mmunodeficiency **v**irus. It is the virus that can lead to **a**cquired **i**mmuno**d**eficiency **s**yndrome, or **AIDS**. Unlike some other viruses, the human body cannot get rid of HIV. That means that once you have HIV, you have it for life. About 50,000 people get infected with HIV each year. In 2010, there were around 47,500 new HIV infections in the United States. About 1.1 million people in the United States were living with HIV at the end of 2010, the most recent year this information was available. Of those people, about 16% do not know they are infected.

- Young people aged 13–29 accounted for 39% of all new HIV infections in 2009.
- With regard to youth, HIV disproportionately affects young gay and bisexual men and young African Americans.
- All young people should know how to protect themselves from HIV infection.

New HIV Infections (Ages 13-29 Years)

- In 2009, young persons accounted for 39% of all new HIV infections in the US. For comparison's sake, persons aged 15–29 comprised 21% of the US population in 2010.

- Young MSM, especially those of minority races and ethnicities, are at increased risk for HIV infection. In 2009, young MSM accounted for 27% of new HIV infections in the US and 69% of new HIV infections among persons aged 13–29. Among young black MSM, new HIV infections increased 48% from 2006 through 2009.

The National Minority AIDS Coalition, which strives to develop leadership among all communities of color as far as HIV. Their website is www.nmac.org

Also the National AIDS Treatment Advocacy Project includes summaries of conversations held by AIDS experts directed towards African Americans and HIV. Their website is www.natap.org

Again, the body.com has extensive resources reliable to African Americans with HIV/AIDS of all ages.

HIV Campaigns (Get Involved)

Rap It Up-is about taking a stand in your life and community to help stop the spread of HIV/AIDS. It's about protecting yourself and those you care about, being informed, by getting tested annually, talking openly with your partner, friends/family, and taking responsibility in your community. Sponsored by BET, to learn more visit www.rapituppresents.com

Greater Than AIDS > Non-Profit Organization

Greater Than AIDS is a leading public information response to the U.S. HIV/AIDS epidemic. Launched in 2009, it is supported by a broad coalition of public and private sector partners, including media and other corporate allies, Federal, state and local health agencies, national leadership groups, AIDS service and community organizations.

Through targeted campaigns and community outreach, Greater Than AIDS and its partners work to increase knowledge, confront stigma, and promote actions to prevent the spread of the diseases. While national in scope, Greater Than AIDS focuses on reaching communities and people most affected. To learn more visit www.greaterthan.org

Act Against AIDS Government Organization

Launched in 2009, Act Against AIDS is a campaign of the Centers for Disease Control and Prevention (CDC). Act Against AIDS seeks to raise awareness of HIV/AIDS among all Americans. It also works to reduce the risk of HIV/AIDS infection among the hardest hit populations. To learn more please visit www.cdc.gov/ActAgainstAIDS

Printed by Libri Plureos GmbH in Hamburg, Germany